'Both a gorgeous romance between
to books and reading . . . This debu
loved it'

'It's a love story and a love letter to reading, and it shows you just how powerful books are . . . a life-affirming, bookishly beautiful novel'

CRESSIDA MCLAUGHLIN

'A gorgeous debut from tremendous Tessa Bickers. It's ahhh but it's also hahahahaha. I loved it'

SALLY PHILLIPS

'Poignant . . . Simply a beautiful story about love, friendship and the restorative power of forgiveness'

JESSICA GEORGE

'An exploration of friendship, love, loss, this is a book lover's dream rom-com'

Heat

'It's *You've Got Mail*, but make it (even more) bookish. A really heartfelt love story about the power of friendship, family, and the written word. Bookworms everywhere will adore this'

NIAMH HARGAN

'Moving and romantic. Tessa Bickers writes with a fresh and warm-hearted voice. What a romantic concept!'

LIA LOUIS

'If you love books and love *love*, you are going to adore *The Book Swap* . . . Heartwarming and hopeful and a testament to the power of a good read'

JULIE COHEN

'A soul-warming tale, perfectly balanced. I cried not once but several times . . . I loved it'

FREYA BERRY

'Celebrating the power of love and literature, this swoon-worthy love story is perfect for book-lovers and hopeless romantics alike'

Woman's Own

'Funny, heartbreaking and achingly romantic. Relatable, multi-layered characters with complicated back stories – highly recommend'

LORRAINE BROWN

Tessa Bickers studied journalism at Bournemouth University, and went on to co-present a breakfast radio show in the South West. Moving into celebrity news, she interviewed some of the biggest names in show business, including Leonardo DiCaprio and the cast of *Sex and the City*.

Tessa started her creative career as a singer-songwriter and, after a few failed *X Factor* auditions, she went on to perform at Glastonbury Festival and Secret Garden Party with her band Tess and the Tellers. These days she has replaced her guitar with a keyboard, and songs for books.

The Book Swap

TESSA BICKERS

HODDER &
STOUGHTON

First published in Great Britain in 2024 by Hodder & Stoughton
An Hachette UK company

This paperback edition published in 2025

The authorised representative in the EEA is Hachette Ireland, 8 Castlecourt Centre, Dublin 15, D15 XTP3, Ireland (email: info@hbgi.ie)

1

Copyright © Tessa Bickers 2024

The right of Tessa Bickers to be identified as the Author of the Work has been asserted by her in accordance with the Copyright, Designs and Patents Act 1988.

All rights reserved. No part of this publication may be reproduced, stored in a retrieval system, or transmitted, in any form or by any means without the prior written permission of the publisher, nor be otherwise circulated in any form of binding or cover other than that in which it is published and without a similar condition being imposed on the subsequent purchaser.

All characters in this publication are fictitious and any resemblance to real persons, living or dead, is purely coincidental.

A CIP catalogue record for this title is available from the British Library

Paperback ISBN 978 1 399 70608 7
ebook ISBN 978 1 399 70609 4

Typeset in Plantin Light by Hewer Text UK Ltd, Edinburgh
Printed and bound in Great Britain by Clays Ltd, Elcograf S.p.A.

Hodder & Stoughton policy is to use papers that are natural, renewable and recyclable products and made from wood grown in sustainable forests. The logging and manufacturing processes are expected to conform to the environmental regulations of the country of origin.

Hodder & Stoughton Ltd
Carmelite House
50 Victoria Embankment
London EC4Y 0DZ

www.hodder.co.uk

For teachers – thank you.

*And for Mum, Dad and Charley, Maria and Penny –
my greatest teachers of all.*

1

Erin

They say it takes one moment to change your life. My moment will happen at twelve minutes past three this afternoon, but there's no way of knowing that when I wake up.

Everything else about this Thursday is the same as any other except for one thing: the date. It's in my mind before I even open my eyes. It's heavy on my shoulders as I get dressed for a breakfast meeting, pulling on a long white skirt, light grey T-shirt and leather jacket, while considering every possible reason I could call my boss, Charlotte, and tell her I won't be going to work today. It stands beside me as I step onto a rush hour tube from Brixton to Oxford Circus and it follows me all the way to The Ivy Brasserie, where I take a seat outside and prepare myself for one of those ridiculous meetings you're forced to have in PR. The ones where neither of you are allowed to say it's a meeting, and instead you spend an hour talking about anything but the reason you're both there, then I pick up the bill, which confirms everything that has gone unsaid. *You will feature our Traitor Fashion label in your magazine and say good things about it.*

Martha isn't even one of the worst editors, but lunch drags the way anything would drag today and I'm relieved when she picks up her hot pink Spring/Summer Jacquemus bag to go.

'You know, the first time I met you, I wasn't sure if you were cut out for this industry,' she says, smiling down at me,

1

handbag already on her shoulder. It can't hold much more than a lipstick. 'But you've got it, Erin. A few more years and Charlotte better watch her back.'

Her eyes are warm as she turns away and I have to wait until she can't see me any more before I shudder.

'Ewwwww,' Cassie says, when I relay the story of being compared to Charlotte, once I've got to the Traitor head office on Oxford Street. It's open plan, with over a hundred people sharing the room. Every day I'm grateful that, out of everyone, I was put next to Cassie. Today she's dressed in rainbow dungarees that look super fashionable on her, but would make me look like a walking tote bag. She opens up her drawer and pulls out a mini bag of Haribo, throwing it at me. 'Are you okay? Do you need a cold shower? Shall I start calling you Char?' Her clear plastic-rimmed glasses hang off the end of her nose.

'I'll just scratch all the skin off my body and then I think I'll be okay.' I put my new-season Traitor handbag onto my chair, and open up the Haribo, turning to leave. I've got to tidy the whole showroom before my ten-o'clock influencers arrive.

'Fuck it, shall we just quit while we're ahead? Set up our own thing, do something worthwhile?' Cassie throws it out there, stopping me in my tracks.

I lean my head back and breathe in, imagining it. 'The dream. A job that doesn't suck out your soul. What though?'

Cassie's bright blue eyes light up, her curly hair dancing. 'Okay, stay with me. We could make tiny little outfits for bees, and then—'

Charlotte appears beside me, her nails freshly painted a bright red, and her roots, which were dark yesterday, blond again. Lucky, given how busy she's constantly reminding us we are, that she has the spare time for self-care. Probably because she palms most of her work off on us.

'Both of you, less of this chit-chat and into the showroom, now.' She leaves, wafting a trail of expensive perfume in our direction as she spins away. Cassie raises her eyebrows as though it's some exciting mystery, but I know exactly what's about to happen. As we approach the glass room, I can see everyone else is already in there, waiting. She's asked the whole team. We've got a meeting together in just a few hours' time, it makes no sense to call another one now.

'Who was the last person in here?' Charlotte asks, her eyes landing on me for a second before scanning across the others. Of course this couldn't wait.

I swallow. 'I was. Alicia Gold could only do nine p.m. last night and I know how much you wanted her, so—'

'And you thought this was an acceptable way to leave it afterwards?'

I look around. There are clothes all over the floor. Last night I made the executive decision that rather than work an extra hour overtime, I'd tidy it in my paid hours today, but that's not exactly something I can say aloud.

'No,' I say, my cheeks turning red as I feel everyone's eyes on me. They'll all just be glad that it isn't one of them. Only Cassie will really care. 'I'm sorry. I'll sort it now.'

'I should hope so. You think anyone's going to post about us if they see our showroom like this? It's an embarrassment.' She looks at me with this expression at least once a day. Like I'm something her creepy-looking bald cat, Boris, dragged in. I wait for her to dismiss everyone.

'Cassie,' she says, instead. 'What do you see that's wrong with this room?'

I can't look at Cassie. She has to answer, and I don't want to make her feel bad. Especially because Charlotte knows we're friends. She's chosen her on purpose.

'The ... erm ... the clothes aren't hung up.'

'Dominique?'

'Bin is full of cans.'

'Sara?'

'The colours of the clothes are all mixed up.'

My whole body's shaking with rage. Charlotte knows how late I worked last night. I thought she might finally compliment me on something.

'Francesca?'

'There's smears on the glass.'

For fuck's sake, now I'll have to clean the windows too and because of this meeting, I now have seven minutes until DIY Duo arrive. Two girls who started filming each other doing their make-up before school and became so successful, they left after their GCSEs to do it full-time. Obviously they're now millionaires, aged twenty.

In my head I scream that if it's *that* bad everyone should help tidy it, given we all use it, but I wait until they're gone and then I bend down and start picking up clothes, desperately fighting back tears at the unfairness of it all.

Suddenly all I want is to get home and see my best friend, Bonnie. She'll make me feel better. She'll help me to laugh about all this. She'll have the wise words no one else will. Frustrated, I pull a lime-green T-shirt towards me, and allow myself to sob into it once, before throwing it into the bin bag, where it belongs.

By lunch I'm already behind and have just minutes to bite my way through a chicken wrap, while staring at my diary.

There's a launch for a new energy drink in there for tonight that wasn't there this morning, and when I see it I choke on a chunk of wrap. Tonight's the only night I have to make my fancy dress costume for the fundraiser back home in Frome this weekend. Everyone has to go dressed as something beginning with 'b'. I'd purposefully kept my evening clear and only one person would have put an event in there. As if humiliating me in front of the whole team wasn't enough. I throw away my wrap, appetite gone.

I don't know what I've done to make Charlotte treat me like this. I'm good at my job. I work hard. I do everything she's ever asked of me and it's never good enough.

I just want to walk out of the office after this meeting and go home to my best friend, drink a bottle of wine or two while I cobble together the world's worst fancy dress outfit. Instead I have to get home, change, and be at the event by seven. I stare at the bin. How quickly can chicken give you food poisoning? The fact that eating off chicken is preferable to doing my job ignites something in my brain. Nothing about this is right.

I'm so full of anger towards Charlotte, I can't even look at her as I take my seat in the meeting. While she talks about figures and plans for the next quarter, I've created a whole rap in my head, made up entirely of the words 'shut' and 'up'.

At ten past three, everyone turns to stare at me because it's my turn to list my 'biggest learning' and my 'biggest win' of the week. They're all wondering if I'll mention the showroom.

Beside me, Cassie has the bell. It's passed around the room so that someone can ring it if anything exciting is announced.

I stand up, clearing the rap from my mind. I'm going to have to say aloud what happened with DIY Duo. I haven't prepared anything else.

'My biggest learning,' I begin, my voice shaking because I always hate this bit, but especially now, 'is we need to change the way we allow people to browse our showroom. The girls from Duo tried to take extra free stuff today and I, erm . . .' I cough and stare down at the table and back up. Everyone's looking at me. 'I told them to put some back, but in future we should probably—'

'What did they do?' cuts in Charlotte, her long red fingernails drumming against the notepad in front of her as she leans back in her chair.

'They . . . They . . .' Out of the corner of my eye, I see Cassie shake her head ever so slightly. She knows what happened. She's telling me to do anything but tell the truth and I know that's the right thing to do, but my mind's completely blank. I can't come up with a lie fast enough, and Charlotte created the 'five-item limit' rule. Maybe she'll actually be proud of me for enforcing it. 'They got really cross and they left with nothing,' I say, forcing the words out as fast as I can.

Cassie visibly shrivels up until she's nothing but a heap of rainbow-coloured clothes beside me.

The finger tapping stops.

Even Charlotte can't believe I've admitted it after what happened this morning. I can tell by the way her head shrinks back, her white neck disappearing under her fake-tanned chin. She's holding her hand out flat in front of her, fingers in mid-air. She doesn't know whether to start tapping again.

'They've got over a million subscribers to their TikTok channel. The last post they did increased our traffic by two hundred and fifty per cent.'

I nod. I was hoping she wouldn't have all the stats. 'But Alicia Gold took some stuff, so . . .'

'Alicia will get us nothing.' This is the opposite of what she told me yesterday, when she insisted I stay three hours late to let Alicia in. 'Whereas the DIY girls . . .' She turns her hand into a fist, displaying huge diamonds on most fingers. 'That wasn't a lesson, Erin. That was a huge fucking mistake.'

Swallowing, I go to sit back down. Cassie tries to replace the bell and somehow it lets out a ring as it hits the table, so she has to jump on top of it to stop it from further celebrating my *huge fucking mistake*.

I bite my top lip, shoulders shaking.

'I'd still like to hear your win, if you have one?' Charlotte says once I'm back in my seat, her voice quiet. For a second I think it's because she feels sorry for how she's treated me today, but one look at her face says the opposite. She doesn't know about the result of my meeting this morning, which secured me a double-page spread in a Sunday supplement, boosting our sales by as much as the DIY Duo would. She doesn't think I have a win and she wants to watch me fail one more time in front of everyone. One more time before I have to dash off to an event *she* put in my diary because she can't be bothered to go herself.

I stand back up, my jaw clenched.

'My win would be . . .' I pause, debating whether to tell her about this morning's successful meeting or let her see it for herself in all its full-colour, double-page glory.

'Of course, if you haven't got one . . .' Charlotte sighs over the top of me. I'm about to do what I always do. Ignore the way she treats me and just try, even harder, to impress her with my win. But something about that over-exaggerated sigh cuts through the final thread holding me together.

'I'm meant to be back home in Frome today, climbing to the top of Cley Hill where the ashes of the person I love most in the world were scattered, before going home to cry my way through reruns of *Gilmore Girls*,' I say before she's finished speaking. 'I should be with my loved ones, but I'm not, because you wouldn't give me the day off work. You didn't even give me a chance to explain why I needed it, you just said we were too busy.'

The smirk falls from her face, but the fact it was even there at all confirms she really doesn't have a heart. All my fear of Charlotte evaporates. I lower my voice to keep it steady. Everything that's been building all day is coming out and I don't know how to stop it. 'I've stayed in this job for seven years, hoping it'll get better. Maybe one day live up to the image I had when I started, but it just keeps getting worse.' A flash of my sister Georgia appears in my head, rolling her eyes at me as I complain, once again, about work. 'I sacrificed everything, waiting for things to change. But now I think staying here might only turn me into you, and that's not someone I want to be. Someone who makes everyone's life a misery and then fucks off home to their bald cat.'

There's a gasp. I don't know who it comes from. Looking around, my eyes land on the bell, which is sitting in front of Cassie shining as though it's about to fulfil all its potential. I'm shaking. 'I did have a win. I got a double-page spread in *Hello Sunday*, but I don't think that's my win any more.' Cassie's eyes are bulging as the others stare at me, mouths open so wide I can count at least ten fillings in the room. 'I quit.' The words feel so good, I smile and pick up the bell, ringing it as I repeat the words. 'I. Fucking. Quit.'

Throwing the bell down, I pick up my laptop and march past Charlotte towards the door. It's only when I catch sight of her expression that I know that really *was* my win, because on her face, amongst all of the anger and shock, there is finally something else. The tiniest glint of respect.

'Jesus, Erin, I wasn't expecting you,' says Callum when I let myself into our shared flat in Loughborough Junction a good few hours before I'm normally home. My flatmate is sitting in front of the television, dressed head to toe in a red Adidas tracksuit, dark brown hair slicked to the side, thick sideburns almost touching his chin. His Sheffield accent is the nicest sound I've heard all day and for the briefest of moments I want him to hug me. It passes.

'Thought you were working today?' I manage to say.

'Gave myself the day off,' he replies, staring at the cycling on the screen. He means he's called in sick to his product design job, the way he seems to whenever there's some sort of bike race happening. In true Callum fashion, he asks me nothing about why I'm back and instead turns the sound up.

'I quit my job,' I shout over the top of the commentator, because I need to say it out loud to believe it.

'Nice one,' he replies without looking up, so I disappear into my bedroom and shut the door.

Bonnie's sitting in the chair in the corner, reading a magazine. It's the one place in my bedroom that isn't completely covered in stuff. All around it are bags of freebies from work and boxes I've only half unpacked since I moved from my last flat, in Stockwell. I found this flat after starting a brief relationship with the security guard on the door of my old place. When he told me he was falling for me and wanted to quit his job, I lied and told him it couldn't work because I was moving out. Which meant I actually had to.

There are the shoes I've kicked off at the end of a fourteen-hour day. Books, everywhere. So many books that they won't fit on the one shelf above my bed and are instead stacked in hopeful 'to be read' piles anywhere that there's space.

'Home early,' Bonnie says, a big smile on her face. She's wearing one of her wigs. The purple one that's so long, it reaches her bum.

'I just did it, Bon. I quit.' I throw myself onto the bed, leaning my head against the wall.

'Shit yeah, you did.' She tilts her head back and laughs. It's deep and throaty. It warms me. 'Finally! How do you feel?'

'Like I might be insane?' I squeeze my eyes shut. 'And also . . . relieved. Like it's the start of something.'

'*Yeah* it is.'

'Like it should have happened years ago.'

'It should have.'

'I just want to reset everything, start again with a clean slate.' I look up at my bookshelf, my eyes landing on a neat white spine: *The Life-Changing Magic of Tidying Up*. I look at Bonnie. 'Can I Marie Kondo my life?'

'Do it, do it, do it,' she says, jumping up and dancing, so I smile for the first time all day. Maybe all week. 'Out with the old, in with . . . well . . . nothing new, yet. But soon. New job. New you.'

I look at the boxes by her feet. What's even in them, anyway? Clothes I clearly don't wear. Books I don't read. Stuff I don't need. I haven't missed any of it since I moved in here. That's got to mean something. I open them up and look through them, hardly even recognising the contents.

Bonnie's back in the chair, watching in amusement as I grab a bin bag and throw some shoes in. Pull a few more things from my wardrobe. I go through the books on my shelf, filling a suitcase with any I know I won't read again. I've never thrown out a book in my life, but I need to make space for the new ones. The ones I'm yet to read. I move the stacks that were on the floor onto the shelf and stand back smiling. Finally, the shelf looks full of promise. Finally, I'm excited about reading again.

I keep going. Half-finished moisturisers, broken hair straighteners and uncomfortable bras. Bonnie claps along, her eyes landing on a bright blue nail varnish I've just thrown in the bin. She pulls it out, resting her left hand on her leg as she starts painting.

I'm on a real roll now. I clear most of the contents of my bedside table. Old batteries. Chargers for things I no longer own. Christmas cards that don't mean anything. A single birthday candle. By the time my phone goes I'm down to my T-shirt, sweating as I ready myself for the inevitable bollocking from Charlotte, but it's Mum.

'Sorry, but you do *not* spark joy,' I mutter, sending her to voicemail. With each small step, I'm starting to feel like, after seven years of moving from shit flat to shit flat, and from shit fling to shit fling, while staying in a job that only makes me miserable, I finally have a bit more control over my life. I'm going in a new direction.

Before the momentum goes, I take the unwanted bags to the wheelie bin outside our flat, and fill my little old Ford up with boxes for the local charity shop. I'll take them on the way to the fundraiser back home in Frome. If I go this afternoon, I'll have enough time to make it to Cley Hill after all. I can still do what I intended to today. It's not like I have a job to get to tomorrow.

First though, the books. I've got another idea for them.

'Back in a sec,' I say to Bonnie, grabbing the suitcase.

'I'll make us a cuppa,' she shouts after me. 'When you're done with all this mad makeover stuff you can tell me exactly what Charlotte's face looked like. I want a wrinkle-by-wrinkle description. And Erin,' she says, waiting for me to turn around, 'I'm so proud of you.'

I smile, tears springing to my eyes. I don't tell her, but she's the person who gave me the confidence to go through with it. I did it because I knew it would make her proud.

A short walk from our flat, just under the bridge towards Ruskin Park, there's a little community library, which sits there apparently 'in loving memory of Eileen Gladys Day'. I've taken the odd book from it when I've passed, but I've never given back any of my own. Not until today.

There's rarely anyone here, and when I reach it the sight of it makes me smile. It's an old repurposed cabinet that someone's added a roof to, so it's like a little home for books. Pale yellow, with a blue door frame and patterned glass panels showing three shelves, sparsely filled. I unzip my suitcase and start pulling books out, putting them wherever there's space. Modern classics. The one about the world ending in twenty-four hours that everyone was talking about last year. A few by the same author who was a good holiday read. With each handful I put in, the more excited I get about the books waiting for me at home. The more this feels like the right thing to do.

Marie Kondo says it's wise not to look too closely now, because this is the moment where I could crack and wheel them all home again.

'They don't spark joy. They don't spark joy. They don't spark joy,' I repeat as I fill the shelves.

As I place the last paperback in and zip up my suitcase, I sigh.

The Book Swap

It makes me happy, to think of someone else reading these books. Finding something in them that I didn't. Taking them somewhere I've never been.

Of course, the suitcase feels a lot lighter on the way home – it's empty – but I'm surprised that I feel lighter too. I've done it. I've just cleared all the baggage from my life, ready to start again. It's so overdue.

Today should never have been the day I changed my life.

I promised Bonnie I'd do it three years ago. I promised her the day she died.

2

James

'All set for tonight, JJ?' Mum asks, when I come back in from my morning run.

I'm so happy to see her showered and dressed rather than curled up on the sofa in a dressing gown that I pull her in for a hug and, standing nearly a foot taller than her, kiss the top of her head.

'If you want to go, we'll go,' I say, releasing her.

Now that Mum's improved, it's my last night here before I go back to London, and she's decided that we should get tickets to the fundraiser for the town's hospice. It's at the local event hall, the Cheese & Grain, and has been held every September for the last three years in honour of Bonnie, a friend of mine from school. There's nothing I want less than to walk into a room filled with fellow ex-pupils, but I'll do it for Mum, because attending events with her is never something that I can count on, and she's so excited.

What makes it worse is she stayed up all night making my costume, and it's ... well, it's good. Too good. Embarrassingly good. Like I'll look like a total twat in it. It's going to feel like I'm back at school. Walking into a room and everyone laughing.

'Isn't it a fun idea, though? Anything beginning with "b"? I might steal it for my own party next year.'

Mum always has high hopes for her birthday when she's out of a bad bipolar episode.

Here she is now with rosy cheeks and a sparkle in her eye, like she hasn't spent the last six weeks unable to get out of bed or eat anything aside from fried chicken. Like she hasn't turned down every single offer to leave the house, while crying so hard, and for so long, that Dad and I both called the doctor at exactly the same time, more than once.

When Elliot and I were little, Dad would liken her illness to the Very Hungry Caterpillar. That Mum goes away and builds a cocoon around herself, before re-emerging as a beautiful butterfly, hungry for life. For all the days she's missed.

'Not sure I'd call this a party exactly, Mum. But you should do it. Patricia opens up a whole world of exciting fancy dress options. Pimp. Pepper shaker . . .' I run out of ideas, but it doesn't matter. She's back at the sewing machine in the kitchen, starting on Dad's outfit.

'I'll just get changed,' I say, grabbing a glass of water. Dad's at the table, playing some diamond crush game. I wish I'd never taught him how to use his iPhone properly.

After a shower I pull jeans and a T-shirt out of the suitcase that's been laid on the floor, packed, for the last six weeks. It's waiting for the day I can fold the two halves back together and return to my other life in London.

I've got used to it now. The switching between my two lives. This childhood bedroom, with the single bed in the corner and the desk in the window, set up for the Zoom calls and the training I do remotely. Books on business wedged in next to all the English ones from my GCSEs and A levels. *The 7 Habits of Highly Effective People* and *How to Win Friends and Influence People*, sitting beside *The Catcher in the Rye* and *A Portrait of the Artist as a Young Man*. My London room in the depths of Penge holds much less of me within its walls.

The Book Swap

Just clothes and a few things in a desk drawer. I rent it from my mate Nathan, from uni, and it's the only thing that's set to change when I get back. His girlfriend, Hannah, is moving in and I need to find a new place to live.

'Consider it an opportunity,' my best mate, Joel, said, when I told him. 'To get out of the arse end of London and start living. It's not like you can't afford it.'

Nothing's more important to Joel than being rich. That's why I've ended up at Big Impressions Training. Totally lost as to what to do with myself, I followed his motto: if you don't know what you're good at, find something that will eventually make you shit loads of money instead.

It turns out it's near impossible to catch up with someone financially when they work in banking, but with my latest promotion I might be one hundredth of the way there.

'Going into town,' I shout at the front door.

Dad appears, dressed in jeans, a T-shirt and a waistcoat. His long grey hair is pulled back into a ponytail.

'I'll join you,' he says, peering into the kitchen. 'If that's all right with you, love?'

He disappears to give Mum a kiss.

We start the short walk from just outside the town centre, down to the little cobbled street that leads to the shops.

'Thought I might check out the bookshop one last time.'

'Closed all the ones in London, have they?' He grins at me.

'If you'd only come up to visit me sometime, you'd know.' I look across at him, so at home here. 'Do you ever miss it?' I ask.

Dad was a true Londoner until he met Mum. She appeared front row at one of his gigs back in 1974, and that was it. He just knew. From that moment on, wherever she was, he'd be there too. Unfortunately, within a few years, just as Dad's career was taking off, that meant Frome – where Elliot arrived, and then me.

'Of course,' he says, waving through the window to one of the staff in the deli at the top of Catherine Hill. 'But missing it reminds me of why I left, and what I have because of leaving.'

Sometimes I try to get Dad to admit the truth about how he feels. There's no way he can be this philosophical about it all. The life he chose means he's forever haunted by the words 'one-hit wonder'. They precede his name in any article ever written about him. The man behind the title song for the multi-million-pound box-office smash, *Nobody Boy*, who never sang again. It's my worst nightmare, but he wears the badge if not with pride then at least without any remorse.

He shows no shame in his career, going from supporting Fleetwood Mac in stadiums to donning a Domino's uniform and delivering pizzas. No shame, even when I took my best friend from primary school, Geoff, home in the summer holidays before we started at Frome College, and he burst out laughing at the sight of my dad running down the stairs in his navy blue polo shirt, with the red dots on the sleeve, sporting a logoed baseball cap.

'I'll bring us back some double pepperoni for tea,' he shouted, patting me on my head. I shrank away from him as Geoff followed me up the stairs, cackling.

By the time we started our first day at college, he'd told everyone. I sometimes feel that it kickstarted the worst few years of my life.

We haven't managed many of these walks, me and Dad. Until just a few days ago, Mum required constant supervision. We took it in turns. I silently berated Elliot for getting away with not helping, purely due to geography. He's a full-time dad in New York and even if he were ever to offer – which he hasn't – bringing three-year-old Jordan would be too much for Mum. She'd hate for him to see her that way.

We've got good at it anyway, Dad and I, over the years. He's stopped feeling bad about asking me. I've started offering my assistance earlier – the moment Mum doesn't reply to a message within twenty-four hours, or if Dad says 'holding up' when I ask how he is. It's a slick operation, devised over time and out of necessity.

'Hopefully it's a good, long spell this time,' I say, as we pass the three-storey second-hand shop halfway down the hill, which has been my main source of entertainment this trip.

Dad shrugs. 'Just got to enjoy every good day,' he says. 'Make happy memories to last us through.'

I look across at him, this man who's so selflessly given up his life to care for my mum. Who never wishes for more than what he's got. I open my mouth to say something. To tell him how admirable it is. What a good man he is. To say, 'the way you've looked after this family is nothing short of heroic. You're the glue that holds all of us together. We'd fall apart without you.' I can't do it. His choices, no matter how heroic, contributed towards making my time at school a living hell. There wasn't a day that went by where I wasn't shouted at or laughed at. Spat on or kicked. Had chewing gum stuck into my hair, or an entire group of boys standing around me, ready to do awful things unless I found some way to stop them.

It also meant that several times a day, someone would come up to me and sing Dad's one fucking song, 'Do You Know Me?', in my face.

We pass the Italian restaurant that was built three years ago. I remember, because it was one of Mum's worst ever spells. I was back home long enough to watch the whole thing rise from the ground. By the time we reach the bookshop, the moment to say something to Dad has passed. One day though, I should tell him.

I put my hand on the door to push it open, shrinking back when I see through the glass panel that there's a woman in there, browsing. I recognise her long, wavy brown hair, tucked behind one ear, the same way she wore it at school. She's wearing a floor-length white skirt, with black DMs and a leather jacket. All the times I've been back in Frome, and not once have I seen her. Not since the day she left school. I hold my arm out to stop Dad and watch as she pulls a book off the shelf and turns it over, immediately engrossed in whatever's on the back. I've been in that shop so many times, I know which section she's in. It's the self-help one.

'Actually, I reckon I'd prefer a pint,' I say to Dad and walk away, leaving Erin Connolly to browse in peace.

Just as I'm about to put on my fancy dress outfit, Elliot makes his daily guilt call. He does it whenever I'm back home with Mum. There was once a time in my late teens where he made no contact for two years, but that seems forgotten now – by him, at least. He calls as though it's what he's always done.

'How's it going in the old mad house?' he asks, TV playing out some dramatic kids' show in the background. It's all creepy high-pitched voices and explosive sound effects.

You'd know if you ever came home. The words fly into my head and stop before they reach my lips. Most of the conversations I want to have with my brother happen in my own mind.

'Better by the day.'

'That's great. Quite a short one this time?' He sounds cheerful. Upbeat. Like life's back to normal again. It didn't feel short when I was up with our mother until three a.m. for weeks, or on the phone to the doctor's surgery the second they opened.

'Yeah. She's doing good.'

'Have you hit up any of the old dirt tracks while you've been back?'

My chest tightens. When I was in sixth form, Elliot used to pick me up after college, bikes in the boot of his car, and we'd travel all around Somerset and beyond, finding new paths to cycle down. The rougher and muddier, the better. It's where we did all of our best talking.

'No time, unfortunately.' *I wouldn't do it without you.*

No one speaks.

'How are you?' I ask, eventually.

He sighs. 'Okay. Could do without Carl spending half his life on the other side of America.'

I flinch at the mention of Carl, the way I always do. I know it isn't fair to blame Elliot's husband for my brother's absence in my life, but I don't know how to stop it. Yes, Elliot left, but Carl kept him there.

'Sorry to hear that.'

'Got your outfit on yet, JJ?' Mum shouts from downstairs.

When Mum handed it to me, she said what a shame it was that Elliot couldn't be here too. That of course he couldn't be, when he was doing such a brilliant job, raising his little boy. Apparently though, it's fine for me to leave my own actual job to come home. Expected of me, even. But not the golden boy. Anyway, Elliot isn't the one who is responsible for her getting ill.

'I better go.' I hang up. How is it possible to miss my brother when I only just spoke to him?

Helena's reaction confirms my outfit is too much, when she turns up at the front door dressed in a tight black dress, wearing a bandana. She looks exactly the same as she did fifteen years ago, when we were both students at Frome College.

'Bloody hell, James. Someone's going for the best outfit prize tonight.'

I'm a book. *Great Expectations*, to be precise. The costume is made of rich navy velvet, the title hand stitched into the front of the jumper in gold. There's even a navy hat with a gold tassel hanging from it, as a bookmark.

I sigh. I didn't even know there was a prize, but now it absolutely looks like that's what I'm trying for.

'Glad you've shaved though. Means I can see that perfect square jaw of yours.'

She reaches up for my chin, pulling me towards her.

'B for bandana. That seems much more the level we should be going for.' I lean forwards, kissing her lightly just as Mum and Dad appear behind me.

'Wow, Trish, you look fantastic,' Helena says over my shoulder. 'Gareth, have you thought through how you'll drink with a dummy in your mouth?'

'Trish made a hole for a straw,' he says, and I'm not sure I've ever heard more pride in Dad's voice.

We walk down to the Cheese & Grain together, my costume acting as a sort of forcefield, its pages blocking Helena from getting too close. Probably a good thing, given I leave for London in the morning. This is only ever a Frome thing, which started a few years ago when I bumped into her at the local Garden Café while getting some space from

Mum. She wasn't at all well that day, and she was taking it out on me. I was useless. She wanted me to get out. She didn't ask for me to come. She didn't need my help. This was all my fault. All of it. Sometimes she wished she'd never . . .

I left before I heard her say it.

Helena had approached me that day. She recognised me from school. She sat down opposite me without even asking and ordered cake with two forks. She told me about the hilarious day she'd had, chasing her umbrella down Catherine Hill and knocking over the local MP as he left his office. Within minutes of being in her company, and after three forkfuls of cake, my home life was forgotten, as was the fact she had been on the periphery of the group who made my life hell at school.

She mentioned it once, when we were in bed together. I could tell it was something she hadn't thought about in years.

'God, didn't people make up a song about you, or something?' she said, and she even laughed. I froze beside her, clenching my jaw as I waited for something. I don't know what. An apology, maybe. 'I had the *worst* haircut in school.'

That was about two years ago now and, over time, I've grown to like her. How at ease she is around my family. How gently she puts up with my last-minute cancellations or urgent demands to see her, when the house feels like it's closing in on me. How readily she appears to return to a life without me, the moment I'm gone.

'All packed?' she asks, once we've joined the queue of bottles and brains, Bambis and Buddhists, birds and balloons.

'Never really unpacked.' I shrug, and she laughs.

'Of course you didn't.'

'What's that meant to mean?'

'Well, unpacking would be like committing to staying. To actually settling into your life here. The only way you can get through it is to remind yourself it isn't permanent.'

I frown at her. Is it true? Do I like to remind myself it's temporary? Isn't that just how everyone feels?

'This is exciting.' Mum leans in behind me, her baboon ear tickling my cheek.

At least Helena's distracted me from worrying about everyone I might see. Not that I can really recognise anyone, anyway. They're all in fancy dress and the hall, when we enter, is dimly lit with disco lights flashing. Loud music playing. Dad hoists his nappy higher and pulls Mum towards him for an immediate bit of dancing. Creating a happy memory to get him through.

Helena sees a group she knows on the dance floor and disappears, as I wander to the bar to order champagne.

'I've got some news,' I shout, once I've joined Mum and Dad, handing them each a glass. I've been waiting until Mum's better to tell them. I wanted to tell this version of her, not the other. 'I'll be able to send a bit more cash home soon. I'm becoming a partner.'

Their faces light up and Mum screams so loud I can feel people's eyes on us, but I don't care. Dad pats me on the shoulder as he glances away for a second.

'Proud of you,' he says, raising his glass. 'Though don't do it for us. We don't *need* the money.'

'It's the least I can do,' I say, and Dad frowns. Fixes his light brown eyes on me. Opens his mouth to speak.

'Last call for anyone to enter the talent contest,' a voice announces, booming across the speakers.

'How about it, JJ?' he says. 'You could read that chapter of yours?' His eyes won't leave my face, so I try not to show my genuine reaction. I roll my eyes, laughing, but my chest tightens at the mention of my chapter. It's the one thing I wish I'd never told Dad, because he's the only person who won't let me forget it. The creative writing course in London I did a few years ago, where I got shortlisted in a 'best first chapter' competition. I've left it to sit there in an unopened document on my laptop ever since. Better to keep it as one perfect chunk than try and finish it and fuck up the whole thing.

'I'll do that if you sing that Christmas single that never got released,' I say, raising an eyebrow at him.

Dad wraps an arm around Mum and raises an eyebrow of his own, turning to talk loudly out of the corner of his mouth. 'Think I touched a nerve, there.'

3

Erin

I squeeze through the double doors of the Cheese & Grain, trying to avoid damaging my already fragile cardboard book pages. I swallowed my pride and called my sister, Georgia, asking for help with my costume. She obliged, with the minimal effort I stated was required. If anyone sneezes, the whole piece will fall apart. On the front, in felt tip, she's written *One Night in Erin*.

Georgia has come as a Barbie, complete with a neon pink boob tube and a long brown wig covering her usual short bob of the same colour. The outfit is so unlike anything she'd ever wear that it feels like I'm hanging out with someone else.

'You do know "Erin" sounds nothing like "heaven"?' I say, following her to the bar.

'Bad puns are even funnier than good ones.' She spins around and winks at me, her pink lips glowing under the lights.

The conversation stops because ahead of me is the photo wall of Bonnie, all the pictures blown up so big it's like she's here in this room. The largest is her proudest photo. The headshot that was taken when, at twenty-six, she became the youngest ever editor of *Voice* magazine. She was in the job for less than a year.

Leaving Georgia at the bar, I walk towards the wall, running my eyes across Bonnie through the ages. As a baby, big bouncing curls on top of her head. As a stroppy teen, arms folded, always in the same combat trousers. There's the one of me and Bonnie in the Frome pub she loved the most, The Griffin. I didn't know they had that picture. It was taken the night she asked to go out one last time, the way we used to. She wasn't well enough but she insisted it was possible, and somehow she made it happen. Within two weeks she was in the hospice. Within a month she was dead.

That night she put on sequins. She wanted to talk about boys and life, like we always did, except there was one big difference in the conversation. We could only talk about my life in the future, or hers in the past. I found it hard to be myself. How could she expect me to act the way we always did, when everything had changed?

'I've got a question for you,' she said. My least favourite of her sentences. 'What makes you happy? Truly happy.'

'You,' I said without hesitation, and she rolled her eyes.

'I was about to say it can't be a person.'

I looked at her. Black curly wig, pretty similar to what her hair used to look like, before she lost it. Her head tilted to one side. The sparkle still firmly in her warm, brown eyes. That was the last thing she lost. They were wide, like they always were when she was really listening. She's the only person who's ever looked at me like that.

'Fine,' I said, taking her hand across the table. 'If it can't be you, then it would be making you proud. That's what makes me happy.'

We locked eyes then, so much unsaid. We both knew I wasn't just telling the truth, I was saying it because there were times when I hadn't done that. When maybe I'd done the opposite.

'Bonnie, I—'

She shook her head. 'I know.' She smiled across at me. 'You don't need to say it, Erin. Just promise me you'll live a good life. A happy one. You're not just living it for you now, you know? You're living it for me too.'

My eyes flooded with tears, as I bit my lip and nodded.

'In case you ever need a reminder,' she said, pushing an envelope across the table. 'Open it now and I'll kill you. I'll tell everyone about the time you kissed Darren Whitcroft behind the science block when you were meant to be dating his brother.'

My mouth fell open, allowing me to feel some happiness through my tears. She always came up with a different threat when she wanted to get her way. Who would do that when she was gone?

'You wouldn't dare.'

'Try me.'

I opened the envelope when I got home. Inside was a card with an A.A. Milne drawing and a quote. On the back, in Bonnie's bold, neat writing, she had just written the words: *Don't forget to make all your dreams come true!*

It's my most prized possession.

Georgia joins me, quietly placing a large glass of white wine in my hand.

'I made the worst outfit to try and hug you in,' she says, patting just above my bum, the only place not covered in cardboard.

'I miss her so much,' I say. 'I thought it would get easier.'

'It might if you took my advice and actually spoke to someone.'

'That's not fair,' I say through tears. 'I tried that therapist you recommended. Dishy Rishi. His office stank of bleach and he left stupidly long pauses after I finished speaking.'

Georgia rolls her eyes. 'Rishi's one of the best out there, but you know he isn't the only therapist in the world. There are literally thousands of us. Everyone's training to be one these days.'

She gently turns me, so I'm no longer staring at the changing faces of my best friend. Behind me, the room is now packed full of people. Everyone who knew and loved Bonnie. The stage is lined with buckets, inviting extra donations throughout the night. In a few minutes there's the talent show, which Georgia's threatening to enter us both into.

There are already some people on the dance floor, and standing amongst them all is someone dressed as another book. It's a way slicker outfit than mine, made from what looks like velvet. In what's the most bizarre thing I've seen in a while, the book is hugging a baby and a baboon.

Georgia leads me to one of the round tables in the corner of the room, placing the rest of the bottle of wine in front of us. I nod towards her dress, which has fallen so low she's close to exposing both, surprisingly pert, breasts.

'Have you had them done?' I ask, horrified.

She lifts her hand, pushing the bottom of her wig. 'Flattered, but no. Used tit tape for the full Barbie effect.' She hoists her dress back up to chest level. 'And don't think compliments are going to stop me from asking,' she says. 'What the fuck did you quit your job for?'

I shrug. In the last forty-eight hours I've started to wonder whether it was a moment of total insanity. Then I imagine walking back through those doors on Monday, or I think about how proud Bonnie would be, and I know I did the right thing.

'I just hated it. Charlotte made my life hell.'

'Oh, for God's sake, Erin. She was just the latest person

you got to blame all the shit things in your life on.' She sounds exasperated, but the words sting.

'What's that supposed to mean?'

'Mum. James. Derek. Charlotte. Even Bonnie. You do know no one except you is responsible for your life?' She lifts her hand and waves at one of our old teachers, dressed as Bon Jovi, as though what she's just said is a casual throwaway comment.

'That's not fair. Charlotte turned on me because she's a bitch who—'

'Charlotte turned on you because you were a depressed hot mess for months and you refused to do anything about it. Still are, in fact.'

I open my mouth and close it again. Ready to defend the story I've told myself since Bonnie died.

'What are you going to do now?' Georgia softens her voice and looks at me with genuine concern. 'I'm worried about you.'

I want to be sick. She's asking the one question I haven't dared ask myself because I have no idea what the answer is. 'You need a plan, because otherwise I fear you might fester away in that disgusting little flat with your very bad-influence, lazy housemate, and reappear aged fifty, having wasted half your life and believing it's all someone else's fault.'

'Is this meant to be a positive, uplifting pep talk?'

'Don't put me next on your blame list.'

'I get your fucking point,' I shout at her, downing some of my wine. She squeezes my hand.

'Can I suggest some things?' I don't even bother replying because I know she's going to carry on speaking either way. 'Talk to someone about Bonnie. And your whole life if you want to. Make some sense of it all. And find a job that you actually bloody well enjoy for once, so I can stop getting those miserable messages every Sunday night.'

'That's not fair. Of course you love your job. All you do is let other people talk and then they leave and you feel like you've fixed their lives for them.'

'There's a bit more to it than that, but yes, it's rewarding. Many jobs are. Find one.'

Bonnie's parents take to the stage, her mum standing at the microphone dressed as a barbecue with a tong in each hand.

'Thank you, all of you, for once again being here to celebrate our Bonnie.' She swallows and looks to Bonnie's dad, a baguette, who's standing beside her clutching her arm. 'We're not surprised to see so many of you here, because we know how special our daughter was, but it's nice to have it confirmed.' She smiles and there's a small wave of laughter and agreement across the room. 'Now let's raise some money for a great cause while doing the thing Bonnie loved best . . . having fun.'

She raises her glass and we all lift our own. Everyone cheers.

The talent show begins, as always, with Bonnie's two younger sisters doing a dance routine. What follows is everything from terrible magicians, to mediocre singers, to one of Bonnie's colleagues from *Voice* magazine belting out a pitch-perfect rendition of a Whitney Houston number. The applause is so loud, there's no way the noise meter won't pick her out as the winner.

Georgia and I separate, talking to a few different people from school or who we know from around town. I bump into Bonnie's parents as I make my way back to the bar. All of us stop and exchange stiff smiles.

'Erin,' Bonnie's dad says, nodding at me.

'H ... hi,' I try to say, but it comes out as a whisper. My cheeks start burning and I lift my glass up, ready to press it against them.

'How are you?' Bonnie's mum asks, tilting her head. 'You see the photos?'

I nod, tears filling my eyes as I try to force a smile. There's a thickness in my throat as I speak. 'I did. Thank you.'

She glances towards the wall, and back. They're both waiting for me to say something and I want to. I need to, but I can't find the words. My throat feels too tight.

'We need to prepare the raffle,' Bonnie's dad says, resting his hand on his wife's shoulder, and giving a small smile.

'Of course.' He holds his arm out to let me pass them, and I push my way to the bar, ordering a shot to go with my wine.

I turn around to see Georgia in a long discussion with Bon Jovi. She had a crush on him at school, despite the twenty-year age gap, and it's looking worryingly like her feelings might finally be reciprocated. I make my way back to the photo wall and raise my shot glass to Bonnie, before downing it.

The night ends with the best and worst dressed prizes, which go to Big Foot and a pair of bollocks, and everyone starts to file out.

Georgia and I are staying at Mum's tonight – I agreed, mostly due to a lack of options since Dad moved to Spain with his new wife and I can't afford a hotel. When we're reunited her eyes are somewhat glassier than when I left her.

As we walk towards the exit there's a big laugh from a group of men, followed by a shout and a loud smashing sound. I hear it at the same time as I feel the sharp pain in my foot.

'Fuck,' I shout, bending down to see deep-red blood spilling out of the flesh exposed in my sandals.

'What?' Georgia asks, looking down. 'Oh Jesus.'

Someone appears beside me with a tissue, and hands it to me. Their sleeve is the deep blue velvet of the book I saw earlier. I look up, and my heart stops as I see the owner of the sleeve is James. I haven't seen him since we were fifteen. I hoped I never would again. I don't even know why he's here, when Bonnie and I hated him, but I'm even more confused as to why he's staring down at me, head tilted to one side and his pale blue eyes wide with concern.

'Are you okay? There might be some glass in there.'

He's stopped bleaching his hair, leaving it a light brown that, combined with the thick black lashes, makes his blue eyes quite piercing. They were hard to look away from in school. Now I tear my eyes from him and scrunch the tissue into a ball, throwing it back.

'I'm fine.' I spit the words out.

He catches the ball and holds his hands in the air, blinking.

'Sorry, I—'

'Oh, *now* you're sorry.'

He steps away, like I've hit him.

'Bit fucking late now, isn't it? But nice to know you finally realise that word exists.'

The lights come up, signalling the end of the night, and I jolt backwards as I take him in. His eyebrows knitted together as he runs a hand through his hair. His eyes never leave my face.

'Come on, Erin,' Georgia says, bending down to take my hand, before pulling me up.

My flesh feels like it's burning. I need to get away from him.

There's a ripple of laughter amongst the men and I frown, looking from them to my sister, bringing my hand to my mouth as I see what they're so amused by. When she bent down to help me she must have stood back up too fast, because she's now standing beside me with her pink neon dress down to her waist, and her tit-taped breasts on display.

Georgia squeezes her eyes shut and purses her lips, then, without saying a word, readjusts her outfit before taking my hand and leading me away.

When I wake up the next morning, I can hear Mum and Derek downstairs in the kitchen, talking. I roll over and pull the pillow beside me over my head.

'Oi!' Georgia yanks it back from me, and I sit bolt upright.

'Sorry. Forgot you were there.'

It's something she used to do, after Mum and Dad broke up. Often she'd find me in bed at Dad's and just climb in beside me without saying anything. It's the only happy memory I have of that time.

'Coffee?' she asks, and I frown because there's no way Georgia's going to get up and make us both a coffee. There's something suspicious going on.

'Ye—' I start to say, as she shouts over the top of me.

'Morning, Mum!'

'Morning, darling. Coffee?' comes Mum's voice from the bottom of the stairs and I roll my eyes as Georgia winks at me.

'Yes please. Erin's up too.'

I can already hear Mum walking back to the kitchen and saying something to Derek.

'Did you seriously think you could get through a whole weekend staying at Mum's house without seeing either of them?' Georgia says, folding her pillow in half and turning to face me.

'I've managed it before.'

'They were on holiday, in Greece.'

'So?'

She bites her lip. Squints. 'Why do you think James was there last night?'

I push myself up and rest my head against the wall behind me, pulling my legs up towards me. I even prefer talking about Mum to this.

'No clue, but it was disrespectful. To Bonnie, and to me.'

'It was a weird decision. I wonder if there's a part of him that—'

'Please don't do some weird therapist analysis. He probably just realised it had been years since he made my life a misery, and it was time to try again.'

'Yes. I imagine it was all about you, Erin. As per—'

'Coffee's down here,' Mum shouts, and Georgia jumps up and pulls on some leggings, before walking towards the door. She stops and waits.

'Bring mine up,' I say, looking down at my nails where the white varnish has started to chip.

'No,' she says, and opens the door. 'We're coming,' she shouts.

I let out an exaggerated cry and fling my legs out of the bed, following her.

Derek's sitting at the table and he's a third of the way through a book that came out last year. It totally divided readers between those who loved it and those who thought it was trying too hard. I was part of the adoration camp and I want to know what he thinks, but I won't ask.

Mum walks up to Georgia and hands her a mug.

The Book Swap

'Thanks, hot stuff,' Georgia says, kissing Mum on the cheek before sitting down beside Derek.

Mum hands me a mug and I take it, going to the end of the table.

Derek puts his book down and smiles at us both.

'Lovely to see it's my wonderful stepdaughters joining us this morning, not the herd of elephants I heard thundering up the stairs last night.'

He stands up, dressed in tennis whites, and pushes his glasses up his nose. Picking up the mug in front of him, he downs the contents before walking over to the cooker, where Mum's placing bacon on a grill pan.

'See you later, darling. I'll pick up the papers on the way back.'

I close my eyes, so I don't see her kiss him.

'Bye, girls,' he says, squeezing Georgia on the shoulder before walking past me and stopping.

'I think so far, it's formidable,' he says, nodding towards the book, which is still resting on the table. 'The way that she's tackled the issue of her protagonist's mental health, by setting those scenes in another world with so much abstract imagery, is very clever. Very clever, indeed.'

I try to feign disinterest even as excitement fizzes inside me. He likes it too, for all the same reasons I do. He doesn't wait for a response. He knows I won't give him one. Instead he walks out of the kitchen and down the hallway to the front door. I pretend I don't notice Mum and Georgia's eyes on me.

'Bacon sandwiches all round?' Mum asks.

'Hell yes,' Georgia replies, sipping her coffee.

My stomach betrays me by rumbling. Everyone hears it.

'Sure. Thanks,' I say, bringing my own coffee to my lips.

Mum puts the bacon under the grill and turns to rest on the oven. I glance quickly up at her. She's letting her grey grow out. Ever since I can remember, she's had the same hair colour as me, returning to the hairdressers every six weeks without fail to get the highlights put back in, and later dye and highlights. Now the colour starts above her ears, and the crown is silver. She can see me looking, and puts a hand to her hair to run her fingers through it. She's self-conscious. I look away.

'So, how was last night?' She's asking me. Looking right at me. I wait for Georgia to answer, but she doesn't.

I want to tell her the truth. I want to talk to her the way I used to, before she ruined everything. To tell her that it was devastating to only have photos of my best friend in a room where she'd normally have been the life and soul. That the only thing that makes it better is that I still see Bonnie as though she's real. I know that makes me sound mad, but Mum wouldn't make it feel that way. She'd understand. When I was younger, she always understood whatever I was feeling. Then, she cheated on Dad and she left us, and suddenly she was responsible for all the bad feelings, and I couldn't talk to her about it any more. She was gone. She tore our family apart, and, rather than stick around to help us through it, she moved out – into this house, with Derek.

'It was fine,' I say.

She keeps her eyes on me, nodding slowly.

My throat tightens and I stare down into my coffee.

'Guess who got their tits out, though? This guy,' Georgia says eventually, pointing at herself with two thumbs, unable to take it any more.

*   *   *

The Book Swap

Later, on the drive back to London, I turn the sound on the radio up every time Georgia tries to bring up Mum. This is why I hate seeing her. Why, if I can avoid it, I will. Because I just leave feeling sad, and I'm sad enough already.

When I drop Georgia in Clapham, she leans her head back into the car.

'Talk to someone. I'll pay.'

I don't tell her that I already talk to someone. Someone I'm on my way back home to chat to now. I talk to Bonnie.

Callum's sitting on the sofa with a friend, drinking beer, when I walk in. It means, in a few hours when the friend's gone, I'll be getting a knock on my door. Letting him in for the tipsy sex we seem to have fallen into over the past few months. There's minimal speaking in between, but if we're both home and one or both of us has had a drink, there's a high chance we'll end up in bed together.

'Hi,' I shout loudly over some sort of sports commentary booming out of the television. He raises his hand in the air by way of response, still dressed in the same tracksuit. I wonder if he's even got changed since I left.

I forgot about my mass clear-out and for the first time since I can remember, walking into my room doesn't fill me with dread. It actually looks surprisingly together. Tidy. Like the sort of room that *should* belong to a thirty-year-old, instead of the mess I was living in before.

I know Georgia's right and I've got to make some changes. The first thing I'm going to do is frame the card Bonnie got me. A reminder to live my life for both of us. Standing on my bed, I go to the bookshelf to find the book I keep it in. It's my other favourite possession. The copy of *To Kill a Mockingbird*, which I studied for my GCSEs and again as part of my English degree, and have kept ever since. Every page has sentences underlined, and notes in the margin. I've kept all of the books I studied, but that's the one I fell in love with. I used to read it most years, but I haven't in a long time. Maybe I will now. I always find something in it that feels like it's speaking just to me. I can't see its spine on the shelf. It's white with black imagery across it. A girl swinging on a tyre. Jagged black writing. I'd know it anywhere. I pull all of the books down onto the bed and rifle through them, my heart in my throat. Some old favourites are there, amongst my to-be-read stack: *Jane Eyre, Little Women, Wuthering Heights.* I can't see it.

'No, no, no, no, no,' I say, looking over to Bonnie's chair, but she's nowhere to be seen.

I try to remember putting all the books in the community library. I'd have seen that book, surely? There's no way I would have put it in the suitcase and given it away, except if, as established, I was temporarily insane. Possessed by a desire to rid my room of unwanted things.

Tears of frustration in my eyes, I burst out of my bedroom and pull open the front door. I run as fast I can up the road and under the bridge to the library.

I yank open the little cabinet door, scanning the spines. I can see some of the ones I donated, and that fills me with the smallest bit of hope. It's got to be here – but as I pull the front row of books out to look behind them, I know it isn't.

It's gone, and the last thing Bonnie ever gave me has gone with it.

4
James

'Excuse me, you dropped this.' A girl who looks a similar age to me chases after me at Bank Station, where I'm meeting Joel for a drink. She's holding my bank card out towards me.

'Oh wow, thank you!' I reach out and take it.

She smiles at me, pushing her wavy blond hair over one shoulder. 'That's my good deed for the day done. Now I can celebrate, with wine.'

I laugh. She's got warm brown eyes and when she smiles, she shows all her teeth. It's on the edge of my lips to suggest I take her for wine as a thank you. I stare too long at her face, trying to figure out how she'd react. A memory comes crashing into my head. Kelly, in sixth form. How she screwed her face up when I invited her to the leavers' ball, saying, 'What the hell made you think I'd want to go the ball with *you*?' I can picture the group she was with laughing as they walked away.

'Well. Thanks again,' I say, holding the card up. Maybe there's a wave of disappointment that crosses the woman's face, but maybe there isn't. I've been wrong before.

Leaving the station, I cross the road towards the pub that sits next to Joel's office. He's so busy with work these days that it's the only place it's possible for me to see him. It's a pain in the arse to get to from Penge, but once I move it'll be easier. I've decided on Brixton. It's got good transport links for when I need to get back to Frome, and every time I pass through it on my way back to Penge it feels alive. Busy. Like things are happening there. It's how I want to feel in London.

Pushing open the door to the pub, I approach the bar and order two pints. Joel will be late. He's always late. I find a table and pull my phone out, checking my work emails. The contract I signed on my return to the office offered an eye-watering commission for bringing in my own clients for training, and a base salary that I could only have dreamed of when I left university with my Business Management degree and no idea how to use it. Everyone had thought I'd choose English Literature. Even me, until I panicked that if I failed at it, it left me with no real way to make money. I could end up in a Domino's outfit, just like Dad. Instead, I googled degrees that guaranteed jobs after uni, and English didn't feature. Business Management did. I switched last minute.

Joel strides through the door looking like he's stepped out of a Hugo Boss advert, dressed in a sharp navy suit and a white shirt, cufflinks sparkling under the bright lights. Every time I see him walk through a door, it reminds me of the way he sauntered into Frome College on the first day of year twelve, just a few months after my friendship with Bonnie and Erin ended, and became the only person to speak to me. His height – which he claims is quite an accomplishment for someone half-Malaysian – meant that not only did I have a mate, but that when I was with him, the bullies didn't bother me. I was close to six foot, but skinny. Joel was six foot five, and built like an American football player. Unbeknownst to him, he became my defence. I haven't let him leave my side since.

'All right, champ,' he says, approaching the table and raising his hand for a high five. I lift my hand and slam it forward.

The Book Swap

He moves his a second before I reach him, and grins. 'Congrats on the promotion. Back in London a matter of weeks and he's got a pay rise.'

'What can I say. I learnt from the best.' I'm not even sure how much money Joel earns these days. If he told me it was seven figures, I wouldn't be surprised. I nod towards the pint opposite me and he clutches his chest, pretending to stumble backwards.

'Finally buying a round. I approve wholeheartedly of this promotion.' I roll my eyes as he takes a seat, undoing the top button of his shirt and leaning back in his chair. 'Welcome back. Gone a while this time. How's your mum?'

I nod. 'Better, thanks.' I trust Joel more than almost anyone else in the world, but I still can't find the words. Still end up saying so much less than I want to say.

'That's good. Your dad?'

'Starting to learn all about his new-found fame in the digital era.'

Joel laughs, showing a row of perfect, white teeth. 'That guy. May he never change.'

'I wouldn't mind if he did a bit.'

'You don't mean that.'

I shrug, downing some of my pint. I do mean it. It's sad to see Dad living the life he does, when he was capable of so much more.

'What about Frome? Still a shithole?' Joel can never forgive his parents for taking him out of school in Orlando and moving him to our small town. Even with all the worst times I had there, I like Frome a lot more than Joel ever could.

'You'd know if you ever came home.'

'Frome isn't my home.' Something passes across his face. He shakes his head. 'So, it was good to be back?'

'It was.' For a moment I see Erin inside the bookshop, gazing lost at the self-help section, and wonder if she's okay. 'Always is, weirdly.' I stare down at the table. 'How's work?'

He grins and picks up his pint. 'Good. Busy. Not getting too much sleep but it's all part of my plan to retire by forty, so I'll take it.' He swivels his shiny silver watch towards him. 'Heading back there after this, actually.'

That's why I gave up trying to match Joel. I haven't got the stamina. Everything in his life revolves around being in the office and making money. It's inspiring and exhausting all at once.

'You go to Bonnie's thing last month?' he asks and I shake my head in mock disgust at him calling it a 'thing'.

'You mean the memorial? The fundraiser held in loving memory of our ex-school friend?'

'*Your* ex-school friend. If you recall, by the time I arrived, you'd fucked things up so monumentally that Bonnie actually *hated* me without ever speaking to me, purely because I was mates with you.' He bites on his thumb. 'You see Erin?'

I nod.

Of course Erin was back in town for the fundraiser. I was so consumed by my own thoughts, I'd not really considered why she might be in that bookshop until I was inside the Cheese & Grain and staring into her raging face. I forgot how she can make me feel. How one look in her eyes can take me back to the different memories of school. The better times, when I had Erin and Bonnie beside me. Friends to hang out with. A short but feisty forcefield to keep me safe.

Maybe I should have been embarrassed, back then, by how we became friends, but I was always too grateful. It was year eight and by that point the bullying had gone from verbal to physical. I was carrying a tray of food towards a table at the edge of the dining hall, and felt their presence before I saw them. The hairs on the back of my neck stood up as I sensed the footsteps behind me.

'Do you know me?' one of the bullies sang, voice high-pitched. Nothing like my dad's singing voice. Then came the next line: 'I'm your Domino's delivery driver.' They had photos and videos of my dad now. They ordered pizzas to the school at lunch just to watch him turn up, and in the evenings, they spent their parents' money on food and then filmed Dad from a window as he tried to deliver it. All the videos would get shared so by the next morning I was the laughing-stock all over again.

On that day I tried to pick up speed. One of them hooked their foot around mine and sent me flying towards the ground, the contents of my tray landing with a crash against the wooden floor. It felt like the whole room burst out laughing. I was so overcome by the humiliation that I didn't realise how badly my chin was bleeding until I heard the voices of Erin and Bonnie.

'I saw what you did, you little prick,' Bonnie said, reaching out and shoving the ringleader, Marky, backwards, in the way I so often dreamed of doing. He was already walking away.

A group of girls passed me and looked down without stopping. Helena, I remember, was amongst them.

'You need to go to the nurse,' Erin said, holding her hand out to pull me up, as Bonnie crouched down and collected the mess around me, placing it back on my tray.

I stood up and took the tissue Erin held out for me, pressing it against my chin. I let them lead me to the nurse.

One of my biggest regrets in life is fucking that up by hurting Erin the way I did. Bonnie remained fiercely loyal to her, even when Erin was no longer at school with us.

'Yeah. I saw Erin,' I say now. 'Wearing some velvet outfit Mum stayed up all night making.'

'I need a pic of that immediately.' Joel holds out his hand and beckons my phone towards him. I bring one up of me and Helena and hand it over. He presses the bridge of his nose with his thumb and forefinger while he attempts to recover.

'That is something else. Still hooking up with Helena, I see?'

'Yeah.'

Joel's never approved of me and Helena. It makes sense that he wouldn't, given who she hung out with during our school years, but he doesn't know how desperate my need is to escape my family home sometimes. How bad Mum can get. There's only so many times I can hear her telling me she wants to die, before the guilt consumes me and I need to get out of there. She thinks it's fine to tell me, because it was my birth that made her this way. She was well until she had me, and then everything changed.

'Just needed some air sometimes,' I reply to Joel instead, pushing the memories away.

'But why Helena, of all people? She was one of them.'

'She wasn't quite. And anyway, she's changed since school.'

'I should bloody hope so. They made your life hell.' Joel's always there to remind me of the things I'd rather forget.

'It wasn't her specifically.'

'What do people say these days? If you're not part of the solution, you're part of the problem. Silence is violence.' He raises an eyebrow and I swallow, pushing the shame down with it.

'Hey, did you see old Mr Marsden has published a book?' Joel changes the subject and a stabbing feeling hits me in the chest. Mr Marsden was the head teacher. How the hell did he have time for that? 'Something about flying worms taking over the world. Wrote it for years, every morning before work, apparently. Mum sent me the article from the *Somerset News*. Made me think of you and that idea you had in school.'

I frown. 'What idea?'

'What idea? Are you joking? The book you were going to write. You had all these little sheets of paper you'd shove into your backpack, with lines and stuff on. It was fucking good. I always thought it would hit the bestsellers list and you'd get invited back to school one day, to talk about it.'

'The ultimate sign of success. Returning to the school stage after you've left.'

'Exactly.'

His phone vibrates and he looks down at it, eyes widening. 'Shit. I have to go. The shares I just invested in are plummeting.' The colour's draining from Joel's face and he's already on his feet, grabbing the last of his pint and downing it. 'Congrats again on the job,' he says, racing towards the door, before turning back, phone to his ear.

'It was something about all that shit with Erin. Your book idea,' he shouts, and then he's gone.

It takes me over an hour to get back to my flat, and throughout the journey I can't believe I haven't considered moving before now. It required Nathan asking me to move out for me to do something about it. Now I can't wait to be out of here. To be somewhere new, closer to town.

I go to the desk in my room and pull open the drawers, rifling through them, trying to find the notes Joel spoke about. How could I have forgotten about the idea? It was what kept me going through my last year of school. Throughout all the bad times, when I missed Erin and Bonnie horribly and hated myself for what I'd done, I'd write notes to myself about the book that would change everything for me. I even met up with the universally popular English teacher, Mr Carter, in a café after school sometimes, to discuss the idea with him. He'd left the school by then, but we kept in touch. I wouldn't let go of the dream the way my dad did, I'd keep going. I'd write a bestseller. A coming-of-age story about a boy who falls for the girl who saves him from the bullies at school, only to break both their hearts.

Finding something hard, I pull it out. It's my copy of *The Perks of Being a Wallflower*. Just seeing the cover, a showreel of memories race through my mind. It was *our* book. Mine and Erin's, and then later Bonnie's too. I flick through it, sentences jumping out at me on every page. Every single moment in this book made sense to me. To us. It felt like someone had written about our friendship. Resting it on my lap, I pull out the box that was hidden behind it. Inside is one of the scribbled notes.

His worst day becomes his best day when he looks up to see her standing over him, holding out her hand.

Somewhere along the way my dream had stopped being about writing a book, and became only about making money. I decided I would never humiliate my future son by ending up in a Domino's uniform. I managed it. I started off working in the gift shop at the Science Museum while I tried to find a job I actually wanted to do. From there I ended up creating and running training programmes within the museum. The only part of it I enjoyed was the storytelling element. I got to write the history of the Big Bang, but in a way children would understand and enjoy. I put my all into those stories. I'd stay late after work with the presenters, making sure they emphasised the right bits. That they knew where to add the comedy, to make all the children howl with laughter. Dorothy, the CEO of Big Impressions, approached me with her granddaughter directly after one of the Big Bang shows and offered me a lot of money to leave my job and join her.

I wanted to do other things too. I didn't want a job that was my life, at first, so I signed up to the writing course. If I was going to sell my soul to the world of corporate training, I'd write on the side. That was the course where I wrote the chapter that got shortlisted. My tutor suggested a master's. Or another course. He really got behind me and I started to consider it quite seriously. Then Dorothy made me a senior consultant. I was making more money than I'd ever thought possible. I was running out of spare time.

Now, here I am, taking another step up the ladder and looking for my very own flat. With that, all the dreams I once had for myself seem further behind than ever. I have to remind myself of the reasons I'm doing it. To help out Mum and Dad. To avoid any chance of being some one-hit wonder. To be financially stable for any future family I might have.

Picking up my phone, I message Dad.

James: All okay?

He replies almost immediately, despite the hour.

Dad: Great. Mum applying for part-time jobs. Look out Frome! Any idea how I download this Tick Tock thing? Apparently someone's done something hilarious with my 'Do You Know Me' video.

He follows up with a GIF of himself dancing. It's one someone's made from his *Top of the Pops* appearance. Did I mention that I wish I'd never taught him how to use his phone?

I open Facebook, my mind back at college. The place it so often goes to, even when I'd rather forget my time there. When I type in 'm' the suggestion comes up immediately. Marky Backhouse. I click on it. He's added a new profile picture since I last looked six months ago. In the films, the bullies always become overweight and bald in later life. They're low lives who go on to achieve nothing, giving the victim a sense of victory, and closure. Not Marky. He works in real estate. Lives in Dubai. His profile photo is him on a jet ski, six-pack rippling in the sunshine with a blond woman behind him, arms wrapped around his neck.

Pulling the note towards me, I read it again.

His worst day becomes his best day when he looks up to see her standing over him, holding out her hand.

I can already see the story forming in my mind.

5
Erin

All I've done since I quit my job last month is scan job adverts from bed while eating peanut butter out of the jar and making several trips to the community library in the hope my book might be returned. I've successfully avoided calls from Mum, Georgia and the office. The last one didn't leave a voicemail, which makes me think it was Charlotte calling to ambush me.

Cassie messages every day, either to check in or to tell me something that'll make me feel better.

Cassie: Reason number 806 it was a good idea to quit your job: Charlotte's just introduced Meat Free Mondays for the entire team. Sara had to throw her steak subway in the bin.

Cassie: Reason number 1014 it was a good idea to quit your job: all but one toilet is currently blocked and we're having to share the men's. What do they DO in there? I'm on a total hunger and fluid strike to avoid ever having to go there again.

Cassie: Reason number 22,314,806 it was a good idea to quit your job: it's Monday. MONDAY. And I'm at work.

I swipe out of my most recent message from her, and go onto Instagram, where my thumbs somehow lead me to the page of my most recent ex-boyfriend, Dylan. We went out for six months after I broke up with the security guard from my old flat, but we mutually ended it a few months before I quit my job. He kept whispering things like 'Let me in, Erin' and 'Where have you gone?', until that turned into angry accusations that I was 'cold' and 'guarded'. I said if that was how he felt, he deserved someone better than me, and he agreed – which I wasn't expecting.

Before I know it I'm down a rabbit hole, clicking on people who've liked his photos and guessing at which attractive blonde might be his new girlfriend. I settle on *Isabella Gordon*, who has the most nauseating bio of all. *Model. Entrepreneur. My heart belongs to my dog. If you don't love* Before Sunset *don't talk to me*.

When my phone rings again I answer without thinking. Anything to take me away from the person Dylan has deemed better than me.

'Are you out of bed?' Georgia asks, as I pull the duvet off and spring up.

After Mum's affair and everything that happened around it, I took to my bed at Dad's house in a pair of tracksuit bottoms, and didn't leave for weeks. Couldn't. No one, not even Bonnie or Georgia, could get me up.

'Very much so.'

'As of . . .?'

'How can I help you?'

'By telling me you have some sort of plan.'

I slump back down.

'I'm looking, but all the jobs I'm qualified for are ones I don't want to do. I think I need a change of career.'

I can hear her heels clicking against the pavement. Georgia's always on the move when she calls me.

The Book Swap

'You can do that, but what's your starting point? Job Centre? Gumtree? Shop windows?'

'The last one. Going to go for a walk now,' I say, looking down at my tracksuit bottoms and T-shirt, which I also slept in. 'I'll take something to tide me over while I figure it out.'

'The pub next door to me needs a kitchen assistant. Urgently. It was written in pen and stuck to the window, so they're probably desperate enough to take you.'

'Well then, perfect.'

She sighs and I know she's squeezing her eyes shut to try and not shout at me. She's done it since we were kids.

'I just want you to be happy,' she says, and her voice breaks.

I frown and pull my phone from my ear to stare at it.

'Are you crying?'

'It's been too long now, Erin.' She's definitely crying. 'I can't help you if you won't help yourself, so please try. I've got to go.'

Before I can say anything, she's gone, and Isabella Gordon's naked model shot reappears, her face looking even more smug than it did before I answered.

An hour later I send Georgia a photo from a shop window I've just passed. Just Stitch in East Dulwich is looking for a sales assistant. No experience necessary. Apply within. The shop's full of beautiful fabrics and carousels of different threads.

I can see your tracksuit bottoms in the window reflection, is all Georgia replies.

I wander to the café opposite and order a coffee. I could apply for that job. With my background in fashion I might even get it. But then what? My mind wanders to Bonnie's postcard. About living my dream. About being happy, the way Georgia just told me to be.

I know I'm not, yet. I've gone against everything I promised Bonnie, but it's not because I'm trying to let her down. She should still be alive and she isn't, so every day without her doesn't seem worth living. Not when she had everything ahead of her and she didn't get to do any of it. She knew exactly what she wanted to do with her career. Where she wanted to live. What clothes she wanted to wear. She knew what her boundaries were. When to cut someone off, or to say no. She respected herself and stood up for what she believed in. The only decision I've made recently wasn't even thought out. I've got no plan. No idea where I'm going in life. How come I'm the one still living?

Bonnie would tell me off for this attitude. It's the opposite of what she wanted for me. If she were in charge of my life right now, she'd put her arm around me so the bright-coloured sleeve of whatever in-season jacket she was wearing hovered in my eyeline, and she'd march me into that shop. She'd say, 'My friend here is the best person for this job and you should hire her immediately or, in the words of Julia Roberts in *Pretty Woman*, it's a big mistake. Big. Huge!'

My life would be so much easier if Bonnie were in charge of it. She lived a life without fear. Had no shame about who she was or what she believed in. She would never have let a woman like Charlotte control her for a day, let alone seven years. The second she wasn't enjoying it, she'd have left and she'd have made sure everyone knew whose fault it was. In fact, quitting my job is the most Bonnie thing I've ever done, and while I'm wallowing in it now, it felt good. It was the right thing to do. Maybe if I start living my life the way Bonnie would have, I'll actually do something with it.

Tapping my foot, I stare at the glass jar of sugar cubes in the centre of the table. Given my current circumstances it

The Book Swap

isn't the worst idea I've ever had. Erin would never walk into that shop and apply for that job, but Bonnie wouldn't think twice about it. Her attitude was to live in the moment and to go for what you want.

Downing my coffee, I stand up, cross the road and walk into Just Stitch.

'Could I take a job application, please?' I say to the woman behind the counter, whose face lights up at the question.

I don't go as far as Bonnie would have on the speech front. I'm pretty sure that's only something someone else can say about you.

When I walk out of the shop, application in hand, I kiss it and smile. My first official Bonnie act is done, and my heart is pounding with excitement. It doesn't feel like I'm living my life, it feels like I'm living hers, and there's something so much better about that.

On the walk home, I take a detour past the community library.

It's the only exercise I've been getting up until now. I've walked here, once, twice, sometimes three times a day, just in case. The book's never there. I know in my heart that it's never coming back, but Bonnie wouldn't give up and so I can't either.

As I reach it, I take in the plaque. I've never noticed the words beneath it before. The dedication to Eileen on the brass plate that sits under the slanted roof of the cabinet, sandwiched between handwritten signs saying, 'Take one, leave one' and 'Everyone welcome here'. I'm staring at the plaque because I can't bring myself to look inside yet. If I don't look, I get to hold onto the tiniest bit of hope that my book could be there. The small print in Eileen's memory reads, 'Her life – and language – were as colourful as this library.'

I look down at what I'm wearing. Grey tracksuit bottoms and a stained off-white T-shirt. The same clothes I've been in since I woke up without a job to go to. I get why Callum does it. Life is so much easier when you don't have to decide what to wear every day. But now I feel both guilty and ashamed. I've been living in greyscale instead of in colour.

The sandpaper-like roof of the cabinet is bubbling up in places. The pale yellow paint's starting to chip, having withstood a few winters. I wonder whether this is what Eileen, purple-rinse set in place with rollers and surrounded by books and love, requested on her deathbed. *Get me . . . a fucking . . . painted library.*

My eyes land on the spine of a book I can see through the glass, and my heart jumps with such force that I can feel it in my throat. It's black and white. It's placed right in the centre, as though it's been waiting for me.

Flinging open the door, I reach in, hands shaking. I can't believe it but it's back. *To Kill a Mockingbird.* My copy with its yellow pages, the first few of them sellotaped into place from my many hours of poring over the words. The inside of the front page is covered in my handwriting, breaking down the themes and characters alongside page references, and home-made tabs are taped in, marking the most important moments. There's no chance Bonnie's note will still be in here – but I flick though the pages anyway, and tears immediately fill my eyes because there, tucked in the centre, amongst pages full of my notes from school, is the card.

Thank you, thank you, thank you.

If anyone could see me now, they'd wonder what's going on. A woman, dressed in what looks like pyjamas, on her knees at the community library, clutching a postcard to her

The Book Swap

chest as she cries freely. But I don't care. She's come back to me. Bonnie's come back.

I'm still holding the book open on the page it was placed in and, wiping my eyes, I catch sight of some red pen scribbled beneath the black. The line about never killing a mockingbird is underlined and to the side in black biro I've written, *Protect the vulnerable – this is why Atticus takes Tom's case.*

Underneath it someone has written in neat, separate letters, so different to my own scrawls, *Is writing in the margins of a book a crime as bad as killing a mockingbird?*

I freeze, running my eyes back and forth across the two sentences. It's almost like they're teasing me or telling me off, but they've written in the book too, so it ends up making me laugh instead.

I swallow, flicking back and forward through the pages. The notes are everywhere. Red words amongst my black ones, breaking up comments that were only ever intended for me. I'm too grateful that they've returned the book with the postcard still intact to be embarrassed or cross, but I definitely feel exposed. At one point I've written, *Such a dreamboat* by a line about Atticus to remind myself of the moment I totally fell for him, and the other reader has obviously seen it, because written beneath it is:

We're agreed Atticus is the best parent in any fiction book ever. Right? If I'm ever a dad, he's my role model.

So the person writing back is a man. Mystery Man.

He's questioned things I've written. Laughed at observations I've made with a, *LOL – so true!* or a, *Ha! Love it.* Towards the end he's written:

I never realised how powerful this line about courage was until I saw your comment.
Got me right in the gut. Thank you.

Heat rushes to my cheeks at that one. It feels like my biggest achievement in days, to have taught someone something about a book I love so much. He's done the same though. The words, *Is this sad or is it kind of beautiful?* written in the last few pages make me see that moment from a whole new – arguably more positive – perspective.

Shaking my head, I flick to the back page to return Bonnie's postcard. Written at the bottom, beneath the words 'The End', it says, *Meet me in* Great Expectations*?*

Somewhere behind me a child shrieks, flinging themselves through the tunnel on a scooter, and I reread the words, a smile spreading across my face. Does that mean what I think it does? I start scanning the shelves, searching for the words. Can I be right? Has he put a book back? I don't know who this 'me' is, but I want to find out. He's made me happy for the first time all week, and in a long time, and maybe reading *Great Expectations* again through his eyes will be like reading it for the first time.

Inside the cabinet I land on the spine. A thick cream one with the word 'DICKENS' in capitals. There's the book, waiting for me, and the feeling is similar to receiving a wrapped present on my birthday. I pull it out and open it on a random page. The red pen has circled a line about life being made of many partings welded together and it feels like a sign somehow. Like whoever this man is, he understands the *exact* place I'm at in my life. Mourning the partings, and terrified of the future. It's like the space beside it is waiting for my response.

'Thanks, Eileen,' I whisper to the community library, taking the book. 'I promise to change into something colourful for you.'

I have a fleeting thought of going out to buy the cabinet a new roof. Giving it a lick of paint. Repaying it for what it's just given back to me.

Standing up, I walk away, and it's as though I'm carrying an opinionated but insightful new friend with me. A parting, welded together by the book in my hands.

6

James

An estate agent meets me outside a house on the edge of Ruskin Park, which is a short walk from Brixton. It's the eighth one I'm viewing and I haven't even seen a photo. Apparently 'demand is so high, we don't have to bother'.

This guy, who looks like he should still be in school with his baby face and fast-talking enthusiasm, leads me up the stairs to a third-floor flat and opens the door to reveal a space that is, for once, freshly painted and a decent size. The kitchen and living room are one open-plan area and beside them is the bathroom, but it's the bedroom that decides it for me.

There's a desk under the window, which looks out over the park. My chest rises at the sight of it. It's so full of hope, if you ignore the Gary Lineker book sitting on top of it.

The appliances look newish, it doesn't stink of damp and it's got a view. The whole place feels hopeful. It feels like a new start.

'How can I get it?' I ask, and the agent's face lights up.

'Transfer me the deposit, right now, and it's yours.'

He's baby-faced, but sharp. He reminds me of Joel, who stepped so effortlessly from his last day in college to a job in the City, as though he'd always been there.

After shaking the agent's hand, I follow my map back to Brixton, unable to believe that within a week this will be my new commute. It leads me down a street on the opposite side of the park, where I step over boxes of toys left on the pavement 'free to a good home' and pass a cat that eyes me suspiciously as I walk too close to the wall it's sitting on. I approach a bridge, slowing as a little community book shelf sitting to the left of it catches my eye. It's the only piece of colour in an otherwise dark corner of London, sitting beside discarded rubbish and in front of a flower bed that's home to every empty crisp packet consumed within a ten-mile radius. I've seen these libraries before but never stopped at one. Makes sense I should try the one in my new neighbourhood.

There's a decent selection. Loads I'd buy if I were at a bookshop, but I'd feel bad taking too many. I'm reading the back of that one everyone raved about last year, where the world's ending, when someone approaches behind me.

'Just popping this back,' says a woman in her fifties, and she pushes the book onto the shelf directly in front of me, before walking away.

To Kill a Mockingbird. I pull it out, turning it over in my hands as I take in how totally destroyed it is. If I were still in touch with the ex-girlfriend who always commented on how badly I treated books, I'd send her a photo. There are pages taped in. Markers on different pages. Sentences highlighted or underlined. My heart starts racing just looking at it. This is what I used to do. I lived for English lessons. They were one of the main reasons I kept going to school, even when I knew the bullies were waiting. Our teacher, Mr Carter, was so good you couldn't help but fall in love with whatever you were reading in his classes. He created a fascination in me for words and their meaning. Within moments of stepping into his classroom, I was transported to another world. When Mr Carter left, just before our GCSEs, it totally shook me. Would I be able to continue loving the subject as much without him?

The Book Swap

That's why, the next year, I came up with the book idea Joel mentioned in order to keep that love alive. I haven't been able to stop thinking about the idea since I found some of my old notes about it – and while holding Harper Lee's masterpiece in my hands, all of it rushes through me again. How intensely I wanted to create through my teenage heartbreak. Even back then, I knew it was going to change the course of my life, to have hurt and been hurt like that. I wanted to remember it all, so I could share my story.

I open up the book, scanning the notes. They're insightful, and in some places touching. It's almost as though the woman behind me has gifted me an education in what makes good writing.

'Excuse me,' I shout after her, and she turns to look at me. 'Are you sure it's okay if I take this?'

'Wasn't mine,' she says. 'I found it in there a while ago and thought I'd give it a go, but all the notes were too distracting. Couldn't get on with it at all.'

She walks off and I look back down at the book, flicking to the opening page, where all the useful quotations are written out, with the page number beside them. This has to be a sign. Maybe I don't have time to do anything creative right now, or to take classes outside of my job, but I have time for this. Reading what someone else has discovered. Learning from the greats. The classics.

A postcard drops onto the floor at my feet and I pick it up. *Don't forget to make all your dreams come true!* it says, and I flinch. How did they know? I turn it over, smiling at Pooh and Piglet, then tuck it gently inside.

'Cheers, Eileen,' I say towards the library, tapping it on its dishevelled roof before carrying my new book back towards the tube.

I stay up way later than usual reading it. I enjoy the commentary on the depth of Harper Lee's characters, or the clarity between good and bad people, but it's the other messages that I keep on reading for. I know, from about halfway through, that it's a woman. She refers to Atticus as 'dreamboat' and wants to change her name to Scout. There's so much personality within her comments that after a while it isn't enough to just read them. I find a pen in a different colour and, for my own amusement, I start replying.

Bit heavy! Time for a tea break at this point, I think, it says.

Nice way to avoid the pain of a good book, I reply. *I see you're an avoidance reader. Does tea taste better with tears in it?*

There is no other book ever written that has better names for its characters. Atticus! Jem! Scout! Finch! Everyone else should just GIVE UP! she writes.

I laugh, and write below in red.

You genuinely mean that because of the names, no one should ever write a book ever again? If that happened, you'd miss out on crackers like ... Jack Reacher?

It doesn't just feel like I'm replying to someone's notes, it somehow feels like I'm talking to a mate. A mate I don't always agree with – she seems pretty hard on most of the characters – but someone I can discuss writing with. I didn't realise how much I've missed it. I used to try with Elliot, but he and his husband had normally seen the film rather than read the book. And Joel would let me talk about it but I could always tell he wasn't interested. He was just trying, because of me. With this person, with Margins Girl, it feels like we could talk for hours.

On the train to work in the morning, I open Notes on my phone and, without thinking too much about it, I start typing. It isn't a continuation of my original chapter that got shortlisted, it's my story from college. The one I always wanted to write. I decide to go with it.

It's everything Joel reminded me of, combined with everything that has happened since. I have people in my life I need to apologise to, and this somehow feels like the beginning of that. It isn't a letter, but it's close. By the time I look up, I've passed Highbury & Islington, my stop, and have sailed on through two more. For the first time since I can remember, I didn't even notice my commute.

When I make it to the office, there's a load of emails in my inbox. A flash of one of the comments in *To Kill a Mockingbird* appears in my mind. Margins Girl had written something about how Atticus just got even sexier for caring about his passion, more than the money. For taking a case he knew he'd lose, because it was the right thing to do. I'd like to think that if I actually cared about the job I did, I'd do the same. I'd choose the right thing over money every time.

At lunch, I go to the local bookshop and stop at the classics section. I run my eyes along the spines. What if, by chance, Margins Girl uses the library regularly? Could I repay her somehow for what she seems to have ignited in me?

Great Expectations. We did a vote on whether to study this book in our English class. We could choose Dickens or *Emma* by Jane Austen. The class was mostly girls, and they went with *Emma*. I always told myself I'd read Dickens in my own time. Mr Carter absolutely raved about him. About how well he could tell a story.

Pulling the book out, I turn it over, opening it on a random page. I don't know if I'll be able to make notes the way Margins Girl has, but perhaps I could try. My eyes lock onto a sentence I can't seem to move on from: 'Life is made of ever so many partings welded together.' My mind passes through Elliot and Mum and Dad, even Helena, before landing on the person I miss most of all. The person I shouldn't miss. For the last few months of her life, taking both of us by surprise, she became my best friend. The biggest secret I've ever had to keep, because if it ever got back to Erin it would destroy her. The person I'd long for one more parting with – because it would mean she was still here. That I'd see her again. My mind lands on Bonnie.

7

Erin

The office never called again, but my last month's pay arrived in my account, followed by a P45 to my email in November, sent by HR. Charlotte's given up and I don't know whether to be proud or disappointed.

'Definitely proud,' Bonnie says one evening, staring down at her nails, which are painted turquoise, a sleek, black, bobbed wig on her head. 'You think she'd have let them pay you if she wasn't secretly in awe of what you did?'

'They *did* pay me up to the end of the month, and I left way before that.'

'Exactly!' She grins at me, pride written all over her face, and, as always, my heart lurches at the sight of her smile. 'You walked out on your awful boss *and* you've managed to get your sister off your back by taking that job – which, by the way, I *knew* you would get.'

'I know you did. That's why I applied,' I say, taking a sip of wine.

'That's my girl. What did Cassie say about it?' Bonnie raises one perfectly plucked eyebrow. Her eyebrows always looked like she'd just been to a brow bar, until the day they disappeared. That night she took me to the pub and gave me the card, they were back, drawn perfectly by hand.

'I haven't told her,' I say. 'I wanted to tell you.'

Bonnie leans back in the chair and folds her arms.

'You should tell her. Invite her out for a celebratory drink.'

'We didn't really hang out much outside the office,' I say, picking up a jumper from my bed and folding it, before placing it in the wardrobe.

'One way to change that.'

I shrug. 'I've been thinking . . .' I try to think of the words to admit the truth to Bonnie about something that's been distracting me. This is the longest I've been without some kind of boyfriend in years, and I don't like the feel of it. 'I might get in touch with Dylan. I haven't met anyone else since him, and—'

Bonnie slams her hand into her forehead, running her long, slender fingers down her face.

'You're just bored.'

I down some more wine. 'I think I'm lonely.'

The moment I say it out loud, I realise it's true. It's the same feeling I have every time I don't have someone in my life – and yet when I do have them, I'm in a constant state of panic. It was always that way with Dylan: *Who's that messaging him? Why isn't he replying? Is he late or is he not turning up at all?*

As if he can read my mind, Callum appears in my doorway. He went into work today, so instead of the usual red tracksuit, he's sporting navy jeans, a T-shirt that says, 'The sea isn't real – it's so big it makes no sense' and a beanie. He's got a silver snake chain bracelet around his wrist, and his eyes are slightly bloodshot, like he went for a pint or six after work.

He hasn't done this in a while. Not since the night after Bonnie's memorial. I thought maybe he was seeing someone, and was growing panicked as to what that meant for me. What would happen to this arrangement I've come to rely on if he met someone?

The Book Swap

He doesn't bother with small talk, or pretending like there's any other reason that he's appeared in my bedroom close to midnight.

'I saw your light was on,' he says, and I move to put my wine on my bedside table, which is the only sign he needs in response.

He reaches for my hips, pulling me towards him. I can smell the night on him. The pints of lager, followed by something stronger. A whisky or two.

'I thought about this all the way home,' he says, pressing his lips hard against mine.

I reach up, pushing the beanie off his head. His lips move down my neck, his hands pushing their way up the inside of my T-shirt.

He moans when he finds I'm not wearing a bra, and bites me, gently, on the flesh between my neck and my collarbone.

He doesn't ask where I've gone or for me to let him in, the way Dylan used to. He doesn't care about any of that. All he wants is this moment with me, and that's something I know I can give.

I turn, quickly, to check Bonnie's chair, and when I know for sure that she isn't there I pull Callum onto the bed.

In the morning he goes to work and I've got three hours before my trial shift starts at Just Stitch. The woman I'd spoken to in the shop called to offer me a paid afternoon and everything in me wanted to say no, but Bonnie would have said yes, so that's what I did. Reaching for my shelf, I bring down *Great Expectations*. I've been trying to take my time reading it because it's the thing that's been giving me the most joy. Mystery Man's notes are sparser than my own.

Sometimes whole chapters go by without a comment, but when there is one, I leap on it, hungry for more. It isn't just comments, it's an insight into his life and I think it's for my benefit.

He's highlighted one quote, which says, 'The broken heart. You think you will die, but you just keep living, day after day after terrible day.' Beside it he's written:

I mean, I do agree, Dickens – but I'd also like to add that the days get better. Might we want to include a little bit of hope in here, for the optimists?

I involuntarily run my finger over the words that have made me laugh out loud. I hope he's right, because so far every day without Bonnie has felt terrible.

Later, beside a line about Pip being washed by his sister, he's written:

Unfortunate love from a caregiver. If ever I complain about my mum, please remind me that she at least didn't aggressively bathe me.

I think back to one of my favourite memories of my own mum, who used to take me out of the bath and roll me up in a towel, then pretend to post me through the side of the bath as though I were a letter. The memory fills me with an unwelcome sense of guilt. I've ignored every call she's made since I came back to London. When I'm there, I feel like I lose all the power. That all the indifference I feel when I'm apart from her disappears, and I'm back to being the child who loved her. Who thought she was the best person in the world.

The Book Swap

I'm not even reading the book any more, I'm just flicking through it and trying to find more comments. On one page, there's a quote he's underlined, and the margin beside it is covered in writing. The quote reads: 'Pause you who read this, and think for a moment of the long chair of iron or gold, of thorns or flowers, that would never have bound you, but for the formation of the first link on one memorable day.'

Finding your book in the library was a first link for me. These margins don't give me the space I need to explain how significant it was. It lit a fire in me. It reminded me of who I am. It woke me ... argh, damn these thin margins! ... up. I don't know who you are, but thank you. Thank you, kind stranger, for forming this link I so desperately needed. I will never, ever forget that moment. It is memorable, and therefore, so are you.

I read it over and over, until my eyes blur. If I hadn't put the book in the library by accident, this would never have happened. For whatever reason, it was meant to be.

I reach the part of the book I always remember. Pip returns to Miss Havisham's house and learns that his childhood love, Estella, is to marry someone else. She tells him not to worry. That she'll be out of his thoughts in a week. 'Out of my thoughts! You are part of my existence, part of myself. You have been in every line I have ever read ...' he says in response, and continues on with a speech that, to me, encapsulates the sheer terror involved in loving someone. That by loving them, you absorb them. Mystery Man's just drawn a box around the passage, with the words 'Holy shit!!' And it's such an accurate summary, I laugh. Does he think the same as me? That the very thought of being so wrapped up in someone else is a reason never to love someone at all?

I know exactly what book I'm giving him in return. Just wait until he sees what Catherine says about Heathcliff. I've even got a copy on my shelf, notes included. Like *Great Expectations*, *Wuthering Heights* is about how all-encompassing love can be. I read each of them with a combination of envy and terror. Is it brilliant to love in that way, or does it destroy you?

Whereas before I was embarrassed that a stranger saw my innermost thoughts on a book, now he's shared his own I don't mind. I *more* than don't mind. I'm excited to share the next book with him. Maybe he'll see it differently. Maybe, given he's clearly an optimist, he can reassure me that the love within these books isn't as scary as it seems.

Pulling a pen from the drawer beside my bed, I turn to the back page of *Great Expectations* and write in my neatest handwriting *Meet me in* Wuthering Heights?

I call Georgia on the walk home from my trial afternoon at Just Stitch. 'Job number two is no more,' I say, smiling as I wait for a car to actually stop on Lordship Lane and let me cross.

'You *quit*? On your first day?'

'An optimist would call it my last day,' I say, my brain immediately landing on Mystery Man.

'Definitely a pessimist.'

'Whatever. It wasn't for me. She did this creepy role-play where she left the shop and then came back in as a totally different character, with a different voice and a scarf around her head, and started firing questions at me. It was ... *so* weird. Anyway, I'm not hanging around in jobs that don't serve me any more. I'm channelling Bonnie.'

Georgia sighs. 'What does channelling Bonnie consist of, exactly?'

The Book Swap

'It's my new mantra. What Would Bonnie Do?'

'Oh God. Are you going to start wearing one of those bracelets like that group of girls who fancied our religious studies teacher used to at my school? Except instead of a J for Jesus, it'll say WWBD?'

'Bollocks. Should have stolen some thread and beads before I quit, and I could have made one.'

'That's the spirit. Stealing *and* quitting. Really make Bonnie proud.'

I walk up the hill towards the big Sainsbury's, swerving around a woman in a woolly hat and scarf charging towards me at quite some speed, pushing a buggy with two babies in.

'She honestly would be proud of this. I'm finding out what I don't want to do. Moving closer towards what I do.'

'Which is?'

'Not PR, and not selling silk.'

There's a pause.

'That's it? That's all you've got? You're good at so many things, you must have some idea?'

'Did you just . . . pay me a compliment?' My joke doesn't land the way it should because my breath is coming in short gasps as I take on the hill towards the flat. Thank God I turned down that job, there's no way I could have done this commute home every day.

'I was channelling what Bonnie would say. Okay, wait . . .' Georgia disappears for a moment, her voice sounding further away when she next speaks.

'Would you describe yourself as talkative, steady, kind, quiet or assertive – and you can only choose one?'

'Is this an online quiz?'

'Just answer.'

'What the hell does *steady* mean?'

'Erin.'

'Fine, kind.'

'I put steady. Okay next . . .'

Georgia proceeds to lead me through a string of questions as I struggle to make my way home, each more patronising than the last. When pushed I'm apparently thoughtful, with good writing skills, a laid-back attitude and slow to change. The majority of those Georgia answers for me.

'Okay, drumroll please . . .'

I'm minutes from home by this point. I've been answering her questions for the majority of the walk.

'According to this you should be . . . Ha!'

'Oh God, what?'

'Well you might need to change that letter on your bracelet back to a J, because it's suggesting you become part of the clergy.'

'Right. Well thank you for wasting minutes of my precious time.'

'Wait . . . I just chose the funniest. There were others . . . Artist. Event planner?'

'Goodbye, Georgia.'

'Teacher?'

I hang up just as I reach the library, and pull both books out of my bag, slotting them in.

8

James

The CEO Dorothy insisted on opening champagne after work to celebrate my win with At One Pharma, which means I'm late home to meet Helena.

She messaged last week to say she was in London for work for a few days and it would be 'fun' to stay at mine, if I was up for it. It was only after I had agreed that she said she 'may as well' stay for the weekend. She's never visited me here before and something about the idea of it puts me on edge. Outside of Frome, our lives are so separate, and I thought we were both keeping it that way on purpose.

She's sitting on the doorstep with a wheelie suitcase beside her, rubbing her hands to keep warm, when I burst out of the park.

'Sorry, sorry, sorry,' I shout, running towards her.

My proposal at work has been taken on as an official part of the training, which means I'm being paid for that on top of the commission. This month's salary will be more than I'd normally earn in half a year. A few weeks ago, that would have been the best news imaginable, but I keep thinking about Atticus in *To Kill a Mockingbird*. How much Margins Girl respects him. Would she respect me and my work, or think I've sold my soul to an industry that profits off other people's poor mental or physical health? *Don't answer that.*

'All good,' Helena says. 'This isn't the worst view to wait in front of. Is it a common thing to run around the park without your top on in mid-winter?'

'Apparently so. Normally just men.' I smile and she laughs and stands up, kissing me on the cheek.

'How was the journey?' I ask.

'Actually, really easy. No wonder everyone's moving to Frome! You can basically commute to London from there.'

'Let's not forget that it's run by Independents *and* has the tourist attraction of the carpenter who works topless with his doors open.'

'Well, obviously that's the main reason.'

We smile at each other and I keep waiting for it. That feeling I get when I've missed someone.

I unlock the front door and grab her bag, carrying it in.

'I can't believe I'm here,' she says, following me up the stairs. We're filling the silences we've never really had to fill before.

I put her suitcase in my room, staring, as I always do, at the few things I've bought for my desk. The notebook, the fountain pen and a book by Stephen King that every author on Twitter seemed to recommend.

'Nice,' Helena says, taking in the view. She walks towards my desk and picks up the Stephen King book. '*On Writing*. What's this for?' She turns towards me, frowning.

I shrug. 'Just research. For work.'

On Saturday night, we meet Joel for food at a pub called The Crooked Well in Camberwell. He and Helena weren't exactly friendly at school, but I've invited him along because spending a Saturday night just the two of us feels too intimate somehow. I've claimed he's keen to catch up with her. I'm pretty sure Helena's seen through it, but she remains polite throughout.

The Book Swap

'Long time, no see,' she says, kissing Joel on the cheek.

He takes the seat opposite us and I start sweating a bit at the neck of my jumper. Does bringing Helena out for dinner with my best mate imply a level of commitment, when I was trying to do the opposite?

'How's life in good old Frome?' Joel asks, raising his hand to the barman and circling the three of us, then clutching at his throat like he's dying from thirst. This draws a laugh from the waiter, who approaches the table.

Of course Joel doesn't just dislike Helena for who she was at school. He dislikes that she stayed put in a town that he resented living in.

'Bottle of champagne please, mate,' he says with his brightest smile when the waiter races over.

'Lush as ever,' Helena says, looking across at me and grinning. 'I forgot to say I saw your mum and dad at The Griffin having a proper romantic meal. This band started playing and they were dancing together, right up at the front.'

'The definition of true love, those two,' Joel says and it's like a breeze of cold air washes over me. If that's love, I don't want it. It's why I've never had it.

Helena saw one good moment sandwiched between calling doctors, quitting jobs, delivering pizzas and losing out on a record deal. One moment where they were equals, having a meal together. Where Dad wasn't a carer, unable to focus on anything except his wife.

I look over for the waiter bringing our drinks. My throat feels tight. He takes longer than seems possible to pop the cork and fill our glasses. I down most of mine in one, as Joel takes a sip, frowning over at me.

'It was so lovely,' Helena says. 'I hope I'm that way at their age.'

She doesn't say 'we'. She might not even mean with me, but I reach back out for my glass, drinking the rest down. I feel awful. Really awful, for having said yes to her staying, because this is a mistake. I can't do it. I already know I can't.

'All right there, mate?' Joel asks, smiling across at me.

'All good,' I say back, and Helena reaches across and squeezes my hand, briefly, before letting it go.

'James tells me you're sickeningly successful and will definitely be picking up the bill tonight, so I'll be going for the fillet steak,' Helena says, reaching for her own glass, a smile playing on her lips.

I freeze, unsure how Joel will take it, but he leans back on his chair and tips his head back, laughing so loud it bounces around the room. *That's all this is, James. All it has to be. Just a fun evening with friends. Stop overthinking it.*

We finish the champagne over dinner and move on to a red with the steak, which costs the amount I'd spend on an entire meal if it were just the two of us. Joel's avoiding any school chat, but fires questions at Helena about her job and what she likes to do in her free time. It feels less like a catch-up and more of an interrogation, but she handles it with good grace and throws just as many questions back. Soon they're laughing and that isn't really what I intended. I don't need for this to go well. For them to become mates.

'Who were your best friends at school, again?' I ask Helena, picking up the glass of red and drinking some.

It's a question I've never asked before because I haven't wanted to be reminded of it, but now I do. Now I think it might be the only way out of this.

Helena frowns, but answers. 'Jess, Benita, Felix, Zoe ... Zoe's the only one I properly still speak to.'

There it was. Just one name, sandwiched between others, that I knew I'd hear. Felix. Felix who was fine at first. Who actually used to speak to me in the first couple of years of school. Three years later, he was one of them – and being reminded that Helena could have actually liked him confirms what I've always known. That having anything more serious with her would be impossible.

'Anyone fancy dessert?' Joel asks. He's got a tiny spot of red wine on the collar of his crisp white shirt. If I tell him, I know for a fact it'll go straight in the bin when he gets home, and he'll buy another. He probably has twenty, brand-new, still in their packets, in his walk-in wardrobe waiting for him. If I'm selling my soul to earn money, then so is Joel. The thing is that he doesn't care – and I'm starting to think maybe I do.

'All good for dessert, thanks.'

'Same. Although ... I should take a look, just in case,' Helena says.

In the morning, I walk Helena back towards the train station. It's like the further we get from my flat, the more I can breathe.

'How come you don't come back to Frome much when your mum's well?' she asks suddenly, as we walk through the park.

'It's just the only way it works for me,' I say, too hungover to be dishonest. 'I have to split my life in two. Frome and London. When Mum's ill, I'm there. When she's well, I'm here.'

'Why do you have to split it though? Who says?'

A group of people walk past, laughing at some silly voice one of them is doing.

'I do.' I bend down for a stick and pick it up, throwing it ahead of me. 'To be happy in one place, I can't think about the other.'

'Wouldn't you say that just makes you unhappy in both?'

I look across at her, smiling. Maybe she's right, but if I admit that, nothing makes sense any more. 'I'd say it makes me happier.'

'Because you don't have to commit to anything, full term. That's why.'

She nudges me on the shoulder with her own and then walks slightly ahead of me, before turning back.

When we reach the bridge, she stops at the library.

'Oh I love these,' she says, crouching down and opening the doors. 'Might get a book for my journey back.'

I stand, watching her. My chest tightens. The library isn't hers. It's mine. And Eileen's. And Margins Girl's.

'Ooooh. *Wuthering Heights* would be a cheery read!'

I can't help looking around, in case the deliverer of my books is approaching the library right now. My heart does a tiny one-two boxing motion at the thought, which is mad. She could be fifteen. Or fifty. She could be a man who says 'dreamboat'. It's stupid to even care about seeing her, but I want to. To say thank you, for everything she's ignited in me.

'Christ, someone's totally destroyed this copy of *Great Expectations*. There's writing all over it.'

I jump down so fast I crack my knee into Helena's back.

'Ouch!' she cries, reaching her hand behind her to rub where I made contact.

'Sorry,' I say, but I stretch past and pull out the Dickens book, flicking straight to the back. Has she done it? I'd understand if not. Maybe it was just me who got something from the notes. But I can already see replies from Margins Girl, on the last page. I scan it until I reach the bottom, warmth spreading through my body as I see the final note, written in much neater handwriting than that which is scrawled across the pages of the book. *Meet me in* Wuthering Heights? I can't believe it. She's replied. Reaching back into the library, I find the book, where Helena just returned it.

She looks across at me now, frowning.

'Might learn something,' I say, shrugging. 'Sorry. Is your back okay?'

The rest of the walk to Brixton is spent as though there's a ticking time bomb in my hand. All I want is to safely deposit Helena at the tube and run home, for a date with Margins Girl, and Emily Brontë.

'You've perked up, suddenly,' Helena says, as I laugh at some comment she's made, my mind on the handwriting I saw in response to mine.

'Mind if we pop into Pret so I can get a sandwich for the train?'

'I think there's one at the station too?'

She's already walked in, reaching for my hand to pull me in behind her. I throw my head back, sighing. I've never known time to stretch as much as it does now.

'Club sandwich?' I suggest, picking it up. She leans forward to read the ingredients, then shrugs, putting it back.

'Their wraps are good,' I add.

'Might get a salad,' she says, scanning the bottom row of the fridge. I open up *Great Expectations* on a random page, scanning it for a response in different writing.

You're SO right, it says, and I smile, trying to see what they're agreeing with.

'Can you order me an oat latte?'

★ ★ ★

It's two in the afternoon by the time I get home and sit down on the sofa, my heart racing.

I read all the replies, savouring them.

It's like you know what I'm going through, the writing says, beneath the passage about partings being welded together. That was the bit that made me choose this book. It resonated with Margins Girl too. Not only that, but she's revealed something personal about herself. There are more:

You've successfully made me feel bad about the silent treatment I'm currently giving my mum ...

And by a line about success and failure, she's written, *At least she has some success thrown in!* Which makes me laugh and feel sad, all at once. Who is this person who feels made up entirely of failures and partings?

There's one bit underlined that I hadn't commented on. The part where Miss Havisham explains what real love is. 'It is blind devotion, unquestioning self-humiliation, utter submission, trust and belief against yourself and against the whole world, giving up your whole heart and soul to the smiter.' *And that's why we don't do it!* she's written.

Greedily, I pick up *Wuthering Heights*. All I want to do is flick through it, and read the book through her comments, rather than Brontë's words, but I know that isn't the unspoken agreement we've made. I skip through the editor's preface, and start on Chapter One, throwing myself into 1801.

By Chapter Three I've got my notebook from my desk, jotting down observations about the writing that might help my own novel. The structure. Any comments from the margins that I want to remember. I shake my head at the skill of the writing. The thought that's gone into how to tell the story. I reply in the margins, marvelling not only at the writing, but how astute Margins Girl has been about the book. A few of the comments are in a different coloured pen, perhaps added at a different time.

Imagine loving someone so much that you'd die without them? To be fair, I'd have made a similar speech about my guinea pig, Hazel, once upon a time. When she died, Mum helped me bury her in the garden and I insisted on lying beside her in a sleeping bag, so she didn't get lonely. Think I lasted ten minutes, but the sentiment was there.

Don't you think people got to wear much better clothes back then? I think my life would be complete, were it still acceptable to wear a bonnet.

She only shut herself away in a room for five days? I managed a whole month once. It actually gets easier, the longer you go without leaving. I don't know why I'm telling you this. I'd cross it out, but for some reason, scribbling out words in the margins is unacceptable, whereas writing is fine. Argh. I'm making myself sound weirder by the second, aren't I?!

Quite the opposite, I think as I read that last comment.

I run, I reply. *I try to run every day because otherwise I worry I might get into my bed and never leave it again. Forcing yourself out every day – that's the harder choice, don't you think?*

I scan my eyes over the words, unable to believe I've written them. I've never told anyone that. How I run because I'm so afraid that if I don't, I'll end up like Mum.

9

Erin

'Honestly, everyone's quoting you,' Cassie says, leaning forward across the table, a grin on her face. 'Your "I. Fucking. Quit" line. Charlotte's even taken the bell away. Now we all have to clap instead – and yes, that's as cringe as it sounds.' She rolls her eyes and pours us both another large glass of pale rosé.

We're indoors at the Hope & Anchor pub in Brixton, escaping the bitter December cold.

'Well if I die, at least I've made some kind of mark on the world,' I say, smiling before I realise what I've said. Shaking my head, I make a silent apology to Bonnie.

'Oh, definitely. Also, and I hate to admit it, she's being a tiny bit nicer. Nothing crazy. Anyone who's started after you left is still terrified of her, but it's like this secret club. For those of us that were in that room . . . we see the change.'

'Right. So I sacrificed my entire career so that you could all have a lovely working environment while I'm unemployed?'

Cassie scrunches up her face. 'Afraid so. But now you get to choose a whole new career that doesn't take over your life.' She reaches out and grabs my hand. 'Oh, it's so nice to see you. I wasn't sure if . . .' She stops. Shrugs.

'What?'

'I just didn't know if I'd see you again. I never knew if it was just . . . you know . . . a work thing.'

Shame rushes to my cheeks, making them hot. How must I have behaved around her, to make her feel that way? It isn't something I'd tell Cassie, but Bonnie and Georgia aside, she's probably my closest friend. What does it mean if a person you think you're close to doesn't even know if you want to stay in touch with them or not?

'It wasn't just a work thing,' I say. 'Sorry. I ... my best friend died three years ago, and I've just, I guess, struggled a bit.' I pick up my wine and down some, so I don't think too much about what I've just said out loud. I never told anyone at work about Bonnie. Largely because I knew that if Charlotte knew, she'd find a way to use it against me.

'Oh my God.' Cassie jumps up and runs around to my side of the table, pulling me towards her for a hug. 'Why didn't you tell me? I'm so sorry.'

'I was just trying to keep work separate.' As I say the words I understand why Cassie felt the way she did. I was treating her as part of that separate life.

'What happened?'

'Cancer. She was the same age as me.'

'God that's so sad,' Cassie says as she returns to her seat. 'Tell me about her.' She reaches across and tops up my wine, her eyes wide as she watches me.

'She was amazing,' I say, stumbling for words. I don't talk *about* Bonnie, I talk *to* Bonnie. This is new for me. The past tense stuff. 'She had this incredible throaty laugh that filled the room. She always had the best advice. Was such a fierce cheerleader of women, and her friends especially. She was loyal. Funny. She'd never let you get away with saying something that wasn't true. You know, like the little lies we tell ourselves to excuse something? She saw right through them.' Smiling, I realise how good it feels to remember her this way.

To share her with someone. With Cassie. 'Thank you,' I say. 'I don't often talk about her. Not like that.'

Cassie smiles back at me. 'Sounds like she was one of the great loves of your life.'

She gets it. 'She is. She was. Speaking of which...' I raise my eyebrows and Cassie rolls her eyes as she lets out a groan.

'I'm not giving up hope. I refuse to,' she says.

'But...?'

'But the last date I had was, well, standard for me. His profile said he was looking for a relationship, and in the messages before we met, he kept saying how important honesty was.'

'Uhoh.'

'So I told him the truth over our first drink. That I wasn't fucking about. I wanted to meet someone. I wanted the rest of my life to begin with the next person I got into a relationship with, and if that scared him then it wasn't going to work.'

A shiver passes over my body, just at hearing those words. How can Cassie know that? How can she be so sure?

I swallow some wine, and nod for her to continue.

'He assured me it didn't freak him out. He even kissed me over the second drink. Then at the end of the night, when I wouldn't go home with him, he told me I was never going to meet someone by being so full-on and stomped off. Not heard from him since.'

'I'm so sorry, Cassie. You don't deserve that.'

'Don't be sorry,' she says, swallowing down some wine. 'It's why I do it. You really get to find out who the arseholes are. Unfortunately, so far, it's been all of them, but there has to be someone out there who wants the same thing I do.'

'There will be,' I say. 'And we'll find them.'

She smiles across at me. The table next to us cheer as their long-awaited pizzas finally arrive. 'I just wish it didn't all have to be online. Why can't I just meet someone in the flesh? Have a real connection with someone, rather than having to force it through words all the time.'

'It'll happen,' I say. 'It's my worst fear, but if you want it to happen, it will.'

By the time I stumble home I want the exact opposite of what Cassie's looking for. I walk straight to Callum's door and knock on it.

'Who are you fucking?' Georgia asks, when she calls midmorning as I'm pushing down the top of the cafetière and scanning jobs on Nextdoor – officially the most depressing neighbourhood website on the internet.

The question seems to come from out of nowhere, but I know why she's asking. She messaged me last night and I didn't reply. I was with Callum, and in the cold light of day the thought fills me with shame. She wouldn't approve. I know she wouldn't.

'What? No one.'

My phone starts beeping as Georgia requests a video. I accept.

'Look me in the eyes and say that again.'

'No one,' I say, bringing my eyes as close to the camera as they'll get.

'I *knew* it! No time to find a job, but enough time to shag the sorrow away.'

'I'm not shagging the sorrow away.'

'So you are shagging?'

'Are you jealous?'

She laughs, looking away from the camera and back again.

The Book Swap

'Oh my God. *You're* shagging too!' I point my finger at her through the screen.

'Let's save this for dinner next week. In the meantime, I need an up-to-date account of your work prospects.'

I push so hard on the top of the cafetière that hot coffee starts spraying out over the edge, down the sideboard and onto my jeans.

'Fuck. Ouch! I'll call you back.'

I drop the phone and reach up for the closest thing in sight to clear up the mess, spying a tea towel and whipping it towards me. I don't realise I must have put the cafetière back on the tea towel until it comes flying towards me, shattering on the floor as it lands. I stare at the ground, watching as glass and coffee spray out across it.

Why does everything feel so hard at the moment? I can't even make a drink right. I put my head in my hands and let out a loud groan.

'You know, you wouldn't cry over things like spilled coffee if you had a therapist to cry to about the real stuff,' Georgia shouts from the phone, where she was supposed to have hung up.

'Fine. Fucking book me one then,' I shout back, sticking my middle finger up at her even though she can't see.

She doesn't say bye, but I know she's hung up. She'll already be on the phone to one of her therapist friends, getting my first session booked in.

'Is that coffee coming, or what?' Callum shouts from his room. I completely forgot he was still here. I guess he's taking the day off again, which means I have the perfect distraction from my own mind.

I walk back into his room, my jeans still lying on the kitchen floor.

* * *

That afternoon, having applied for a couple of jobs on Nextdoor – including a woman locally who needs some help walking her dog and another who wants some handwritten notes typed up – I make my way to the library. It seems to have taken ages for Mystery Man to return the book this time, and I'm starting to wonder whether he's given up. I don't like how low my heart sinks at the thought of it. That last book came at a moment when I really needed it. Now, I feel that way again. Bonnie's heavy on my mind and I've got no idea what I'm doing with Callum. I've got no job and I feel like everything in my life is just completely fucked. I'm trying to think the way Bonnie would, but sometimes it's hard. If I get too down, I can't seem to get into her mindset. I don't have the positivity.

Approaching the library, I reach the bridge just as a man's walking away. I've never seen anyone here before. I know they must come, because new books appear and get taken, but I've let myself think it's just me and my Mystery Man. I take in the back of the man walking away. Could he have just left something? Could he be the person I'm writing to?

Pulling open the door, I see my copy of *Wuthering Heights* sitting there. With shaking hands, I take it out and turn straight to the back page. When I see the handwriting, my heart leaps to my throat. *Meet me in* Mansfield Park? I smile. It's an interesting choice. Instead of *Pride and Prejudice,* or *Sense and Sensibility,* or *Emma,* he's gone for the Jane Austen novel that divided the public, and I like him more for it. I can see the indent of more writing through the page, and turn it over. There are questions laid out, under the heading 'Questions for Mystery Book Club'. They're for me.

I slam it shut, desperate to get home to the comfort of my own bedroom so I can take it all in. Instead, I turn back to the shelves to pick up my Austen. I can't see it where the other book was. Can't see it on the other shelves either. Pulling them out, I start littering the pavement with every book from the library.

'Sorry, Eileen. I'll put them back,' I say, scanning the titles, but it isn't any of them.

You fucking well better, I imagine Eileen replying.

I replace them all, picking up my book. What are the chances that . . .?

Closing the door, I turn around and start running in the direction of the man I just saw walk away.

'Excuse me,' I shout, chasing his navy waterproof mac up the road and around the corner, away from the park. 'Sorry, excuse me, sir,' I shout, as though I'm in an Austen novel myself.

The man stops and turns around, just outside a little café on the corner of Coldharbour Lane.

My heart's pounding. Now I've reached him, I don't know how to ask for the book back without sounding weird and possessive.

He's in his fifties, with piercing grey eyes, his head tilted to one side as he frowns at me.

'Sorry, did you just take a book from the library?' I say, struggling for breath. 'I know this is really weird, I just . . .'

He puts his hand into the large pocket of his coat, and pulls it out. An involuntary shriek comes from my mouth as I take in the cover.

'This is going to sound even weirder,' I say as he holds it. 'But please could I have that? It's part of a . . . an *exchange* I'm involved in and I was meant to pick it up earlier, but I just—'

'No,' he says, forcing a smile that doesn't reach his eyes. 'Sorry, but my daughter is studying Austen and she's really struggling with English. These notes look helpful.'

He turns to walk away. 'Please,' I shout, frozen to the spot. 'I don't know how to explain, but I need it. I'll ... I'll teach her about the book myself. Those notes you think look so helpful – they're mine.' I hold out my copy of *Wuthering Heights* and flick through it, showing him the notes I've actually written. 'I have a degree in English Literature from Durham Uni. Admittedly not a first. Have to have *some* fun, am I right? Anyway ... I can help with her studies. I live locally and ...' The man is staring at me, his head on one side again. Possibly wondering whether he wants someone who must seem mildly unhinged teaching his daughter.

He reaches into the back pocket of his trousers, and pulls out his wallet, opening it.

'Fine,' he says, removing a business card and placing it on top of the book, before handing both to me. 'Email me and we'll set it up.'

He turns and crosses the road briskly, disappearing into Loughborough Junction station, leaving me with two books, his card and a triumphant flush to my cheeks, the likes of which I haven't felt in years.

'I think you've now officially lost it,' says a voice in my head, and this time I'm not sure whether it's Bonnie, or me.

10

James

'Oi, oi!' Joel shouts, as he jogs towards me, a tight top stretching across his chest muscles, his hands in big grey gloves.

He's wearing one of those woolly hats with headphones in the ears and he lifts it up when he reaches me, leaning forward to stretch out his front leg and run his hands down it towards the icy ground.

'All set, running partner?' he asks, rising back up.

He's met me in Ruskin Park after declaring we need to bring back the running club we started in sixth form. The only time I ever felt safe was when I was out on my bike with Elliot, or running with Joel. The bullies left me alone when we were together, and seeing him in front of me now gives me that same feeling.

'Depends if you can keep up,' I say and he grins, racing away from me, towards the outskirts of the park.

'Helena's good fun,' he says, when I reach him. 'She—'

'I'm going to end it,' I interrupt before he can say anything more.

He shakes his head, running past the corner I'd normally turn down, and continuing up the hill instead. The hill of the ultimate thigh burn.

'She reckons I don't commit to anything.'

He laughs. 'And you intend to prove her wrong by ... ending it?'

I can't talk for a minute as we reach the steepest section of the park, both of us slowing to a near walk as we round the corner. My throat is burning and my legs are throbbing.

I haven't told Joel about the book swap and I'm not going to. I can't think how to explain it without it sounding weird, but it's on my mind so much, I'm glad he's brought up Helena, so I don't just blurt it out. Ever since *Wuthering Heights* I keep thinking about the comments. About the person behind them and how, through Margins Girl's gentle observations on each book, and the insight she's given me into her life, she's brought a new part of me alive. She's brought my love of fiction alive, and that's got me writing again.

'Is it true?' Joel asks, interrupting my thoughts. 'That you don't commit to stuff?'

It's the same question I've asked myself, and I've already come up with the answer.

'No,' I say. 'There's loads of stuff I commit to.'

'Go on,' Joel says, as the ground flattens out and we increase our speed slightly with longer strides.

'Mum,' I say. It feels good to vocalise it. 'Whenever she needs me, I'm there. I drive her to her appointments. I organise her medication. Do the laundry, clean the house, bring her healthy food so she'll eat something other than fried chicken.'

'You do,' Joel replies, loyally.

'I committed to Jenny for a bit, at uni. Not for long, it has to be said, but a few months counts.'

Joel's slightly ahead of me now. He doesn't reply.

Taking a deep breath of the freshest London air I'll probably get all day, my mind shifts to Bonnie.

'Bonnie,' I shout.

She's the reason I try to enjoy these deep breaths – to take notice of them, because she told me, towards the end, how lucky I was to just breathe in and out with ease. How much people take that for granted. How much we take everything for granted.

'I was committed to her.'

He's too far ahead of me now, unable to commit himself to the word 'partner' when it comes to running.

I showed up to take Bonnie to chemo, every time that she needed me, ever since that first time.

Mum had been having a particularly bad day, in the depths of several really bad days, in the early spring, almost four years ago. 'I don't want to be here any more, James. I can't cope,' she said, squeezing my hand. 'Make it stop. Make it stop, or I will.'

'It will get better, Mum,' I said. 'It always does. Just a few more days and the medication will kick in.'

'I don't want to rely on that. I just want it all to end. If I had a knife right now, I'd do it, James. I would.'

I nodded. I ran downstairs, grabbing a bag. I filled it with every single knife I could find in the whole house. Anything that looked remotely like a knife and could be used as a weapon. I found Dad in the sitting room, putting Mum's pills into a day-by-day pill box. I told him to get upstairs and then I packed all of the knives onto the back seat of the car, and I started driving.

I didn't know where I was going. Helena was at work, and I needed to go anywhere that wasn't home. Dad could cover it for a minute. He was good at that bit. He didn't feel like it was his fault, the way I did.

Rounding the corner on Bath Street, I saw her. Bonnie. At the bus stop outside Westway cinema. She was always so distinctive, even at school, with her halo of natural hair and her brightly coloured clothes. When I realised she was crying, I pulled into the side road, parking right on the zebra crossing, and I ran to her without even thinking. Her pain distracted me from my own, and in that moment, it was all that I wanted.

'Are you okay?' I asked, before remembering she wasn't Bonnie from school. She was adult Bonnie, who hated me as much as Erin did. Who hadn't so much as spoken to me since before our GCSEs.

'Depends who's asking,' she said. 'If it's you, then I'm fine.'

She looked up at the electronic timetable. The next bus going anywhere was in nineteen minutes.

'Fuck,' she muttered, wiping her eyes.

'Do you need a lift? My car's right there.' I pointed over to it, just as a traffic warden pulled out his electronic device. 'Shit.'

I ran back, shouting as I did. 'Sorry. I'm moving it right now.'

'You can't park it here,' he said, as though that wasn't obvious.

'Sorry. I know. I'll move it.'

I jumped in and drove up to the end of the road. When I turned it round and started driving back the other way, there she was, standing on the corner with her thumb sticking out of the end of a jacket that was so vivid, it looked like the technicoloured dream coat.

'I'm doing this because I have no choice,' she said, climbing in. 'I can't walk that far, and Mum and Dad couldn't get today off work.'

'Understood.' I nodded and turned out onto the main road, driving back past the cinema. 'Where are we going?'

'Bath Royal United Hospital,' she said, her voice steady.

'The old RUH,' I replied in a voice that sounded a lot like my dad's, and she looked across at me, shaking her head.

'Well, if I wasn't sure it was James from school, I am now.'

'If you weren't sure, it was pretty risky climbing into my car,' I said, smiling as I settled into the chat. 'I don't think most men who pull over at the sight of a woman hitchhiking and fling open their passenger door should be trusted.'

'I think anyone can probably be trusted more than you,' she replied, and my face turned so hot I had to put the window down.

We drove the rest of the way in silence. When I dropped her off, I asked if she wanted me to wait. She said no. I did anyway. It was that or going home, and I was too afraid of Mum. When Bonnie walked back out and saw me still sitting there, she shook her head and laughed, pulling open the door.

'You're a sucker for punishment,' she said, climbing in and turning slowly around to face the back of the car, before looking at me. 'Did you just go out and buy that bag of knives, or was it there all along? And please know that I'm not sure which answer is going to make me feel better.'

I swung my head back to look at the knives. I'd completely forgotten they were there. Jumping out of the car, I opened the boot and ran around to the back seat, grabbing the bag and locking it away out of sight.

'You can have the long answer that will take us all the way home,' I said, climbing back into the driving seat. 'Or the short answer.'

'James,' she said, smiling sleepily across at me. 'We were in English together. All those infamous long essays you used to hand in. You're a storyteller. Tell me the story.'

Bonnie rested her head back against the seat and closed her eyes, and I told her. I told her everything she missed knowing about Mum after we stopped speaking at school. I'm not even sure she was awake for all of it, but it didn't matter. God, it felt so good to tell someone. Someone who knew me, but didn't. Someone who had even cared about me, once. I parked up back at her house, lightly touching her on the shoulder.

'If Erin asks, I haven't seen you,' she said, climbing out before leaning through the window. 'But thanks. Minus the knives. And James?'

'Yes.'

'I had no idea about your mum. I mean I knew enough, from what you said at school, but it was a lot harder for you than you ever made it sound. That, plus Marky and his mates . . . You've become a much nicer man than you could have been.'

Bonnie walked inside and I watched her disappear through the dark green front door. I watched her disappear through that door so many times after that, but that time is the one I remember.

Now, as I turn up the path towards the top of the park that leads me back to my flat – to see Joel standing and waiting for me without so much as a glistening forehead – I pull out my phone. I need to message Helena, and I need to do it now.

It isn't that I won't commit – I just won't commit to her, and the sooner I tell her that, the better.

On my lunch break at work, I walk to the local bookshop and head straight to the classics section. *Wuthering Heights* was such a gift to me, and I want to repay Margins Girl with something. I don't have the knowledge that she does. It feels like both books she's given me have been carefully selected, but that can't be true. I picked up *To Kill a Mockingbird* by accident. It wasn't meant for me, it was meant for anyone. She couldn't know that *Wuthering Heights* would make me feel more energised and inspired than I have in years. Perhaps, without me knowing, my books are helping her as much as hers are helping me.

Scanning through the titles in front of me, I keep coming back to the same one. A book I've heard of but never read. I reach up for it, and as I did last time, I open it to a random page, laughing and shaking my head at the first words I read. A character in the book is talking about London: 'We do not look in great cities for our best morality.' My mind immediately jumps to Joel and his job, then to me and mine. I pay for the book, wander to the little green that splits Angel in two, and sit on a bench there.

Pulling *Wuthering Heights* and a pen out of my bag, I open it to the final page of text. Beneath the words 'The End' I write *Meet me in* Mansfield Park? As I go to close it, I can't help but notice the four blank pages that sit before the final page listing other books by the same publisher. An idea appears and I immediately dismiss it. I'm probably reading way too much into this exchange. Maybe for Margins Girl, it's just a silly thing that entertains her for a second during the day. She might be put off, even horrified, by me doing something more.

Closing the book, I stand up, then sit straight back down.

If we'd met in person there's no *way* I'd do it, but she's a stranger. A stranger that I've already found myself able to trust, somehow. She replies to my notes. She's open and honest. She's funny. I don't feel like she's judging me. I have a feeling that maybe, in her own way, she's as lonely as I am.

I could try it. It's not like she has to reply, but the notes in the margin don't feel like enough now. I want more.

Before I can question myself further, I start writing. Once I've started, I have to do it.

Questions for Mystery Book Club, I write, underlining my title at the top of the blank page.

1. Why do you write in the margins?

It's an easy question. Or *I* would find it easy, anyway, but perhaps there's more than one answer. My heart starts its familiar one-two boxing motion just at the thought of what she'll say back to me. It's surprising me, how much I've come to love our exchange.

I tap the biro against my lip, staring towards the tree in the centre of the tiny green. Different to the trees in Ruskin Park, but my mind drifts back to my conversation with Joel during our run this morning, as I write out the next question.

2. Is it better to listen to other people's opinions of you, or your own opinion of yourself?

Helena thinks I can't commit. I don't agree. I don't know which of us is right.

3. Why Wuthering Heights*?*

I want to know why she chose it. The subject matter isn't exactly uplifting. My hand keeps moving as I think about the person on the other side of this exchange.

4. Do you ever feel like this is the only thing in life you have to look forward to?

The Book Swap

Jesus, James. Way to scare someone away. I can't tear the page out because it's on the back of the final words of the book and I don't dare ruin the aesthetic by scribbling a big black line through question four. It shows I've thought about it too hard. But it just came out – it felt like I could ask. Like maybe Margins Girl was somewhere out there checking the library every day, the way I do when I'm waiting. That these books and the notes within them might be something that brings her joy too. I've no idea, and I want to know. I can't finish with that question, though. Way too intense. Need one more question to lighten the mood.

5. Do you use the word 'dreamboat' often?

Putting the book back in my bag before I can do any more damage, I open up *Mansfield Park* and scan the introduction.

While Fanny Price may not be everyone's first choice when it comes to Austen's heroines, I decide I'm going to make her mine. I'm going to use her to study what makes a popular or unpopular heroine. I need to know that because somehow, every time I sit down to write my book, it seems to be about this mystery woman who I can't get out of my head. She's become the main character in my story. She's opinionated and funny, open and honest. She studies things and asks big questions. She calls people out, even though she's not totally sure of who she is. She holds a mirror up to the male hero and shows him where he's gone wrong in life. What mistakes he's made, and what he needs to do to make up for them.

She's becoming more and more like the girl in the margins, with every response I get.

11

Erin

The last place I thought I'd find myself on a Sunday afternoon is in the bedroom of a fifteen-year-old girl who seemingly has quite an unhealthy obsession with Harry Styles. There isn't an inch of wall that isn't covered with pictures of the famous pop star. Even the tiny cracks where you might see the paint break through are instead plastered with miniature images of his face. It's actually quite impressive, and if she'd only put as much dedication into her learning, I imagine she'd be an A-grade student. The centrepiece, which all other pictures sit around, is a framed photo of Harry – a couple of years younger, his face pressed up against the face of my new student's with an expression of ecstasy so pure that I hope he never does anything to let her down. Then I see the photo next to it, which shows him with his arm around someone in a floral skirt. The woman's face has been completely destroyed with biro.

It was only as I turned up at this house two streets over from my own and rang the bell that I realised I could have just never emailed him. I've already safely secured the book from the girl's father now, and the chances of me ever seeing him again were minimal. Yet here I was, having booked myself in for a Sunday lesson a few weekends after Christmas. I don't know how to teach English. I've never done a day's teaching in my life. Hopefully I'll do this one session and be terrible, and they won't invite me back. The girl's father did at least say that, as well as letting me keep the copy of *Mansfield Park* that was intended for me, he would also pay me fifty pounds, which is so needed I didn't even try to protest. My savings and final month's pay have seen me through the last few months, but now I need a salary again and I've no idea where to start. Cash-in-hand jobs are helpful, but not enough to sustain a London lifestyle, even when all you're doing is reading free books and very occasionally shagging your housemate.

My student, Savannah, greets me with a shy smile from the desk in the corner of her room. She's lost the chubby cheeks from the framed photo and her long brown hair looks as though it's been straightened with a very hot iron. Bonnie and I went through that phase. I remember her howling with laughter as she laid my hair under a tea towel on an ironing board, while shouting, 'I don't think this is working.' She laughed even harder when I stood back up and my hair was half waves, half so straight the ends looked sharp enough to slice a loaf of bread.

'I hear you might need a bit of help with English?' I say to Savannah, as though her dad approached me, rather than that I hunted him down like a maniac. 'Your dad tells me you didn't get the grade you wanted in your mocks?'

'I didn't get the grade *he* wanted,' she says.

'You don't agree?'

'I just don't like it. It isn't my subject.'

I try to still my features so she doesn't see the dagger as it lands in my heart. How can anyone not enjoy English? I used to live for English classes back in school. I had such a good teacher. I already loved reading, but Mr Carter helped me to understand books. To respect them. To fall in love with the language the authors used. To get right to the heart of what they were trying to say. Shuddering, I push the memories away.

'More into maths,' she explains. 'My dream is to be the girl on *Countdown*.'

So it's true. We have no hope of finding a cure for cancer when even the smartest kids want to use their intelligence for fame. To stand there as the woman hired to wow men by proving we can be smart *and* beautiful.

'I've already got my own TikTok. I go live and people give me these mad sums to do. The videos get thousands of views sometimes.'

'Wow.' I nod, aware that we only have an hour and all the questions I want to ask her about this are in no way related to the reason I'm here. 'You know Jane Austen, who wrote that book,' I say, pointing to the copy of *Pride and Prejudice* sitting on her desk, as I struggle for a way to bring the conversation back to English. 'She made so much money through her writing, she didn't even have to marry unless she wanted to.'

It's tenuous, but Savannah scrunches her nose. 'If I can't marry Harry, I'm never getting married,' she says, with such conviction that I think I believe her.

'And that's your decision to make in the age we live in. But back when Jane Austen was alive, you sort of had to get married. Hardly any women could make their own money. *Countdown* didn't exist back then, unfortunately,' I say, trying to keep any amusement out of my voice. Who am I to mock someone else's dream? At least she has one.

'That sucks.' She glances at the book and back. 'So, what if they didn't want to get married? Then what?'

'They might be forced to, or set up with someone. They might be cut off from their family if they didn't. It's sort of . . .

what the book's about,' I say, carefully, trying to limit the enthusiasm in my voice. 'Read the very first line.'

She frowns as though I'm trying to trick her and picks up the book, opening it at Chapter One, her jaw dropping as she reads the words about single men and what they want.

'How did you know that, without even looking?'

I laugh. 'The same way you know how to do maths. It interests me.'

She keeps reading, without me even telling her to. There's a lightness in my chest at the sight of her. Her eyes skimming the words and a slight smile forming on her face. It's the same feeling I get when Mystery Man replies to my comments in the margins. When he says that I've taught him something about what he's reading.

'And what do you think Elizabeth Bennet's role is in the book?' I ask Savannah.

She shrugs, looking up. 'She's there to shine a light on how no one should have to marry for anything but love,' I explain.

Savannah nods.

'This is the kind of stuff they're going to ask you in your GCSE exam this summer. I promise I can help it to make sense, if you'll let me? We've got four months.'

A small smile spreads across her face, making her look younger than when she's confused or concentrating.

'You're accepting the challenge?'

'I think it might be the best challenge I've ever been offered,' I say, smiling back.

She shrugs, but I see through it. It's the shrug I'd give Mum after she left Dad, and would ask if she could pick me up from school. My shoulders saying I'm not bothered, while the rest of my body is screaming at me internally that I am.

'Fine then.' She picks up the book and places it in my hands, and I swallow down the lump in my throat.

By the time we're done with our first session, I don't think I've given Savannah any particular love of reading, or English, but I've at least helped her to understand what the story's about. The humour in it. The comments the author was trying to make on society at that time. I've made her fall, just a little bit, for Jane Austen, and in one session, that's so much more than I could have hoped for. I think about my old job. It never made me feel like this. It didn't give me the sense of achievement that now dances in my chest, nor did it give me the smile on my face. I want to do it again. I want that rush of helping someone to make sense of something I love.

When I get home, I send a message to Cassie – it's the type of thing I'd usually have sent to Bonnie.

Erin: I taught a Harry Styles-obsessed teen about Jane Austen today. Her room was COVERED in photos. How's your Sunday?

She starts replying immediately, and just seeing that she's typing causes heat to radiate in my chest.

Cassie: Erm . . . JEL. If it were appropriate for me to have Hazza posters all over my walls, believe me I would. You wouldn't like him though. Apparently he doesn't read books.

Erin: How do you even know that?

Cassie: I'd love to say it's because of my youngest sister, but I'm afraid I still read Heat Magazine. It was a fact he gave about himself.

Erin: Well I won't be passing that on to Savannah or she'll never read again.

Georgia insisted on booking me in for a therapy session on the day we've already arranged to have dinner at a little brasserie in Covent Garden. When I approach the table she's there, her dark hair in a sleek bob, looking a lot shinier than usual. No doubt she's just discovered some new serum she's about to force me to buy on my non-existent salary.

'Big day,' she says, standing up to hug me.

'Are we talking about my ten *a.m.* with Philippa, or my four *p.m.* dog walking appointment?'

'Both.'

'Well, the dog was so fat it nearly pulled me into a puddle of mud, and metaphorically it was a similar experience with the therapist.'

Georgia laughs. 'That actually sounds positive. You must have discussed something important.'

I call over the waiter, not ready to answer. Dinner's going to be on Georgia and I intend to make the most of it.

'Can we get a bottle of your finest champagne please?'

'No thanks,' Georgia says, as I knew she would. I just wanted to wind her up. 'I'll have a sparkling water.'

'And your largest glass of dry rosé for me then, please.' I hand him back the wine menu.

'What happened to ordering Deliveroo at your place?'

Flinching, I shake my jacket off. 'More fun to abuse your bank account at a fancy restaurant,' I reply, as she watches me. Her mouth falls open as I watch her slowly trying to piece together why we're not meeting at my place, and that the reason might be to do with Callum.

'Do *not* tell me—'

'Philippa thinks I have deep-rooted abandonment issues,' I blurt out. If there's a chance she's guessed about Callum, I need to get her off the scent, and the only way to do that is to get her on to her favourite subject. People's psyches, especially mine. '*And* I made her laugh, which I'm pretty sure is basically illegal.'

'We're allowed to laugh. We're not robots.'

'If you say so.'

I reach up for my wine from the waiter, and bring it directly to my mouth.

'And what did you learn about this abandonment?'

'That it started with Mum, the day she walked out of our house and left us,' I say, lifting my chin. 'And continued into adult life, and now I just expect people to leave.' I think about how panicked I got that Mystery Man might not leave me another book. It didn't feel healthy at the time. Perhaps that's all part of it.

'And did she say what impact that might have?'

'Clearly you already know the answer.'

Georgia shakes her head. 'Not necessarily. There's no one right answer, just someone's point of view.'

'She said maybe I struggle to let people in now, in case they hurt me. Which is *so* textbook,' I reply, downing some more wine.

I don't add that it did feel good, to have a label for my responses to things. To understand a little bit more about why I might behave the way I do.

'I'm proud of you. For doing it,' Georgia says. 'I guess just . . .' She stops. Shakes her head.

'What?'

'I promised myself I would not get involved with your therapy.' She holds her hands up, leaning back. 'I'm just glad you're talking to someone. That's all I've wanted.'

'But . . .?'

She tries not to say it, but she can't resist. She's never been able to stop herself giving her opinion. It's a reason to either love her or hate her, depending what the opinion is.

'But just try to look at your own behaviour as well as other people's. It's sometimes more helpful to think about how you can improve, than to focus on what other people have done wrong. You can't change them, but you *can* change you.'

'Great!' I throw down my napkin. 'So I'm even failing therapy.'

She stares up to the ceiling.

'You're doing brilliantly. That's all I'm going to say. I'll leave it there. Let's order.'

She calls the waiter over, going straight for the steak tartare and then, stumbling, she switches to the fish pie. I order a chicken escalope, eyes on Georgia.

'What's going on with you? A fish pie?'

She's never been able to order anything but steak tartare when it's on the menu. I wait for her to make some joke, or say something offensive as she usually would, but instead she throws her head forward and bursts into tears.

'God, I'm sure it won't be that bad,' I say, looking around me. 'That woman over there's eating it, and she's smiling.'

'I'm not crying about the fucking pie.' Georgia rubs her fingers under her eyes and looks at me for confirmation she's fixed her make-up. I shake my head and reach across with my fine linen napkin, clearing the black smudges away.

What could she *possibly* be crying about? Georgia has a job she loves and a fancy one-bed flat all to herself. She has more than enough money, and men on tap whenever she feels like it. There's only one reason I can come up with.

'Are you dying? Because if you've waited until now to tell me, *especially* after what I just mentioned about abandonment issues, I will *never* forgive you.'

'Nice,' she says. 'If I was dying, that would be just the right response.'

I look down at the table.

'I'm fucking well pregnant, aren't I?' she says so loudly the woman with the fish pie flings her head up.

A laugh escapes me before I can stop it. 'What? No you're not. How? With who?'

I think back to the last conversations I've had with her. Georgia mentioned she'd hooked up with someone a few months ago, but it hadn't come up again. I just assumed it was over. That she couldn't fit it in. She works with her clients, checks in on me and ensures she's favourite daughter to both parents. That's all she has time for.

'How am I only just finding out about this? A baby? Whose baby? How pregnant are you?'

'God it's just so ... *embarrassing*,' she says. 'To get accidentally knocked up at my age.'

'Answer the questions before I scream them.'

'Seven weeks. And, Rishi,' she replies, as my jaw drops.

'Rishi? Therapist Rishi? Dishy Rishi who you insisted I go to for counselling, only for him to sit there in total silence. *That* Rishi?'

'Yes.'

'You're having a baby with *my therapist?*'

'Your ex-therapist. My colleague.'

'Fucking hell. That is going to be one intense baby.' I look at her. It's as though the whole restaurant has fallen silent for this conversation. 'But a brilliant one. Obviously. It also explains why your hair looks so fabulous,' I add. 'And it isn't embarrassing. A *lot* of things are, including chasing a grown man down the street and stealing his book, but getting pregnant is not.' I reach across and take her hand. Georgia's never needed me before. I don't know what I'm doing. 'Are you . . . okay?' I ask.

'Obviously not.' I haven't seen her like this before. Tears spring to my own eyes.

'You know this is the kind of news most people cry happy tears about,' I say, smiling.

'Most people aren't single in their thirties when they find out, and are therefore less likely to be accused of tricking the person they're having casual sex with into impregnating them.'

'He didn't?' My mouth flies open.

'No. I haven't told him. But if I do, he will.'

I shrug. Maybe she's right. Men do tend to think the moment we hit our late twenties we're after one thing. Callum even made a joke about it the other night. He said I better not be trying to have his curly haired babies. I laughed it off at the time, but thinking back, he definitely meant it.

'Are you . . . do you want it?'

She nods, then shakes her head, then nods again.

'I don't know.'

She drinks some sparkling water, then reaches across and takes a gulp of my wine. 'Wait . . . did you say you chased a grown man down the street?'

And so, to distract her, and because I can't seem to fight the urge to talk about it, I tell her about Mystery Man. She listens, mouth open, smiling, and when I'm finished she leans forward.

'Please God, write back and ask for his number, so you can stop fucking your awful housemate.'

12

James

On my way to work, I open up the library doors, scanning the shelves for the familiar spine of *Mansfield Park*. Once again, it isn't there. Once again, I've totally misread the situation and freaked her out by coming on too strong. I got greedy, wanting more than just her notes in the margins, and if I'd just left it, maybe I'd have another book back by now.

Walking away, I cross under the bridge towards Brixton tube station and call Dad.

'All okay?' I ask when he picks up after a few too many rings.

'Great thanks, son. Was just waving off your mum. She's off to the carpet shop.'

Mum got a job a couple of weeks ago and, by the sounds of it, Dad spends the time in between her leaving and coming back just . . . waiting for her.

'That's good. How is she?'

'Showing an appropriate level of enthusiasm to decking out the entire house in new carpet, but I'm keeping an eye on it.'

I feel the familiar pang of concern. Sometimes, when Mum starts to get fixated on something, it can be the start of a manic episode that leads to a decline. It's hard to know at times whether she's excited about her new job in the way most people would be, or if it's something more.

'Sounds promising. Could be a good time to line up some more of your motivational talks? *How I made it to the Top* by Gareth Parr.'

'Yeah, I'll give it another week while she settles in and then I'll get in touch with my agent. I don't want to disappoint anyone if I have to cancel, so best to be sure first.'

I rub the bridge of my nose. 'May as well call now, though? They might have some universities that need a talk in the next few weeks. I can always come down to help out if anything does happen, but it sounds like she's doing well?'

I can hear the kettle clicking in the background. The sound of pouring and then the 'tink' of the spoon against the china.

'She is. And how's your job going?'

I open my mouth to say what I always say. It's paying the bills, so it's good. Except, since I've started my writing, I don't know if I feel that way any more.

'Keeping me busy. I'm learning a lot.' It's close to the bookshop, which is another reason I don't include.

'That's good. Must feel fun, to learn.'

I laugh. 'I suppose it does.' I pause. I want to check in properly. To ask if he's really okay. I often wonder how it must feel to Dad when his purpose is taken away. Who is he, when he doesn't have Mum to look after? 'So you're all good then?' I say eventually, but it ends up sounding like more of a statement.

'All good,' he replies, and tears sting my eyes. I don't even know why.

On the journey to work I immediately pull out my phone, open my notes, and start typing. It's become habit and now I even look forward to it. When I go running, I'm thinking about my characters. Where I want them to go next. They're falling for each other, the way Erin and I did at school. It's impossible not to think about us when I write about Carmen and Arthur. It brings all those familiar feelings rushing back.

There were a couple of days, a few months into our friendship, when Bonnie wasn't in school, because her youngest sister had just been born. We'd only ever hung out as a three, so when Erin came and sat beside me in English, I grinned at her and her face lit up as she smiled back.

'Tell me you've read this,' she said, pulling a copy of *The Perks of Being a Wallflower* out of her bag.

My eyes widened and I laughed, pulling the very same book out of my backpack. 'Are you joking?'

Her mouth fell open, her warm green eyes dancing. I had thought she was pretty from the moment I saw her, but that was the moment I went from just thinking it to feeling it.

She nudged me on the arm. 'What are the chances?'

I had to look away because I knew my cheeks were turning red. The feel of her against me had completely killed my train of thought, and confirmed that I liked Erin in a very different way to Bonnie. I could hardly speak for the rest of the class, which was unheard of in English. All I could think about was what her touch felt like. How much I wanted her to do it again.

'I want this book added to the syllabus, Mr Carter,' Erin said at the end of class.

He beckoned her towards him and I followed.

'Every kid in school needs to read it.'

He scanned the title and smiled. 'I couldn't agree more. It's a fantastic portrayal of the awkwardness of adolescence.'

'It's so much more than that,' I blurted out. 'In finding people who understand him for who he is, Charlie is able to grow.' I glanced across at Erin, hoping she knew what I was saying. That the reason I loved the book so much was because it reminded me of what I'd found with her and with Bonnie. Erin was watching me, her eyes wide. Lips slightly parted. 'That's what I got from it anyway.'

'But what about the love story?' Erin replied. 'It's loving Sam the way he does that opens him up. That's why he grows. It's more than just acceptance and understanding. It's love.'

Mr Carter looked between us, and his face broke into a smile. 'That's the great thing about books. They're there to teach you whatever you want to learn. They're for all of us.'

We ended up spending the whole of those two days together. She started calling me 'Wallflower' and I started calling her 'Nothing' – both in-jokes from the book we were so obsessed with. We scanned the lunch hall, locking eyes and waving when we found each other. Racing to fit all the words we could into the hour we had before our next class. She could quote *The Hunger Games* from memory. Didn't care about anything except English class.

Erin wasn't sure if she'd ever leave Frome, because she never wanted to be far from her mum. I told her all I thought about was leaving. That my mum had walked out of the house naked that morning and my dad had to whip off his dressing gown to cover her up and bring her back inside. She reached across and squeezed my hand and all I could do was stare down at her slender fingers on top of mine and wish for the world to stop. We walked home together, laughing and shoving each other. Sometimes our shoulders would touch and we'd look at each other, something passing between us. Even though I loved Bonnie, I hated the day she came back to school and those moments became memories.

Now, as I write, Carmen's touching Arthur. He's braver than me. He does what I could never do. He takes her hand

The Book Swap

and pulls her towards him. The scene moves to the present day. Arthur's trying to apologise to Carmen for the mistakes he made. Until this moment, you think my book is about the strength of love. That it's purely romance. Then it changes. Sometimes redemption isn't just about saying sorry, it's about how you recover from the mistakes you make. Bettering yourself is the best kind of apology you can make.

I think about the message sitting on my phone from Helena, awaiting a reply. She's asked why she wasn't enough – and I can't think of the right answer. She sent it yesterday.

As I pick up my phone to try and write back, it lights up with a message from Joel.

Any chance of a beer tonight?

I haven't seen him since our run, but it isn't really like him to ask to see me on the day. My plan was to go home and keep writing. I've written nearly half the book. I can't seem to stop. Might do me good to actually see another person though.

Sure, mate, I reply.

I get to the pub first, ordering us each a pint and using the time to think about what my character Carmen can do to shock the reader and Arthur in the next chapter. The problem is that Carmen is merging with the girl from the margins, so thinking about my protagonist leads me straight to what Margins Girl might be doing. Hopefully answering some questions in the back of a book.

I know so much about her even though I've never met her. I know her sense of humour based on what she laughs at in the books. I know her opinions on wealth. Her morals and values. That she seems both terrified of, and ready for, an all-consuming type of love. I know what kind of man she's looking for. Kind and wise – but firm when he has to be. Someone who stands up for people who deserve it. The type of man I hope I am.

I'm so lost in thought that I don't notice Joel until he's standing right in front of me. He looks completely different to when he's jogging towards me with a giant grin on his face. Today he's pale, except for the dark bags under his eyes. He runs his hand through his hair as he sits.

'Thanks for coming,' he says, downing some of his pint. 'Needed to see a friendly face.'

'No worries.' I smile. 'Everything okay?'

'Not really, mate, no.' Despite his appearance, it isn't the answer I'm expecting, because Joel always says he's fine. He always has. 'The guy who's sat opposite me for four years took his own life yesterday.' Joel stares straight at me. 'I knew something was going on, but all we ever did was smile at each other. Talk about our weekends. He jumped from the roof of his building.'

'Mate, I'm so sorry.' I don't know what he needs from me, so I treat him the same way I do Mum. I listen.

'I should have asked him, just once, if he was okay. If he'd spoken about it, it might have helped. I might have been able to help him.'

'You can't blame yourself. You didn't know.'

Joel shakes his head. 'But my point is, I should have.' He looks around the room, licking his lips. 'What is it with us men? Why don't we talk to each other? There shouldn't be any shame in it. Ask me.' He nods. 'Ask me how I am. Properly. And I'll answer. Then you do the same. Let's just try it.'

He sits back and waits. 'How are you doing, Joel?'

The Book Swap

'I'm shit, thanks. Someone I should have made way more effort with just died and I blame myself. I was so focused on my job, I didn't notice a human being beside me was struggling.'

I let out a breath, my forehead hurting from how long I've been frowning as I listen.

'That felt really good,' he says. 'Your turn. How are you doing?'

I look around me, sighing. 'I think I've got feelings for someone I've never met, and I feel like my job is suffocating me.' I'm shocked by the words that come out. Joel leans back on his chair and laughs, gently.

'I've been waiting years for you to say that.'

'What?'

'About your job.'

Frowning, I stare across at him. 'You told me to take it. You know the whole "if you don't know what you're good at, find something that'll eventually make you shit loads of money instead." That thing?'

He sighs. 'Mate, that saying was never about you. Fuck, I'm so jealous of what you have. What you've always had. That passion for writing. That talent I've seen in all those passages you showed me back at school. If I had an inch of that, do you think I'd be doing this job? I do this job because I can't do anything else.' He stares at his pint and looks back up. 'You know the last time we were here? When you couldn't even remember you had those book ideas at school. It made me sick. That you could forget it so easily.'

Swallowing, I look down at the table. Joel feels like he doesn't have a choice, but he's telling me I do. He's never said anything like that before.

'I've actually started the book,' I say, and he flings his head up, eyes sparkling.

'Yeah? For real? You're writing again?' It's the first pure happiness I've seen on his face for ages. 'You need to tell me these things. Talk to me more. I get that it's different for you. I don't have any siblings, whereas you've got Elliot, but—'

'I haven't talked to Elliot properly in years.' Is that really how little Joel and I speak, that he thinks I'm still close to my brother? He's remembering the Elliot who used to pick me up from school. Who took a gap year just so that I could have him around for my final year.

I spoke to my brother about everything back then, as we cycled down dirt tracks, mud flying into our faces. Then the summer I left college, he took another gap year and went travelling. That year became two years. He didn't come home. He didn't even contact us. Not Dad, or Mum, or me. He just . . . disappeared. He went on this journey of self-discovery and left me behind. By the time he'd re-emerged as my brother again, he had a whole new life. A husband and then a baby. Someone else to talk to.

'So who do you speak to about stuff?' Joel asks, and the only person who comes to mind is Margins Girl.

'I'm not sure. I thought it was you, but apparently not.'

'We talk, but it isn't deep, is it? I know you don't want to commit to Helena, but I don't really know why. I know you must miss Bonnie, but I don't really know how it makes you feel. I know you blame yourself for your mum's illness, but I don't know how heavy that burden is.' He undoes a button on his shirt, pulling at the neck. 'Isn't that mad? When you think about it?'

I laugh. 'I guess it is.'

'Come on.' He stands up, downing the rest of his pint. 'There's a decent Thai place around the corner. Let's get dinner. Talk some more.'

The Book Swap

By the time I get home, it's after midnight and my evening with Joel has given me the courage I need to send the message I should have sent weeks ago. Not just the courage, but the answer I didn't even know I had. I pick up my phone and open my last message from Helena.

James: I need to move on from the James I was at school, and I can't do that with you. I'm really sorry. I think you're amazing. You deserve to be with someone who sees their future when they look at you, instead of their past. X

13

Erin

There's no one way to grieve. This was a sentence my therapist threw in during our last session, and knowing it has cracked open something inside me that I closed on the day Bonnie told me about her diagnosis.

We'd both been living in London for four years by that point, and she'd messaged me earlier in the day to ask what time I finished work. She did that sometimes. Always one for a last-minute plan. When I walked out of the Traitor building she was leaning against a bollard, waiting for me. She was wearing this long tie-dye skirt in brown and green, with a matching crop top. She was the most striking person I'd ever seen. Laughing, I ran towards her to hug her and she held on longer than she normally would. I was so happy to see her. She'd been so busy with her promotion at work I could hardly get her to answer her phone, let alone see me in person.

She looked amazing. Her eyes were done up with liquid eyeliner and she was definitely wearing eyelash extensions. Her tight curls were loose, the way I loved them the most, filling the space around her, much like the way she filled the space of any room she walked into. Just looking at her was like bathing in sunshine. She warmed me.

'It's *so* good to see you.'

She bit her lip. 'You too. What are these?' She pointed at my purple velvet dungarees. They were a new Traitor Fashion release I had to wear while meeting a couple of influencers. They didn't suit me, but I thought I'd wear them home so my Spanish boyfriend, Pablo, could have a good laugh at them before he hopefully removed them altogether.

'Hideous, aren't they?'

'They're one of the worst things I've ever seen. And they clash with my outfit, but I'll take it.'

She held out her arm and I linked mine through.

'Where are we going?'

'Just thought we'd walk a bit.'

I turned to look at her, frowning. Bonnie didn't go anywhere without a purpose. She didn't waste a second. Something was up with her. She'd come to tell me something.

'What's going on, Bon?'

It was at that moment I stopped, my skin turning cold, because the guard she had been wearing when she turned up slipped away. Her face crumpled. A police siren rang out in the background. She looked down at me and she was already crying.

'I'm not well. I'm really not well.' She turned and reached down for both my hands, squeezing them. 'I've got lung cancer and it's stage four.'

My hand flew to my mouth and I tried to steady myself. It couldn't be true. There was no way.

'That's treatable though, right? You can treat it?'

There was a flash of recognition in her eyes. As though she'd been there. Asked those same questions of someone else.

'I can try. I'm going to try, but they're not sure if it'll work.'

'It will.' I was nodding my head. Trying to convince the both of us. 'It has to. You're young. You're . . .' I couldn't find the right word. 'Bonnie. The world makes no sense without you.' My voice broke at that. I was trying to hold it together, but it was too hard.

She smiled back sadly, as though she knew something I didn't, and I started shaking.

'I'm so sorry,' she said, her voice breaking.

I shook my head. 'Don't you dare say sorry.' I pulled her towards me and held on so tight, a group of men walking past us wolf-whistled.

'I'm going to go home to Frome for treatment,' she said, pulling away.

'When?'

'Tomorrow.'

It felt too close to a goodbye. I was nowhere near ready. She'd only just told me.

'I'll come down this weekend,' I said, squeezing my eyes shut because I could hardly see her.

'Great,' she said, forcing a smile, and seeing that broke me. I knew it was for my benefit. That she didn't have the same belief as me.

'It's going to be okay. You're going to be okay.'

The smile had left her face. She'd already been overtaken by something else. Fear. And pain. She was gone before she was gone.

Philippa told me a lot of people respond in that way when a loved one is diagnosed with cancer. They feel forced to start the grieving process before that person is even gone. They start imagining a life without them. Preparing themselves, and then feeling guilty for being able to even consider it.

Walking to Burgess Park, wrapped up against the late winter cold, I realise that life without Bonnie is so different to how I thought it would be. I was expecting this huge gaping hole where she once was. That's what I prepared myself for. It's the opposite. She still fills that space. She's still so present in my mind that the aching for her is constant. I told Cassie that at dinner last night and she hugged me tight.

'I can't imagine it,' she said, not letting go. 'The pain of missing her must be exhausting. She was lucky. So lucky to have a friend like you.'

I squeezed my eyes shut, fat tears dropping onto Cassie's thick lime green jumper. She wouldn't say that if she knew the truth.

Approaching the park, I send Georgia a message. Nothing with any pressure. Just casual.

Erin: How are you?

She replies straight away.

Georgia: Aware what you're really asking is am I keeping the baby, and the answer is . . .

I wait, staring at the screen.

Georgia: Tell you tonight. Mum's birthday. 7 p.m. I'm paying.

I thrust my phone into my coat pocket, tighten my scarf, and keep walking.

Once I reach Burgess, I let myself into a little enclosed garden at the edge of the park, sitting myself down on a bench under a tree.

The Book Swap

Earlier I copied the questions Mystery Man had written in Emily Brontë's novel into the back of Jane Austen's, and now I'm ready to answer them. Excited to. Pulling out my pen, I turn to the back page, already smiling.

1. Why do you write in the margins?
I always have. Don't you think books would go way closer to the edge of the page, if they didn't want us to write in them? I always think of the author, and how sad it must be to have someone read your words and then move on, as though they meant nothing. I can't do that. Books teach us, and I want to make sure I'm learning everything they're offering. I write in the margins to remember the book. To keep the words in my heart.

2. Is it better to listen to other people's opinions of you, or your own opinion of yourself?

I laugh at this one, wondering where it came from. I think about the way I'm living right now. Ignoring all of my own instincts to live my life more like Bonnie would have pushed me to.

Oh, definitely other people's. I think they're probably kinder about us than we are to ourselves.

I get the feeling that isn't the answer he wanted. I don't know why, but I also know that he wants honesty from me.

3. Why Wuthering Heights?
It was the only choice that made any sense after Dickens. Estella and Pip vs Heathcliff and Cathy. Dickens vs Brontë. 'You are part of my existence' vs 'He's more myself than I am.' Passion vs

unrequited love. I think both books, while so different, teach us everything we need to know about love. That no matter the set-up, it involves either heartbreak or optimism. Sometimes both. I hadn't realised how similar they were. Or, rather, how similar the response was that they provoked in me. Why do I find a love like that so terrifying? That's a rhetorical question. If I don't know the answer, I'm fairly sure that you – Mystery Man – won't know either.

4. Do you ever feel like this is the only thing in life you have to look forward to?

The answers have come easily until now. At this one, I hold *Wuthering Heights* towards my chest, pressing it hard against me. I'm surprised he's written it, but mostly I'm relieved.

You have no idea. There's so much more I could write, but those four words say it all.

5. Do you use the word 'dreamboat' often?

Clearly, he was trying to lighten the mood, and I'm glad.

Only for Atticus. He's the only man who will ever deserve that title.

I tap my pen against the book, staring at the space beneath, which is crying out for a few more questions. I decide to add some of my own.

6. What kind of person do you think Eileen was?

The Book Swap

It's something I've thought of often and I wonder if he even knows who I mean. If he's even noticed the plaque on the library.

7. If you could be a character from any book, who would you be, and why?
8. How often do you visit the library?
9. Do you think, in real life, we'd get on?
10. Do you ever wonder what the hell you're doing with your life?

Well, he'd been vulnerable, so I may as well match him.

When I return to the library, I crouch down and place *The Great Gatsby* on the ground while I flick to the back of Brontë, running my eyes over the answers I've given, and the questions I've written beneath them. I want to check I haven't completely embarrassed myself, but then I realise it doesn't matter. I don't know this person, so I can be exactly who I am. There's such a freedom in that that I pick up Fitzgerald and scribble on a blank page at the end. I write, *Thank you for giving me the freedom to be myself.*

Georgia's booked Megan's in Clapham for Mum's birthday. I arrive late to find them both already seated. Mum's all dressed up in her London get-up. Jeans with a shiny belt, and a hot pink top tucked into them. Her freshly coloured hair falls in waves around her face, which lights up the moment she catches sight of me. She's obviously changed her mind on growing out the grey. I want to comment on that. To ask why. The grey suited her, but I like it both ways. In the past, she'd have come to me first. Asked my opinion before going to the salon. It stabs at my chest that she grew out her colour, and then dyed it again, all without me knowing.

She holds her arms out for a hug and a wave of guilt hits me, because I haven't brought a card or a gift. At the time I decided it was a good idea. Another way to hurt her, but now, seeing her across from me, all happy that I've even bothered to show up for her birthday, I think a small present might have been the right thing to do. When we were little, I used to go to so much effort for her birthday. I'd make Dad take me to Anokhi, her favourite shop in Bath, so I could pick her a necklace or something to wear. She cried every time. I think the belt she's wearing might even be one of the gifts I got her.

'Happy birthday,' I say, leaning into her hug without raising my arms, before I grab Georgia, whispering in her ear.

'Yes or no? It's the only reason I came.'

She hugs me back. 'Yes,' she whispers, and my heart surges at her answer. I hadn't realised how important her response would be. I squeeze her tight before sitting down opposite them both.

'Had a nice day in the big smoke?' I ask Mum, staring at my menu.

'We ordered for you, given your tardiness,' Georgia says, forcing me to put my menu down and look at Mum.

'Lovely, thank you. *Matilda* was brilliant. It's a shame you couldn't make it.'

I glance towards Georgia and she gives a small smile in return. She didn't invite me to the theatre. She knew how much of Mum I could handle.

'Now that Erin's finally here, we can give you our gift,' Georgia says. 'Erin, care to explain it?'

It's amazing how quickly adoration can turn to hatred where my sister's involved.

'No, you go,' I say, smiling sweetly. 'You had a whole speech prepared.'

The Book Swap

'Okay, Mum,' Georgia says over the top of me. 'This is from me and Erin.'

She hands Mum a box, with ribbon tied around it. I try to think of all the possible things that could be inside. Georgia isn't a good gift giver. Not the way I am. She'll either google 'gifts for mum' and buy what's at the top, or she'll throw money at it and get something extravagant and unwanted.

Mum unties the ribbon and lifts the lid, pulling out a frame. She looks at it for a really long time, then holds it to her chest.

'Thank you, girls, that's so thoughtful.' She puts it down on the table facing her, so I still have no idea of the photo Georgia has chosen.

'You're welcome,' I say, smiling, and Georgia grins across at me, finding the whole thing hilarious.

Mum's eyes land on me.

'I'm sorry to hear about your job,' she says. 'You didn't mention it when you stayed so Georgia's been filling me in. How are you?'

'Actually, good.' I've always felt that my mum lost the right to know what's going on in my life when she became responsible for blowing it up, but I'm filled with a sudden urge to impress her. To feel her arms around me as she congratulates me on what I'm doing. To have her hold me the way she used to. This is why I didn't want to come. Because I knew this is what would happen. It's a lot easier to keep up the pretence that I don't care when I can't see her. 'I've got a load of job interviews lined up. New boyfriend. I'm hardly home.'

She purses her lips. 'I thought you must be busy. I've called. A lot.'

I picture myself at home on my bed with no boyfriend and no interviews, watching the word 'Mum' flash on my screen until it disappears, telling myself I can't answer because my hands are smeared in peanut butter. My throat hurts and I swallow.

'Yeah. You know me . . .' I shrug. 'Always busy.'

Georgia's watching me, elbows on the table and her hands pressed together.

'What interviews?' she asks. 'I didn't know about these.'

'Because I don't tell you every tiny thing that's going on in my life, actually.' I do.

She raises an eyebrow, as Mum looks between us.

'I've been teaching this girl, Savannah, some extra English. She got a D in her mocks and she's got her GSCEs coming up in May. I go there for a couple of hours each week. Last week when I arrived, she'd actually read some Shakespeare without me forcing her to, and had *opinions* on it.' I can feel my pulse quickening as I speak, and try to tone it down. I've already told Mum more than I normally would, because Georgia's here.

'That's amazing, Erin.' Her face lights up and I shrug, picking up my fork. I start poking it into the wood of the table and Mum reaches across to grab my hand to stop me. I drop it and am moments away from rolling my eyes, the way I would have in my teens.

She keeps her hand on mine. 'Can we just talk honestly, Erin. I can't stand this, I just—'

'Okay, I've got a Buddha Bowl and a Salmon Grill,' the waiter says, and I could jump up and kiss him.

'Buddha Bowl for me,' Georgia says, raising her hand, and Mum looks down at the ground. I'm conscious of every movement she makes, my chest constricting as her shoulders slump forward.

'Salmon,' she whispers, pushing the frame towards me to

The Book Swap

make space for the giant plate she's being served. It turns as it moves, my heart thumping as I catch sight of what our gift is. It's a photo of me and Georgia when we were little, both clinging to either side of Mum, kissing her cheek and staring at the camera as she laughs. Being in a room with Mum used to be one of my favourite ways to spend time. Now it just hurts. It hurts inside and all over my body.

'Chicken Open Kebab,' the waiter says, returning.

'Perfect – thank you.' I smile across at Georgia, who has guessed my order perfectly.

'Thought you'd like that,' Mum says, satisfaction washing across her face and erasing the hurt that was previously there.

'Thanks, Mum,' I say, my throat tight. A rush of love flows through all the resentment and words that have gone unsaid and I look up, cutting into my kebab. 'Your hair looks really lovely,' I say, pushing the food into my mouth before I can regret it.

14

James

My book has a rough title. I'm calling it *Ten Ways to Say Sorry*. The drink with Joel has added another element I'm trying to tie in: the guilt we carry for things that aren't our fault. The times we say sorry when we shouldn't. When we have no need to.

I was twelve years old when Mum first told me her bipolar started after I was born. That for a long time everyone presumed it was post-natal depression, until Dad insisted on a diagnosis from the doctor. I fixated on that fact. That if I hadn't been born, she would never have been this way. She could hold down a full-time job. Laugh whenever she felt like it. I apologised to her once, during one of her really bad spells. She hadn't been able to leave her room for three weeks. She had this blank expression on her face, like she didn't even know who we were. Dad sent me up to invite her downstairs to watch a movie and she just shook her head. I ran towards her and squeezed her hand, desperate for her to be well.

'I'm so sorry,' I said, 'that I made you this way.'

In the movie version of my life, she squeezed my hand back and said that it wasn't my fault. That she'd go through it a thousand times if it meant having me. In reality, her hand sat like a cold rock in mine, until she pulled it away and turned onto her side.

It was stupid to look for forgiveness, and I never dared again. Instead I live with the knowledge that she is the way she is because of me. My life marked the end of hers as she knew it.

The thing I feel most guilty about is my relationship with my mum, I wrote in a comment to Margins Girl.

Thank God for siblings, don't you think? she'd replied. *They're the only people who can understand our fucked-up family dynamics. If I didn't have my sister to speak to, I think I'd be estranged!*

'To what do I owe this pleasure?' Elliot asks, when I call him on Saturday afternoon. I haven't been able to stop thinking about what she said. Maybe I need to try harder.

'Just thought I'd check in on my brother and my favourite nephew. Hey, Jordan!' Elliot gets up with Jordan about six, so even though it's early in New York I know he'll be awake.

'Who's that?' comes a voice in the background and I flinch. He'd recognise my voice if I called more. I don't know why I find it so hard to pick up the phone.

'It's your Uncle James.'

'I don't know James.'

Elliot looks at the camera and grimaces. Something about him looks different. I frown.

'What's happened to your face?'

'You mean these?' He shows me his teeth, which are about ten shades whiter than when we were kids.

'Yes. And . . .?'

'Botox,' he stage-whispers as I shake my head.

'You're thirty-two.'

'But I look younger.'

The Book Swap

'You also only laugh with the bottom half of your face. It's very disconcerting.'

My brother laughs, his forehead remaining stationary. There it is. The easy banter we slipped into when we were younger. When we talk like this, it reminds me of the good times we shared as a family. The times when we'd all go to the beach and Mum would bury us in sand and buy us ice creams. Dad would throw us around in the sea. Elliot and I would get told off for fighting. The days when we were just like any other family.

'How's life in New York?' I ask, changing the tone.

'Oh you know ... same old. Carl's still away a lot. Closing some big advertising deal in LA. Jordan started football lessons and I'm pretty sure he's the next Tom Brady – aren't you, buddy?'

I've noticed how much he does this. I ask Elliot about himself, and he responds by telling me about Carl and Jordan, in the same way that all Dad has to talk about is Mum.

'Nice one, Jordan,' I shout, unsure how close he is to the phone.

'And what do football stars eat for breakfast?' Elliot says, moving from the sofa and walking through to his kitchen. 'Protein. Bacon. Eggs. Pancakes. Coming right up.'

'At what point do you become an official American? When you marry one or when you have pancakes and eggs for breakfast?'

'I think it's when you catch yourself ordering a "soda".'

We both screw our faces up, mine creating many more wrinkles than Elliot's. We both burst out laughing.

'Do you ever think about coming back?' I ask. Since reading Margins Girl's comment about siblings, I've been wondering what it would be like if he was here too. How it might change things.

He looks directly into the camera and I try to read his expression.

'All the time,' he says. 'But I've been gone so long it's almost like I don't know how to.'

'There's this thing called an aeroplane . . .'

'Ha ha.'

I don't want us to make this a joke, I realise. I want him to come home.

'You know you can always come visit us, too?' he says. 'I'm always here. I don't go anywhere.'

'Yeah . . .' I bite my thumb, thinking again about the time that he wasn't there.

He nods, glancing away from the camera and back. 'I should. Listen, I . . .'

'No problem.'

'Bye, Jordan,' I shout, just as Elliot hangs up, silence ringing out louder than his voice for a moment before there's no sound at all.

We've run out of words. It happens every time. Once we've covered my work, our parents and his life in New York, we've got nothing left. Or we've got everything left, but neither of us want to bring any of it up. I don't because I'm too afraid of his reaction, and he doesn't because he's spent his whole life trying to separate himself from the atmosphere in our home. To move on.

Pulling on my Barbour jacket with the big pockets, I leave the flat. I've been trying to figure out when the latest pair of books might be returned to the library, and I've decided that it probably happened this morning. Saturday morning is the perfect time to wander along to Eileen's library. Margins Girl probably had a coffee while she finished off her notes, then walked through the park – because that's always the route I

The Book Swap

imagine – and put them on the shelves on her way to ... Pilates, or something. I've waited until three, just in case she needs more time, but I can't wait any longer. I've sort of got my heart set on the books being there. If they're not, I don't know what I'll do with my weekend. My plans focus around writing my book, and reading hers.

Leaving the park at the bottom exit, I throw my scarf back around my face and put my hands in my pockets. I imagine the two books sitting in the library, waiting for me. My heart's pounding with anticipation, and I'm sure this can't be normal. To be so excited to receive something from a stranger. Someone who could be anyone. That's what's driving me towards the library though. I'm hoping that these next books might give me some of the answers I need. If she's replied, maybe I'll get closer to finding out who she is.

Reaching the corner of Northway Road, I'm ready to cross over to the library when I see there's already somebody there. Stumbling backwards, I move behind the last parked car on the street, ducking slightly. There's a woman crouched on the ground with her back to me. She's got a rainbow tote bag on her shoulder and one book on the pavement to her left as she balances, bending over something on her lap.

I can't seem to catch my breath, and I duck further, resting my head against the boot of the car. This could be anyone. Just one of the many people who use the library. It doesn't mean it's her. Glancing back, the woman picks up the book on the ground and rests another in its place. I catch sight of the black cover with the image on the front as she puts it down before I turn away again. *It's her.* That's the book I chose. It's *Mansfield Park.* Fuck! I'm metres away from Margins Girl and I don't know what to do. I'd never considered that she could be sitting there waiting for me instead of the books. Do

I introduce myself? I try to picture it. The woman turning around, pushing her long brown hair away from her face and looking straight at me. And at that point I say . . . what exactly? What if she doesn't like the look of me? Or what if she's been doing this without any actual desire to ever meet me? The second I show my face, our exchange is over. She might even take the books away with her, and then I'll never know what she said back. If she's even replied. Squeezing my eyes shut, I try to gather my thoughts. All I've been able to think about since this started is meeting the woman behind these comments. Finding out who's on the other end of the notes in the margin – but now she's there, I don't think I can. I'm not sure I'm ready. Edging back towards my viewing point, I look again at the library. Its doors are closed, and she's gone.

I can hear the sound of footsteps – except they're getting closer. Spinning left to right, I expect to see the owner of the rainbow tote bag, but instead it's a man walking towards the bridge. He slows at the library and bends down. No fucking way. Straightening, I run across the road.

'Sorry, mate – something in there for me,' I say and he frowns, shaking his head, his wax jacket squeaking.

'What is it with this library? It makes people *very* weird.'

He walks off in the direction he came from, and I lean back on my feet, staring at the plaque.

'Hi, Eileen,' I whisper, opening the doors and reaching in for my books. Maybe I'm going mad but I'm sure I can still smell the scent of the woman's perfume in the air. Something floral, like roses, and sweet.

I glance quickly towards the bridge, just in case she's still nearby, but there's no one to be seen.

I turn to the back of *Mansfield Park*, smiling as I scan the page. *Meet me in* The Great Gatsby. A book I've been meaning to read but never have, so *of course* that's what she's chosen. I can see handwriting pressed through the page from the other side. She's replied to my questions.

Pulling out the Fitzgerald book, I can't help but flick through it quickly. My eyes are hungry for her words. For anything. There's one note right at the end. After the last page. I stare at it.

Thank you for giving me the freedom to be myself.

A lump forms in my throat and I swallow it down. What was I thinking? I just got the chance to meet her, and in true James fashion I blew it. I was so afraid it wouldn't be perfect that I didn't dare try, and now I might have lost my only chance. I close the doors, tapping the roof of the library, and then I look around in case I can see her somewhere, but she's gone. At least I haven't lost all of her, I think, as I put the books in my coat pocket. The most important part of her is still with me, and now I know a bit more about her.

I know she wears a black Puffa jacket. That she's got long brown hair, and a colourful bag, just like Eileen would have wanted. I know she worries about her comments. Takes time, in the freezing cold, to read through what she's written before she puts the books back. Those things are more than enough, for now, until she responds again.

The sun comes out as I carry the books home, and I turn my face towards it, breathing in the air from the park and thinking of Bonnie, as I often do.

This time I see her across from me in the car, sun shining through the window and lighting her up, so she's glowing. It was the third or fourth time I'd driven her to chemo.

'Thank you,' she mouthed, closing her eyes, and I knew, in that moment, that while Erin might never forgive me, Bonnie had. I nodded and looked away to hide the tears in my eyes, and I drove her home. Whenever I think of Bonnie now, she's got the sunshine blazing down on her, lighting her up like an angel. She'd probably *hate* that. She wouldn't want to be an angel.

She messaged me once, a few weeks after the first time I drove her to the hospital. Childcare had fallen through for her younger sisters, and she didn't want her mum to drag them with her to the hospital. Was I, by any chance, free? I jumped at the message. After that, we set up a rota. Tuesdays and Wednesdays, to ease the pressure, I'd take Bonnie.

'Come in if you want,' she said as she stepped out of the car on our fifth drive to the hospital, slamming the door shut behind her. I couldn't pay for the parking fast enough. Jumping out of the car, I ran after her. She glanced across at me, shaking her head and laughing.

I didn't hold her hand that time – just watched in awe as she had her IV fitted into her arm, chatting away to the nurse as though she was there for some kind of jolly. They were laughing because Bonnie was wearing fluorescent running trousers and looked as though she was going straight on to a marathon.

Maybe they treated all their patients the same way, but I got the impression Bonnie was their favourite. How mixed that feeling must be, to look forward to seeing someone who you wished didn't have to be there.

'What do you need from me?' I asked, once she was sitting in a comfy-looking brown chair, and hooked up to the bag of chemo that hung on a stand beside her.

The Book Swap

She shrugged, then her eyes lit up. 'Show me a selection of the worst YouTube videos you can find.'

I rolled my shoulders, sitting straighter. 'That, I can do.'

Back at the flat, I walk straight to the sofa and take the books out of my pocket before I've even taken off my coat. I turn to the back of *Mansfield Park* and there, rewritten, are my questions and her answers. At the back of *The Great Gatsby*, she's asked five more.

I digest them slowly, pausing as I read the answer to my first question. Her reason for writing in the margins has surpassed everything I expected, and my heart feels like it's trying to climb out of my chest and onto the page. As I learn more about Margins Girl, I can feel a sensation growing inside me that's worryingly close to what some people might describe as love. It's not something I've felt before, but that's how I know what it is. This pounding in my chest. The way my body vibrates at the sight of her words. The desperation for another book. All of it growing with every answer I read. I definitely thought she'd answer the opposite for question two, and tell me we must always listen to our own opinions of ourselves above other people's. The fact she hasn't makes me laugh. It's true. Other people probably are kinder.

Then I reach the answer to question four.

Do you ever feel like this is the only thing in life you have to look forward to?

And she's written:

You have no idea.

Everything stops for a moment, my ears ringing. She feels it too. Relief washes through me. I sink more deeply into the sofa.

With just those four words, I already can't wait to hear back from her. The waiting is getting too long. If I can read the entire *The Great Gatsby* in a few days, then I can return it. Would she even check the library that quickly? Will it be obvious that while I've been waiting for her to reply, I've already lined up my next book? I took a chance that she wouldn't choose it, and it's annotated and ready to return just as soon as I'm done. But what if I put it back too soon, and someone else takes it? I dismiss the thought. Somehow, I know she'll get back to the library before anyone else can.

Turning to the back of *Gatsby*, having not yet read a word, I point her towards my next book. A book that had so many lines in it to comment on, but which contained a quote that made me think only of my girl in the margins. It said: 'One can begin so many things with a new person! Even begin to be a better man.'

I don't know how a near stranger is making me feel that way, but she is. Since we started leaving notes for each other, I want to write better. Create a book full of quotes she'll want to underline and study. That she'll want to – what did she say? – keep in her heart. I want to be a harder worker. A better son. A better brother. A *much* better uncle. I want to fix all my mistakes. Make my apologies the way I'm trying to, through my novel. I want to turn myself into someone new, so that if – or when – I eventually meet her, I'm a better man.

I reach for my pen and write: *Meet me in* Middlemarch?

15

Erin

Boiling the kettle, I reach for the box of teabags in the cupboard above to find that Callum's returned it, empty. It's my turn to buy more and normally I wouldn't think twice about it, but right now I'm surviving on cash from teaching and dog walking and the last few pennies of my overdraft. I feel a pang for Georgia's lifestyle, and the one-bed flat she has to herself. It's looking worryingly like I'll have to ask her to lend me this month's rent, and last time my finances were mentioned she said she was sure Mum would be happy to help. Basically, my sister is playing hardball to get me back into any form of employment, but I don't want to settle for anything. I want it to be something I love.

On my way to meet her at the hospital for her twelve-week scan I pass by the library, and as though Mystery Man knows I need some kind of pick-me-up, my book is back. A grin breaks across my face as I reach in and select *Gatsby*, greedily flicking to the back of the book to see what he's offering in return. *Middlemarch*. It's almost as though he doesn't *want* me to reply for weeks. It's the biggest book I've seen. The biggest in the library – but my pulse quickens because I haven't read it, and I'm already looking forward to discovering what he's pointed out. The things he notices that I might not. Flicking through it, I try to find a reason why he might have chosen it. There's one line that's underlined, where the page is bent right back.

'One can begin so many things with a new person! Even begin to be a better man.'

I feel a bit dizzy for a second, but I tell myself I mustn't read into it. It won't be about me. He just liked the line. *So true!* he's scribbled beside it.

I'm desperate to sit down and read through everything now, but I'm going to be so late. That one line is enough. I put the books in my bag and walk to the hospital, trying to shake off everything to do with Mystery Man, so that I can be fully present for Georgia.

'No way,' she shouts from outside The Phoenix pub, when she sees me walking towards her. 'Don't bring me your shit, Erin. Not today.'

Apparently, I didn't do quite the job I thought of shaking it off.

She's so unlike herself. There's a nervous energy about her. She's biting her lip and her left leg is constantly moving, even though we're standing still. I take her arm, trying to steady her. I channel Bonnie. She'd take charge.

'It's down here on the right, second floor,' I say once we arrive at the hospital. She raises her eyebrows but allows herself to be led.

We go up in the lift, squashing ourselves beside a woman who looks like she should be on her back in a labour ward, rather than walking around freely. Georgia's eyes bulge and I gently turn her away. For her own sake, and for the sake of the woman who's clocked Georgia staring.

I think that for the first time ever, I'm more equipped for this situation than Georgia is, and it feels ... empowering. She's out of her comfort zone, and that's the zone I've been living in since the day I walked out of Traitor and into this new weird existence. It's almost as though being out of my comfort zone *is* my new comfort zone.

I walk up to reception and check Georgia in. She takes a seat on the first chair she sees, clutching her hands between her thighs. It reminds me of a photo we have of her when she was little and was waiting to hold me as a newborn baby. Nervous. Excited. Afraid to love.

I walk towards her, surveying my sister, and stop for a second, not sure why I have and then realising all at once.

'Come with me a sec,' I say, leading her towards the sign for the toilets. She follows me, mute, which is how I know just how nervous she really is.

I pull her into the disabled toilet and close the door.

'What was your plan with this?' I ask, signalling towards her outfit.

She looks down and back up.

'I mean, don't get me wrong, you look amazing. But it's a full-length, skin-tight grey dress. For a scan. Were you just going to hoist it up to your boobs and lie there almost naked?'

Georgia raises a hand to her mouth. 'I didn't think. Fuck, I haven't even shaved my legs. Or my vag. Surely they won't need to see those bits?'

'Well, they won't have much choice currently.'

Her lip starts to wobble, but I'm already pulling down my jeans and wriggling out of them. I hand them to her and pull my T-shirt and jumper off in one.

'That was impressively fast.'

Georgia takes her dress off, and hands it to me. She's so nervous. I try not to think about the sweat patches I'm about to press against my own armpits. She'd do it for me. I think.

We walk back out, me feeling entirely unlike myself in this dress, and Georgia wearing a grimace that might be to do with the scan, or the outfit. A male nurse appears and gives a warm smile.

'Georgia?'

'Yes.'

He nods and we follow him around the glass railing, definitely enough to give me vertigo as it gives a clear visual right down to the ground floor. He takes us into a room, which has a bed and screens at the ready.

A female radiographer turns to stare at us from the computer.

'I'll be doing your scan today and my colleague here will be assisting,' she says.

'We're not a couple, she's my sister,' Georgia blurts out, moving to sit on the bed. 'There's no dad. Or there is – obviously! – but he doesn't know, and—'

'She's nervous,' I interrupt. 'I think if you do this as quickly as possible, it'll be less painful for everyone involved.'

Georgia mouths a 'thank you' at me and sits there, mute.

Once she's finally in position, jeans pulled down and T-shirt and jumper pulled up, the radiographer begins to scan Georgia's flat, toned stomach.

I've heard people joke that you can't see anything clearly on these scans. How it doesn't look like a baby, just a blob – but the moment my niece or nephew comes into view on that screen, I see it. Gasping, I cover my mouth and look over to Georgia. She's biting her lip, staring at the screen at the end of the bed.

'We have a heartbeat,' the radiographer says, looking towards us, smiling. 'Now I just need to do a few standard checks, but so far, it's all looking good.'

I move towards Georgia and grab her hand. It feels cold, and I grip it tighter, rubbing it to warm it.

'H . . . how big is it right now?' she asks.

'It's about the size of a lime, more or less,' the radiographer replies, eyes fixed on the screen as she starts muttering sentences to the man who came to get us, as he dutifully types them into the computer.

'Haven't you got an app?' I frown. 'For the baby? All the "today it's making its own eyelashes" stuff? The girls at work used to *live* for them.'

Georgia shakes her head and I don't say anything more. Finally, I understand what she's been doing these past few weeks. She's been living in denial. I think she's only just realising there is definitely an actual baby in there. Maybe there was a small part of her that was wondering if she'd got it all wrong. Maybe even hoping she had.

'Would you like me to read to you, while she does this?' I ask, and tears fill Georgia's eyes as she nods. I pull *Middlemarch* from my bag, desperate to flick to the back and see if any questions await, but thankfully I have just about enough self-awareness to know that now isn't the time.

I start at the Prelude, and Georgia squeezes her eyes shut as I read about the 'little girl walking forth one morning hand in hand with her still smaller brother,' but then her forehead softens. The lines disappear from her brow. Her hand still grips mine, but less strongly.

She stares at the screen, half-listening to me, half to the doctor, while internally I suspect her brain is questioning what her life is about to become. I see every emotion moving across her face, only glad I can be part of it all. A little bit glad, as well, that somehow Mystery Man has become part of this too.

* * *

Georgia leaves soon after her scan to see a client – probably the perfect remedy for her right now is to focus on someone else's problems – and I go straight home to reconnect with my books. Thankfully, Callum has decided to go into work for once, and I don't have to deal with us ignoring each other in the flat. Without any discussion, neither of us have knocked for the other in a while.

Landing on the bed, a rush of happiness fills me as I catch sight of the new blanket I've added, to give the room some colour. It's a Habitat throw, bright yellow, broken up with dashes of white.

'You're learning, girl,' Bonnie says, grinning at me. She's wearing a bright orange T-shirt, a rainbow headband covering her sleek black bob.

Cassie messages and I pick up my phone with a wave of hope. She had a date last night and I messaged to check in, but she's only just replying. That's got to be a good sign.

Cassie: DISASTER! Knew I didn't fancy her from the moment she sat down, but I'm so used to starting a date with my speech that I went for it anyway, hoping it would put her off. TOTAL OPPOSITE. She was delighted, and took it to mean we were basically girlfriends already. I had to feign a dramatic message about my non-existent cat being ill and leave. She sent so many lovely, worrying messages that I've only just dared come back on WhatsApp, and now I have to tell her the truuuuuth. Save me.

Laughing, I type out a reply telling her to keep going with her mission for love as I reach for *The Great Gatsby*. I flick to the back of the book to read Mystery Man's answers. I haven't been as excited about a book since James and I discovered our mutual love of *The Perks of Being a Wallflower*. We took it to school with us every day, eyes wide as we both read out new lines we'd discovered. 'What about what Patrick says to Charlie. About the way he understands him?' 'Don't. I get teary just thinking about it.' We spoke about it so much that Bonnie got herself a copy, claiming she felt left out. We promised each other that the second one of us passed our driving test, we'd go through a tunnel late at night with our favourite song playing. That's the moment the three friends in the book realise they feel infinite. We wanted to know what it felt like to be infinite, too.

'You'll definitely be the one screaming, like Sam does,' James said, nudging me as Bonnie laughed. I moved away. I didn't want Bonnie to see what happened to my face when James touched me.

Bonnie was the first of us to pass her test, and by the time she did we weren't friends with James any more. We never did drive through that tunnel.

6. What kind of person do you think Eileen was?
I think she smoked like an absolute trooper, swore every other word and spoilt her grandchildren rotten.

So he'd noticed the plaque on the community library, in the same way that I had. We both had the same idea of her.

7. If you could be a character from any book, who would you be, and why?
Atticus Finch, for obvious reasons. My new purpose is for someone to call me a 'dreamboat' before I die.

8. How often do you visit the library?
Yours was the first book I ever took, from my very first visit. And since then? More times than Eileen could swear in an hour.

9. Do you think, in real life, we'd get on?
From our limited exchanges (of which I hope there'll be more), you have the qualities I enjoy most in someone. Funny. Smart. Opinionated without being embarrassed about it. Can I be honest? Argh! I'm going to be. You've taught me more – not just about fiction, but also about myself – since we started this Mystery Book Club than I've learnt in years. So ... in real life, I'd say if you were patient while I humiliated myself through pure admiration, then once we got through that, we'd get on.

Swallowing, I put the book down, my heart sinking with it. He's got me all wrong. The version of me he sees in the pages of these books isn't real. I know because of that, I can never meet him. I'd only disappoint him. The way he's describing me is how I'd describe someone else. It's how I'd describe Bonnie. That might be why, subconsciously, I chose this next book. It was Bonnie's favourite: *Beloved* by Toni Morrison. Reading it now, it's as though the message within it is her way of saying goodbye. I've already underlined one line. 'Something that is loved is never lost.'

I move to his final answer. The one I've been looking forward to the most.

10. Do you ever wonder what the hell you're doing with your life?
Until recently, no, and I've since learnt it is much better to wonder than to just make your way through life without questioning anything. Now, when I panic, I have this vision of what I want my life to look like in the future. Actually, it's you that's made that possible for me. You've reminded me that I love to write. I want to be an author. Until the day I picked up To Kill a Mockingbird, *I'd left that dream behind. The postcard in your*

book about not forgetting to live your dreams, coupled with all your comments, pushed me forward. They kickstarted my determination to work towards my dream. Everything I do now is about moving closer to that. Admittedly, I seem to have side-stepped right now, by taking a promotion at the job I think I hate, but there has to be a reason for everything we do and everything that happens to us, right? Or that's what I tell myself to get myself through, anyway.

There *has* to be a reason for everything. For this book exchange. For Savannah's dad picking up the book Mystery Man left for me, leading me to start teaching. Since Bonnie died, all I've thought about is living my life for her. Doing what she would have done. Jumping at every opportunity. Trying out all these random jobs to see if one sticks – and now one has. If I were to have a vision for my life in the future, it would be to continue what I've started here. To teach people to love books the way I do.

16

James

Since our chat, Joel and I have started running alongside each other when we meet in Ruskin Park. We have more to say.

'*Middlemarch?* Mate, even I know that's a huge book. I remember it from school. She'll think you don't want her to write back!'

'I know. I don't know what I was thinking.'

But I do. I wanted to prove to Margins Girl that it isn't just the chatting with her that I'm enjoying, but the reading as well. I thought if I chose a big book it would prove that, but now I'm really regretting it. I should have chosen something with far fewer pages. *Animal Farm* or *Lord of the Flies*. Something by John Steinbeck. They're all thin enough to fit in the back pocket of a pair of jeans, and therefore wouldn't involve endless wasted journeys to the library and back.

'This whole passing books to her where you've asked her questions and written little notes in the pages? You're basically telling her you love her.'

I laugh, and Joel holds out his arm to slow me down.

'Woah. You heard me, right? I said *love*. You know, that four-letter word that left you running for the hills after that Jenny declared it at uni.'

I push his arm down and jog on. 'It doesn't make me want to run quite so far, with her,' I shout back, waiting for him to catch up with me.

I've done nothing but think about her. The girl in my own novel now has brown hair and carries a rainbow tote bag. I've created a face for her in my mind. Blue eyes, warm and kind. Always laughing. A small nose. Ears that are slightly too big – because everyone needs a flaw, and I don't want the version of her in my imagination to trump the real thing. I think it might be impossible, anyway, to create someone who tops the living, breathing writer of these words. She's captured something in me. I can't think about her without my entire body fizzing with excitement.

'I read the chapter you sent me,' Joel says, back beside me, and I turn to look at him. He's letting the other stuff go, for now, and I'm fine with that. I didn't really think he'd ever read what I sent him, and now he has, I want to know his thoughts. 'It's brilliant, mate. It's really powerful. I knew you could write, from everything I read at school, but this is a whole other level. It reads like a proper book. Like a Dan Brown book.'

'Thanks. I'm glad you like it.' He's right. Even I can see I'm getting better. Maybe it's because I'm in the flow, but mostly I think it's all the learning I'm doing with Margins Girl. 'I emailed that agent who judged the first chapter competition. The one who voted for me.'

'Yeah?' Joel's grinning across at me, the way he does whenever I mention my writing. 'What made you do that?'

'Margins Girl,' I reply. 'She asked me if I ever thought about what I was doing with my life, and I wrote this answer back to her, and I realised how much I meant it. How much I want to be an author.'

'Finally,' Joel says. 'I mean, I've been trying to tell you that for *years*, but I'm glad this stranger can manage it in one question. You're still coming tonight though, right?'

The Book Swap

Joel's trying to build in a bit of work–life balance since the death of his colleague, and he's intent on including me. Running club, trying new restaurants – and now a double date. I feel like I've got more than enough balance already with the job and the writing and the book swap, but after all he's done for me, at school and ever since, I can't find a reason good enough to say no.

'I'm coming,' I say, already dreading it.

A senior executive at work has handed some of his workload over, and it includes more client management, so I'm hardly getting a break. Everything else is slipping. Where I used to call Dad on my way to work, now I'm using that time to write or read or plan a new training programme. Where I used to go out, now I'm at home at my desk, writing and plotting. And annotating books for a stranger.

On my way to meet Joel and our dates, I finally call home. Mum answers.

'Oh darling, we were just talking about you. Flying so high with your job, while we sit here planning to tear up all the carpets!'

'Oh, it's going ahead, is it?' I frown, massaging the back of my neck.

'Well, we can't turn down a thirty per cent discount.'

'Is that *it*? You work there. You should get at least—'

'Your dad's a bit worried I'm going too whacky with the colours, but I think a deep maroon will be lovely in the lounge. I've been googling lots of celebrities and did you know that Melinda Messenger has light purple *everywhere*. And Sandra Bullock has bright blue, so—'

'Those are probably not their real homes though, Mum. They'll have just been paid to pose there.'

I can hear footsteps as Dad approaches.

'Hiya, James,' he shouts in the background.

'I was just telling him all about our house plans.'

'I heard.' There's an impatient edge to his voice, which means Mum has probably been talking about nothing but carpets for days. That isn't a great sign. My heart sinks at the thought of losing Mum again, so soon.

'For the bedroom I thought maybe a turquoise, so we've got some samples to test how that looks.'

I want to see if I can reason with her. If she's open to suggestions, maybe she's not as bad as she sounds. An ambulance passes me, and I turn to watch it drive by before I start speaking again.

'Mum, it might be worth keeping some of the money they're paying you? Otherwise you're just putting it all back into the shop, which sort of makes the job pointless. Well, not pointless, I'm glad you're working, but—'

'You don't mind if we do your room, do you? You're hardly here.'

'No, that's fine. Can I speak to Dad?'

'Typical of you two,' she says, her voice shifting tone. She hates it when I ask to speak to Dad. She knows I'm trying to check up on her. 'No doubt wanting to whisper about me, while I try and do something nice for us all. You two with your nasty little team, trying to ruin my plans. You're both just holding me back, all the time – don't do this, don't do that.' She puts on her worst impression of me. The voice that used to make my skin turn cold. 'Well, I'll do what I fucking like. It's just a bit of carpet. Why would you stop me from doing that? It's like you both enjoy hurting me. Putting me down—' There's a thud, and I can hear Dad saying something before coming to the phone.

'You okay? Sorry about that.'

'Don't you fucking apologise for me,' comes a voice in the background. 'What am I? An embarrassment to you?'

I hear a click as Dad closes a door.

'Nearly time for me to come back, I think?'

'Not yet,' he says. 'You won't believe me, but she's been all right until just then. I'll call the doctor. See if we can make some alterations to her medication.'

'Okay.'

'You stay. You're not long into that promotion. I can cover things here.'

'All right, Dad.' I squeeze my eyes shut. 'Sorry.'

'Don't be sorry. Don't ever say that,' he says, his voice thick with emotion.

'I just . . .'

'You've got nothing to be sorry for. Nothing.'

There's pounding on the door, and more shouting of words I can't decipher. 'I'll call you tomorrow,' I say, forcing the words out.

'Okay. We love you.'

Dad hangs up and I stare at the phone.

I imagine him now, stopping whatever he was in the middle of doing to once again prioritise Mum. Calling her doctor to organise out-of-hours pills. Trying to calm her down while she screams an endless slur of unforgivable things at him. As he wholeheartedly commits to his vows to take my mum for better and for worse, in sickness and in health. You have to love someone entirely to be the husband he is to Mum. For the first time in a long time, amongst all the fear and anger I have towards their set-up, I feel something else. Admiration and respect. Dad makes it work because he loves my mum. Maybe it's everything I'm experiencing with Margins Girl, but suddenly there's something beautiful about that.

It's all I can think about throughout dinner at the Turkish restaurant opposite the Union Chapel with Joel and our dates, Dana and Jodie, as we share a mezze of meats and hummus.

Joel's taken a definite liking to Jodie and is draping one arm around the back of her chair. He leans closer towards her, laughing at something she said. I'm trying with Dana. She's really nice – she's a yoga instructor from Clapham, and she's interesting to talk to. But as we make small talk about jobs and our favourite south London pubs, I can't stop the voice in the back of my mind asking myself if I could love her. If she were to get ill, could I give up my life to look after her? That's become my measure of what it truly means to love someone. Looking after them the way Dad looks after Mum.

We leave the Turkish and walk towards the Union Chapel. A car stops beside us at the traffic lights on Upper Street, windows down and music blaring. My dad's voice rings out into the air. 'Do you know me?'

Jodie starts dancing across the road as Joel's eyes dart towards me. The car drives off.

'That's such a banger of a remix,' she says, when we've crossed.

'Remix?' I can't stop myself.

'What? Where have you been, James? DJ Tenderbass? It's all over the clubs at the moment.' She sidles up to Dana. 'Not sure he's for you, this one. He doesn't appear to go out.'

Joel catches us up. 'Did she just say there's a remix?'

'Not sure he's for you either,' Dana says back, nodding at Joel.

The Book Swap

'Apparently so,' I say to Joel. Someone's rereleasing Dad's song. They're putting it all back out there. Opportunities could open up to him. It could be his chance to prove himself. To rid himself of the one-hit-wonder title.

The rest of the evening is spent at a gig, mainly trying to make out the quite beautiful harmonies of an emotive acoustic folk duo over the sound of Joel and Jodie whispering to each other. Dana and I sit awkwardly, nodding our heads to the music. I run for the tube the moment it's over, and when I pop out in Brixton at the other end it's pissing it down with rain. I dash across the road, jumping on a bus that stops close to my flat. If I get off a stop early, I can even pass the library on my way home. Just in case. If it isn't there maybe I could write Margins Girl a note to find when she puts the books back. Maybe I could even tell her my name. Leave her my number? That's an idea I'll definitely regret in the morning.

Taking out my phone, I check my emails, heart jumping as I see the name of the agent I reached out to.

Hi James,
Please do send over three chapters and a synopsis when it's ready. I'd love to read it.
All the best,
Sophia

I scan the words over and over, unable to stop smiling. I've told her that it's something new – nothing like the chapter she read and enjoyed from the competition – but she's still said yes. I'm half-filled with excitement and half total terror.

At the next stop, the bus starts filling up with people and someone squeezes in next to me, apologising. The soft cushion of a Puffa jacket squidges against my arm, at the same time as I take in the familiar scent of perfume, trying to remember where I recognise it from.

The person beside me shifts, moving their arm so a rainbow tote bag swings from their shoulder and onto their lap.

My chest tightens. I can't take my eyes off that bag. My forehead starts sweating, and I turn away to look out of the window as I try to calm myself. *It's her.* The jacket. The bag. The scent. I have to see her face. I can't even control my body as I turn back, a smile forming as I lift my head to lock eyes with her: my girl from the margins.

17

Erin

It's only after I've squashed down next to him that I realise who it is. *James Parr*.

I'm closer to him than we ever sat in English class. Closer than we've ever been, except that one time I touched his hand back at school. Our shoulders are touching. I can feel the warmth of his breath and the strength of his gaze as he realises it's me.

His eyes widen, reflecting the shock I feel. He must have got caught in the shower too, because his light brown hair's slicked back with rain and tiny droplets cover his thick lashes. His jaw's covered in a stubble I've never seen before and it sends my brain spinning in a way it didn't at Bonnie's memorial. It's James, but so much older. He's a man now and it's like I've only just realised it.

He swallows, his Adam's apple moving up and then down. He keeps glancing at my arm and back to my face, before he holds his hands up, edging towards the steamed-up window behind him and creating a space between our shoulders. 'Hi, Erin,' he mumbles, swallowing. He runs his eyes across my face and shakes his head, a smile dying on his lips.

In my last session with Philippa, James was the main subject. She made me relive what happened between us, and go over my reaction to him at Bonnie's memorial. How strong my response was, after so many years. How it might have been a shock to him, in the same way this chance meeting appears to be. It's like this is some kind of test, and I feel like I'm failing, because I can't move on and be civil. One look at his face and I'm back in my childhood bedroom. The room I didn't leave for weeks, after what happened. I just lay there, staring at the wall, wishing my life could go back to the way it was before.

My heart is filling with pain at everything I lived through as a result of what James did.

I can feel my body starting to shake, and I move my tote bag further onto my lap, gripping it so hard my fingers go white. I turn my face away and into the arse of the man who's blocking my exit. Shrinking backwards, I stare straight ahead, checking my watch. It's too late at night to walk, but I can't stay on this bus. Can't sit this close to him, feeling the heat of him against me. A flash of memory appears, hitting my cheeks. We were at a house party, back in the days when we were close. I had got myself locked in the bathroom. I was pulling at the door, but I couldn't get it open. Someone was on the other side trying to help. It was so loud, I couldn't hear who it was. I pulled extra hard just as they pushed – and the door flew open, James catapulting his way towards me, slamming hard against me, against the wall. Both of us widened our eyes in surprise. I remember liking the feeling of his weight on me. Instinctively lifting my head towards him. Wanting, more than anything else, to know what it would be like to kiss him. Then Bonnie burst in, cackling about someone being sick on the kitchen floor.

Swallowing, I press the button once, twice, three times, just as the bus stops at a red light. James's eyes are on me.

Why is he even here? I thought he was in Frome. It's one of the reasons I love being in London. I hate going back there, and the thought of bumping into him – and yet somehow I've managed it, just metres from home. How?

My legs are shaking. Heat is pulsating through me. I need to take my jacket off but there's no space. James glances across at me again and opens his mouth. Whatever he has to say, I don't want to hear it. I just need air.

'Excuse me, mate,' he says, reaching past me to tap the man who's blocking me on the arm. 'Would you mind moving? I think this lady wants to get off the bus.'

'Sorry,' the man says, his voice gruff. He pushes further back and opens up a space, which I immediately jump into.

'Thanks,' I mutter, squeezing through the row of people taking as many breaths as I can until I reach the wider area for wheelchairs and pushchairs. The bus lurches forwards and I slam into the window, holding out my hands to steady myself. Out of the corner of my eye I see James jump up, before he sits again. Why is he so obsessed with trying to help me? First the cut on my foot. Now a tumble on a bus. If he wanted to save me, he should have done it back when he had the chance.

I wait so long in the rain for the next bus that by the time I reach the flat I'm soaked through and leaving puddles of water with every step. Closing my bedroom door, I strip off my clothes, fingers shaking – from the cold or from James, or both.

Bonnie is in her chair, reading *Beloved*. She looks up at me, long blue hair over one shoulder.

'All right, love?'

'No,' I say, pushing my hair away from my face, panic rising in my voice. 'I just saw James.'

She frowns. 'In London? Why?'

'I don't know why. He's here, apparently.'

She screws up her face. 'Gross.'

Does she remember the party? Walking in on us in Isla's bathroom? It felt the same, just now, sitting beside him again – the closeness, the messiness, the nerves. I need to forget the feeling. Get rid of it somehow.

Bonnie puts her book down and watches me. 'How weird, though. To see him now. In London.'

'I know.'

'On the same bus.'

'Yup.'

'Side by side.'

'Yes.' I reach for my tracksuit bottoms and pull them on, picking up Callum's 'The sea isn't real' T-shirt, which has somehow become mine.

'Don't you think that means something? Like, of all of the people in the world? It's like a message from the universe to deal with your past.'

I shake my head, swearing as I struggle to get my arm through the sleeve.

'Absolutely not. When the past comes knocking, don't answer.'

'I think that's only in horror movies.'

I finally get the T-shirt on and pull it down. 'I'll never forgive him.'

Bonnie shrugs. Locks eyes with me. 'Then neither will I.'

His blue eyes were so warm for that split-second before I looked away. His hair was all messed up by the rain. A wave of sadness flooded his face as I moved away from him.

There's a knock at my bedroom door. It swings open, banging against the wall behind it. Callum's standing there, bleary-eyed, swaying slightly.

'Oh. You look like you need cheering up,' he says, walking towards me wearing just his boxers. I can't believe I've never

The Book Swap

noticed before how skinny his legs are. I almost let out a laugh at the realisation. They're so pale, and popping out of his pants like two little matchsticks – but I do want a distraction from what's just happened. It's like he senses it. He stumbles slightly and I shift upwards in bed. I catch sight of *Middlemarch* on the table next to me, and my heart thumps in my chest. I have more fun hanging out with Mystery Man than I ever have with Callum. We actually have things to say to each other.

'I know just the trick,' Callum says, the word 'just' coming out as though it has a few too many s's in it. He reeks of beer. Normally I don't care. I want it to happen. But now I can't stop looking at *Middlemarch*, thinking about the questions that lie waiting in the back of it. I'm ready to answer them.

I involuntarily screw my nose up as Callum gets closer, pushing his boxers down to the ground, to reveal a penis as noticeably skinny as his legs. What the fuck have I been doing?

'I'm seeing someone,' I blurt out and he stops, stumbling backwards, his chin landing against his chest.

'Nah, mate. I'd know.' My revelation only slows him momentarily. Why would he be deterred by such a statement, when he's pissed and wants to have sex with me? He needs more.

'I don't want to,' I shout, pulling the duvet up around me and backing up against the farthest wall.

'You know what you are?' he says, pointing his finger at me. 'You're a fucking prick tease.'

'If you can call that a prick,' I say furiously, flinging my hand against my mouth after I say it. I didn't mean to get nasty, I just want him to leave. I want to be alone with Mystery Man.

He spins and storms out of my bedroom, slamming the door behind him and leaving his skid-marked boxers on my bedroom floor. Jumping up, I pincer them between my thumb and forefinger and chuck them out of the door, shutting it firmly behind me. I pick up *Middlemarch*.

I've finally finished it and I definitely didn't give it my full attention. I just wanted it to end so I could reread *Beloved*, answer his questions, and ask him some more. I wish we'd chosen poems so we could do this every day. As much as I want to deny it, this isn't really about the books any more, it's becoming only about learning more about him. I don't know how or when that happened.

While my responses to his most recent questions have been taking shape inside my head for the last couple of weeks, I'm yet to answer them, and now it feels like the only thing that will get me through what just happened – the run-in with James. Then I read the first question again, and I don't know if I can do it. I glance towards the chair that Bonnie's no longer in, and back to the book. I can't answer the first question yet. It hurts too much. I skip straight to question twelve.

11. What's your greatest regret? (You can thank Gatsby for that one!)

12. What's your dream job?
You got me thinking about that, with your answer about what you're doing with your life. If the author thing doesn't work out, you should consider being a life coach! In the future, I see myself helping people to fall in love with books. I want to be a teacher. You're the first person I've admitted that to.

13. What makes you happiest?
Wine. Books. Eileen's library. Cider ice lollies (seriously – have you ever tasted one?). Beating my sister at ANYTHING. Long walks. Making myself proud. Every memory I hold of my best friend. The new memories of her that appear and keep her alive. Putting the 'z' on a triple letter score in Scrabble. Imagining my sister riding a penny farthing. Don't know why. Her enjoying her life and achieving her dreams (but ideally it would be while on a penny farthing). Doing this with you. This makes me happy.

14. Are you a fast reader? (I really hope so, because I've just given you Middlemarch*!)*
What were you thinking?! Luckily, yes, but do not test me on that book. I was somewhat distracted by your questions at the end of it ...

15. What is your favourite thing about living in London?

I pause, biting on the end of my pen. This question is the reason I wanted to answer tonight. Because after what's just happened, and with the wine emboldening me, I want to write an honest response.

It used to be the fact I could escape my past here, but that changed tonight. So instead, I'll just admit it's you.

18

James

I can't believe how fucked-up this is. The novel I'm writing has always been for Erin. My small way of trying to apologise for what I did – and the only reason I've been able to write it the way I have is because of Margins Girl. And Margins Girl is also Erin.

My brain starts running back through everything she's said in the books, the pieces slotting slowly into place. Her comments on Atticus. How strongly she related to that quote about grief in *Great Expectations*. Her relationship with her mother. Now that I know it's Erin, everything about our exchange makes sense. Who else could it ever have been, but the girl I forced myself to stop loving the day I broke her trust?

It was raining then, too. Torrential rain that didn't stop for twenty-four hours, so every memory I have of what happened is set in grey. I was hiding behind the art block, cowering under my raincoat as I waited for a moment it was safe to get home. At some point I ducked through to the photography darkroom. Tried to dry off. Some black-and-white photos of dead birds were hanging on pegs. I don't know whose they were, but they were mesmerising. I pretended I was in an exhibition, and stood in front of each one, taking it in. The feathers flat against the ground. The wings that would never fly again.

When I re-emerged, that's when I saw them. Mr Carter, our English teacher, kissing the neck of a woman against the corkboard that proudly displayed the latest lino prints from younger years. I could only make out her back as he moved his head down her body, burying his face into her chest before moving lower. The woman squealed. He spun her around, pushing her against the prints and shifting her legs apart, as his kisses kept moving lower and lower down her body. I noticed her shirt first. It was open, one breast hanging out of a white lace bra, the other still within it.

She started breathing heavily and I finally took in her face, my hand slamming to my mouth as I saw who it was. Erin's mum.

'Oh, Derek,' she moaned as I fumbled towards the door as quickly and as quietly as I could. I edged out of it and closed it gently behind me, before I started running through the rain.

My brain was so full of what I'd seen that I didn't check for any signs of big groups the way I normally would. By the time I heard their voices, it was too late. They'd been waiting for me, and because I'd taken longer than usual their punishment would match.

'Trying to hide?' Marky said, standing in front of me and pushing me backwards, a hood pulled up over his head. 'Fucking pussy. What are you so scared of?'

He nodded towards one of the others, his eyes shining.

I felt my legs kicked out from under me. I landed on my knees, and then my hands and face. The wet concrete pressed against me as I tried to push myself up.

A foot hit me hard in the stomach, lifting me up and flipping me until I was on my back, my head slamming against the ground beneath me. Rain started hammering into my

The Book Swap

face so I could hardly see. There were eight of them, standing around me, hoods up, staring down.

'We're going to play a little game I've just made up. It's called "spit or piss". Do you want to know the rules?'

All the others started sniggering the moment he said the word 'piss', in case I needed a reminder of the type of people I was up against.

Shaking my head, I rolled onto my side, trying to get up. Another foot cracked me under the ribs.

Marky was the first to undo his flies and pull out his penis. I caught sight of Felix. He was always who I looked for in that group. I needed to see if there was any regret and I knew he was the only one I might find it in. He swallowed, and then copied Marky. They all did, clutching their penises and hocking up spit in their mouths, which hovered above me. Marky made a sound as though he was clearing all the snot from his entire body and getting it into his mouth. The first shot just came firing straight at me. I could make out the yellow tint to the saliva as it flew through the air, landing on the corner of my mouth. I shook my head. Another sharp boot in my side so I coughed. I swear some of the phlegm went into my mouth.

'The game goes like this,' he said, raising his voice above the rain. 'Each of my boys here gets to make a choice. They can either spit or piss. On you. It's my idea, so I get to do both,' he said, and I watched as he moved so he was directly over my face, taking hold of his penis in both hands.

'Wait! You need to go to the art block now. Erin's mum is fucking Mr Carter. She's got her tits out.' I yelled the words as hard and as fast as I could. I tried to use their language. I needed to do whatever it took to stop the game from continuing.

I saw Marky pause. He looked around his circle of boys. Felix was looking longingly at the art block. Whether he was hoping to see Erin's mum naked or to get out of what he had to do, I'll never know.

Marky zipped up his trousers and kicked me hard in the shoulder.

'If you're lying, we're fucking coming for you,' he said, and he signalled the others before running off in the direction of the classroom.

Shaking, I jumped up as fast as I could and I started limping, wiping the rest of the spit from my face. My legs kept caving under me. Tears were streaming down my cheeks. Rain rolled from my head and down over my body. Everything ahead of me was a blur. I just needed to make it home before they caught up with me again. I didn't know if Mr Carter or Erin's mum heard me leave. Whether they were even still there. I didn't know how long I had.

I only found that out the next day, when the videos came out. Marky was the hero of the year for capturing it all on his phone. It was the only sound you could make out in assembly. Everyone was so absorbed, they didn't even look at me when I took my seat. But all I could think about was the letter for Erin in my pocket. I just needed to get it to her before anyone said anything. I was fairly sure Marky wouldn't. He was far happier with everyone thinking he discovered them. I saw Felix next to Helena, whispering to her. She whispered to Zoe. They were all looking over at me. I looked around. I couldn't see Erin or Bonnie. Everyone was on their phones. Sweat was prickling at the back of my neck. I stood up and walked out of the assembly hall – straight into Bonnie, who was comforting a crying

Erin under an umbrella. She was crying because of me, and there was nothing I could do to fix it. Guilt consumed me, and I pulled the letter out of my pocket and walked towards her.

She started screaming at me the second she saw me, with Bonnie at her side trying to pull her away.

'Felix said you told them. That you sent them there. How *could* you?'

'Come on, Erin! He isn't worth it.'

The words hit me as hard as the expressions on their faces, contorted in pain and disgust.

'I'm sorry,' I shouted, rain dripping from the top of the hood of my waterproof jacket onto my lips. 'I'm so sorry, I only told Marky and his mates.'

'That's the same as telling the whole school and you know it.' Erin pointed a finger at me, her face screwed up.

I walked towards her, hand outstretched. 'Please, Erin. Can we go somewhere and talk about this?' I was close to tears, and grateful for the rain. 'I wrote you a letter.'

'She doesn't want to talk to you,' Bonnie shouted. She was holding a bright purple umbrella over the two of them. Just days earlier, the three of us were sharing it.

I threw my arms out. 'Please. I really am sorry.'

'It's too late for that,' Erin said, and she was crying so hard my heart ached with a need to make it better, but I couldn't. I was the reason she was so upset. 'Everyone knows. You heard them in assembly just then. They're chanting at me that my mum's a "teacher fucker". It's never going to stop.'

'It will,' I said, my voice weak.

She laughed. 'The way it has for you, you mean?' Shaking her head, she fixed her eyes on me for the last time. 'Can't you see that that's why this hurts so much? You knew what would happen to me if they found out. You *knew*, more than anyone, and you still told them. I'll never forgive you for this. Ever.'

'Neither of us will,' Bonnie added, and the two of them turned their backs to me, walking quickly away from college. Erin never came back. She started at Matravers School in Westbury soon after.

If she ever finds out I'm the person writing in those margins, it's over.

Passing Camberwell Green, I cross at the lights and walk down the high street, avoiding a crowd of drunk people eating McDonald's in a sheltered doorway.

I think about what Erin said to me in the back of *The Great Gatsby*.

Thank you for giving me the freedom to be myself.

The irony of it. That in allowing her to be herself, I have to be anyone but me.

Is that even possible? I could deliver the books in the dark of night. Never reveal anything that gives away my identity. Just thinking about it fills me with guilt, but the alternative is worse. The alternative is never writing back, and I don't think I can do that. She doesn't know it's me. Putting an end to the conversation in the margins would only hurt her more than I have already.

In the morning, as though the universe isn't done mocking me, *Middlemarch* is back. Next to it is a book I've never heard of, called *Beloved*. Swallowing, I run my eyes across the title, then flick to the back of George Eliot to check I've got the right one – and sure enough, there it is.

Meet me in Beloved*?*

The Book Swap

I try not to read into it. It's just a book title. She didn't choose it on purpose. Putting the books in my pocket, I jog to the bus stop. I pull them out once I'm on the tube.

As before, I go straight to the back where the answers to my questions are waiting. I can't think about the fact it's Erin writing back to me. If I can keep them separate, somehow, then nothing has changed. And then I read the answer to question eleven. Her greatest regret.

I let down a friend when she needed me the most and I'll never forgive myself. She died and I think I'll spend the rest of my life trying to make it up to her.

Closing the book, I squeeze my eyes shut. It feels too personal now. How can I let Erin live with that pain, when I know that Bonnie forgave her? That she understood? But I can't tell her, because I'm not meant to know it's Erin, and because of the promise I made Bonnie – to take our friendship to the grave. I never imagined it getting so complicated.

It's only as the train stops at Oxford Circus, and the carriage empties and then fills with even more people than before, that I notice the P.S. in *Beloved* and my stomach clenches.

What's your name, if it isn't too personal to ask? I'm not sure how much longer I can refer to you as 'Mystery Man' in my head for.

I slam the book closed. For the rest of the journey my brain isn't filled with my novel, it's filled only with how I can avoid answering that question. At some point she'll find out, and when she does, I lose everything. All I can do is keep that from happening for as long as possible.

As I exit at Highbury & Islington, I see a giant advert. It's a picture of the Statue of Liberty, with the words 'New York misses you'.

That's the answer. Of course it is.

I pull out my phone and message Elliot.

19

Erin

'I'm gonna move out,' Callum says with a cough when I have the displeasure of bumping into him in the kitchen mid-morning. It's a weekday, when once again he should be at work, and isn't.

'How have they not fired you?' I ask, as the kettle boils.

He reaches above me and takes a mug, putting it beside mine and nodding towards the coffee. I'm not sure how I could ever have had sex with him.

'How do you still not have a job?' he fires back.

I move my body as far away from the cafetière as it'll go before pushing the plunger down. He frowns at me and shakes his head. I couldn't be happier that Callum's moving out, but there's also no way I can afford this rent on my own. I'm hardly surviving as it is. I'll have to start putting adverts up. End up with some total random living in the flat with me, just to afford to stay. Callum knows that. He's taking pleasure in doing it.

Pouring myself a coffee, I walk back towards my room, leaving Callum's mug empty.

'There's no need to be a bitch about it,' he says, and I spin around.

'I'm not being a bitch, I'm prioritising myself. There's a difference – which you'd understand, if you had any respect for women.'

'Fucking hell, Erin,' he says, pouring a coffee for himself, and his accent, which I used to quite like, suddenly sounds like the most irritating thing in the world to me. 'You've got some serious problems, mate.'

'You shouldn't even be here,' I shout. 'You should be at work! Like normal people.'

'You can fucking talk.'

'I'm unemployed, not lazy.'

He shakes his head, wrapping his hands around his mug but not moving.

'You're like ... a child trapped in an adult's body. Sending little love notes to some boy in the back of a book. Quitting your job because your boss was mean to you. Sitting in your room, crying or talking to yourself. Your only friend's your sister. At least I live in the real world – I'm not hiding in my bedroom, living in the past. Like ... get a life, Erin.'

I turn away, taking in a shaky breath. My head spins for a moment and I close my eyes. Try and shake off everything he's said. It's *Callum*. Of all the people to have an opinion on my life, his should matter the least.

He stares at me, the corners of his mouth suddenly twitching. 'Can I have my T-shirt back? I need to pack it.'

I look down at myself, shaking as I realise I'm wearing something of his. Pulling it up over my head, I throw it at him and spin around, walking back into my room and slamming the door.

'And the sea *is* fucking real,' I shout, chest heaving, as I lean against the door.

My phone flashes from the bed with a message, from Cassie.

The Book Swap

Cassie: I felt so bad about lying about the cat I went on a second date with her! Yes I'm insane. No, I still don't fancy her. Yes I told her the truth. Onwards and upwards.

Cassie. She hates where she lives. She always used to say if she had more time, she'd find somewhere else.

Erin: Can't believe you went back in for another date!! Sounds like your day might need some brightening up, and I MIGHT have just the thing . . .

??? she replies.

Erin: My awful housemate is moving out. Don't suppose you want to move in with me?

I bite my lip as I send it.

Cassie: OMG!!!! This has made my YEAR. Proper reply later. Charlotte is ON ONE today! LIVING for my lunchtime Zumba class so I can get the hell out of here Xxx

There were moments throughout living here when I thought Callum and I might become friends, before the ridiculous night-time antics begun. He could make me laugh sometimes. Showed brief moments of kindness, in amongst all the silence and TV watching. Then I would realise that I was pinning too much hope on him, because of James.

James is probably the only and the best male friend I've had, until he wasn't. His one moment of betrayal destroyed three years of good, but before then, he was up there with Bonnie. Seeing his face out of the blue on the bus like that put him back in my thoughts, and while at first all of those were bad, flashes of good keep coming through. Especially now, after Callum. James would never have spoken to me or Bonnie like that. He used to say things that made me believe I could do anything. He's the one who convinced me, at the start of fourth form, that I could stand up in front of the whole school and read an excerpt from *The Hunger Games* in an assembly. I was obsessed with those books. It was the bit about hope being stronger than fear. He read it and I thought for a second he'd welled up. He handed it back to me.

'Do it,' he said. 'It's powerful. It could change someone's life without you even knowing.'

'He's right,' Bonnie said. 'Giving someone hope is like giving them the wings they need to fly through life.'

'All right, Bon. No need to take my words and shit all over them with your poetry,' James said and the three of us burst out laughing.

When I stood on the stage at school and read it, there were the two of them – in the front row, mouthing along to every word.

It's been too painful, ever since, to remember those times. But now the good memories keep appearing. I can't even fight them, because having them back is like having more of my best friend back too. When James told everyone about my mum, I didn't just lose him. I lost all the moments that also included Bonnie.

In the afternoon I make the short walk to Savannah's house, my stomach fluttering. Ever since I wrote the words *I want to be a teacher* in the back of the book, I've been unable to stop thinking about it. I've googled courses. But I haven't gone any further, because what if these sessions with Savannah are a total fluke?

The Book Swap

She lets me in and for the first time she leads me down the hallway and into the kitchen, instead of up the stairs.

'Was just making a squash. Do you want something? An old-person drink? Like tea?'

I roll my eyes and smile. 'I'd actually love a tea.'

'Course you would.' She busies herself at the kettle and I look around, seeing this part of the house for the first time. There's a corkboard covered in photographs, and drawings curled at the edges, some of the ink faded. It looks like it's been there for years, and, judging by the age of Savannah in the photos, it hasn't been updated in quite some time.

'So, did my dad tell you?' she asks, barely allowing the teabag to touch the water before she removes it and flings it in the sink. Quite a good shot, actually. She's grinning at me, and I don't know why.

'Your dad's a man of few words on email.'

She nods. 'Figures. Well, you know that essay I had to write on *Pride and Prejudice*?'

'Of course.' It was Savannah's last essay before the exams start. I've been helping her with preparation work for questions that might come up, but she has to write all the essays herself.

'I got my first C+. It was about what qualities Jane Austen seems to value in a person, based on the book.'

I want to pick her up and hug her, but I'm aware that, even with such an unofficial arrangement, it would be unprofessional.

Instead I break into a huge smile. 'Oh Savannah, that's amazing. Congratulations,' I say, my voice a higher pitch than I've heard it in quite some time. 'I'm so proud of you.' I'm proud of myself too.

'Thanks.' She hands me the tea, keeping hold of the handle so I have to burn my fingertips gripping it by the middle. The colour of it is so pale I swallow down a lump in my throat. This would for sure win the 'monstrosi-tea' competition Bonnie and I started, where we'd send each other photos of terrible cups of tea other people had made for us. Didn't realise I ordered a cappuccino she'd send, with an accompanying photo of a tea with white frothy milk. I loved it. I always felt like I was part of even the smallest moments of her day.

'That's my mum,' Savannah explains, nodding towards the photo I'm staring through while I think about Bonnie. I squeeze my eyes to focus on it. Savannah's about . . . ten-ish, grinning with braces on her teeth. Her mum's hair is blowing across her face as she laughs, one arm around Savannah and the other held out towards the camera.

'She's beautiful.'

'She was. She died six years ago.'

I haven't ever seen Savannah's mum or heard her mentioned, but I didn't want to presume something bad had happened to her. I'm more upset than I expected to find out that something has.

'I'm so sorry.'

Savannah shrugs, but the nonchalance of the action doesn't match the expression in her eyes. 'It's shit, not having her around.'

'I bet.' For the first time in a long time, I experience a small rush of guilt, that my mum *is* around, but that I choose to act as though she isn't. There are similar photos of us together. Hundreds of them, like the one Georgia gave her for her birthday. Ones where I'm looking up at her in total admiration, back before I realised she could do anything wrong.

The Book Swap

'Oh, before I forget,' she says, turning to me, her mum seemingly forgotten. 'A few of the girls in the year below are doing their Year Ten mock exams. I told them about you and loads of them want to book you in. My school's in East Dulwich so I told them you charged one hundred quid an hour. Believe me. They can afford it.'

My eyes widen at the prospect of making that amount of money for talking about books.

'Wow.'

'Shall I give them your email? Dad said I should check with you first.'

Swallowing down all the responses trying to compete to come out of my mouth, I take a moment to calm myself. This all feels so fragile. I'm worried if I show the level of enthusiasm I'm currently feeling, it could all come crumbling down. 'Yes. Please. That would be great.'

She mutters, 'Cool,' and turns to leave the room.

'Right, Savannah, we have just weeks to make you an expert before your exams start. I'm banning all Harry Styles chat from this lesson.'

She turns around and rolls her eyes at me before stomping up the stairs.

It would be way too fast, but I still feel a wave of disappointment when I walk home from Savannah's via the library and my books aren't there. I've stopped caring about what he's written about the books themselves. Now all I can think about is his answers to my questions. I just want to know him. I took a photo of the questions I asked him, and I bring it up on my screen, trying to remember whether I've written anything offensive. Anything that means he might not write back.

16. How did you know you wanted to be a writer?
17. Do you have brothers or sisters?
18. Are you close to your parents?
19. If you could live anywhere else in the world, where would it be?
20. Who is your favourite person in the world?

I can't see anything that might upset him, but there's so much I don't know. Maybe he has a sibling who died, or he hates talking about his family? Maybe he's married and doesn't want to answer who his favourite person is, in case he hurts my feelings? Or maybe – which I've only just thought about because I was so focused on Bonnie – I've terrified him by giving him a book called *Beloved*. I know I'm being ridiculous for thinking any of this. It's been three days. The chances are he's still reading. It's just that last time he put it back so quickly, I thought maybe he'd do the same thing again.

My mind starts to spiral. What if something happens to him and I never find out because I don't know who he is? The books might just stop coming one day, and I'll never know why. I should have asked for his number. Or given him mine. I'm just afraid of what that would mean.

It would be one step closer to meeting Mystery Man in person and the thought of that terrifies me as much as it excites me, if not more.

For the first time I'm starting to understand what Cassie means. Why she's so desperate to have that connection with a person. I want it too. I just want it with Mystery Man and no one else.

20

James

Elliot opens the door to his penthouse apartment, and I laugh as I take in the panoramic views of Manhattan from his living room. You can see everything from the Hudson River to the Empire State Building, all set as a backdrop to some of the most luxurious (and least child-friendly) furniture I've seen. A navy blue velvet sofa, red suede chairs around a giant glass dining table. The least child-friendly, that is, until Jordan barges past me and dives onto the blue sofa, bouncing up and down.

'Not now JJ, it's bedtime,' Elliot says and my heart jolts. I didn't know my nephew had the same nickname as me. That Elliot's carried it on with his son.

The warning falls on the deafest of ears as Jordan keeps launching himself higher and higher. Elliot shakes his head at me and checks his watch – something so shiny it distracts me, for a moment, from the view.

'Is that a—'

'Rolex? Yeah. Gift from Carl.' He glances towards the sofa. 'Better get that tub running.'

'You mean bath,' I shout after him, before walking towards Jordan.

'Reckon if I take one of these fancy cushions off and put it on the ground, you can jump from the arm onto it?'

Jordan nods, his floppy light brown hair dancing in and out of his eyes, a big grin breaking across his face.

I take off all the back cushions, placing them on the ground, a safe distance from the glass table.

'It's pretty hard,' I say, as he climbs onto the arm. 'You sure you're ready.'

'Yeah,' he shouts, and before I can even start a countdown he propels himself into the air, landing with a squeal of delight on the pool of cushions beneath him. 'Again!'

'Bath time, buddy,' Elliot says, reappearing, causing Jordan to break into tears so dramatic you'd think all his favourite toys had been taken from him and destroyed. 'We try to keep it pretty low-key from six o'clock onwards.' He glances down at the cushions and back at me, causing heat to rush to my cheeks. *If I saw them more, I'd know that.*

'Got it.' I pick the cushions up and throw them back onto the sofa as Elliot collects a kicking and screaming Jordan and carries him through to the bathroom. Minutes later loud cackles of laughter are coming from the same direction, and soon after that Jordan bursts back into the room, dressed in Spiderman pyjamas.

'Will you read me a story, Uncle James?' he asks, and my heart fills with love as I remember that I'm not just here because I'm running away from my problems. I'm here to get to know my nephew, and there's no better way of doing that than by sharing my favourite activity with him.

'I'd love to,' I say, meaning it.

He runs off to his bedroom and I follow, shaking my head at the view from his room. At age three he's got some of the best real estate in the city and, to add to the extravagance, a double bed that sits opposite a rack of books, and a blue wooden chest of toys.

'Wow . . . this all yours?'

He nods, thrusting a book into my hand before doing a

very energetic roll into bed, as Elliot appears in the doorway with a ball of Jordan's clothes in his hand.

'Ooooh. *Be Kind*. Good choice, buddy. Good luck with that one,' he adds to me, smiling.

Jordan pats the bed and I go to lie beside him, reading to him all about a little girl who's sad because she's spilled grape juice on her dress.

By the second to last page, I'm wiping under my eyes as I try to keep my voice from breaking.

'. . . So that we can be kind,' I say. 'Again. And again. And again.' I turn to Elliot. 'Fucking hell,' I mouth at him, blown away by the power of a book with fewer words than the first chapter of my novel.

'Told you,' he says, laughing. 'Okay, night, JJ.' He walks to the window, pressing a button to close the blinds, and then bends down to kiss him. I lie there for a second, unsure what I should do, but Jordan throws his little arms around me.

'Night,' he says, kissing me, and then he rolls onto his side.

Swallowing, I stand up and leave the room. He looks like Elliot as a boy and that, combined with the emotion from the book – and the jet lag, and the past thirty-six hours – is enough to almost tip me over the edge.

'So where is Carl?' I ask, once Jordan has stopped coming out and being put back to bed and has actually, finally, fallen asleep.

Elliot hands me a glass of champagne and sits down on the big white chair opposite the sofa.

'LA,' he says, raising his glass and downing some.

'Must be hard.' I glance towards Jordan's room. 'Having him away so much.'

He shrugs. 'I'm used to it, I guess.' He starts spinning the watch around his wrist. 'I think it's harder for Carl. Missing out on so much. It's like he's away, and JJ and I find our own way of doing things – and then he comes back, and it's like he can't find the place where he fits in, you know? He gets pretty down about it. Beats himself up. Wants to be able to do it all. Businessman. Provider. Perfect dad.' He sighs, staring into his glass. 'He doesn't seem to get that he doesn't have to be perfect, he just has to *be* here. To give JJ some attention. Not time, but attention. He fools himself into thinking that giving Jordan his bath, while on his phone, is quality time, but Jordan notices that stuff. Kids are scarily smart.'

'I'm just starting to learn that,' I say, glancing off towards Jordan's bedroom.

'How's stuff with you, anyway? Dad said you're writing a book.'

That's the thing with Elliot. He'll tell you something heartbreaking. Something that definitely requires many more conversations, and then he'll shut it down. I know him. If I push further on what he's just said, he'll backtrack. I just have to leave it. His admissions about his life never come from me asking about them. They come when I least expect them.

'Yeah,' I say, going along with this avoidance tactic. 'I am. Or ... I was.' Thinking about *Ten Ways to Say Sorry* now only leads me to Erin, which leads to the library and onwards until all I can see is her disgusted face on the bus. 'Stopped for a bit.'

'How come?' He finishes his champagne and walks across to the kitchen to top up his glass.

'Just not sure it's any good. There's an agent who said she'll read the first three chapters though, so that's something.'

He sits back down. 'Have you got three chapters?'

'Yeah, I've nearly finished the whole book.'

The Book Swap

'Can't you just send her the chapters now? Then you'll know if it's any good.'

I forget how Elliot is. He never really sees problems. It's why we had such different experiences at school, and why he has so much to offer career wise. He could be doing so much with his life. Probably making as much money as Carl, or more, if he really put his mind to it. I never understand why he doesn't.

'I suppose I could,' I say. I've rewritten those first few chapters so many times, I'm pretty sure they're as good as they can be. Would it be crazy to send them when the book isn't finished? Just thinking about it makes my head start to spin, and I don't think the champagne or time difference is helping. 'How about you and work?'

He shakes his head. 'No time.'

'But Jordan's in nursery now, right?'

He looks at me. Holds my gaze. 'Pre-school, yeah. For a few hours, and while he's there I have to prep meals, do housework, get Carl's clothes dry-cleaned. I already need more hours in the day, without throwing work in.'

I squint. 'That's why you moved here, though? To become some big shot in finance.'

The sound of horns beeping far below distracts me for a second, but Elliot doesn't even notice. 'That's what I thought I wanted, but it wasn't really. I just wanted to get away. Go somewhere new where I could be completely myself.'

His words sound like they've been written by a PR team. I'm finding it hard to believe anything he's saying, and I know if we continue on this topic we'll fall out before I've even been here a day.

'Oh my God,' I say, instead, changing the subject. 'Did you hear someone's released a remix of Dad's song?'

Elliot's eyes light up. 'Good on him. Let's find it.'

We pull out our phones in a silent race to be the first to track it down, as though it might be impossible to find. It's not. It's everywhere. There's even an 'unofficial' video, which has got thousands of views.

'Jesus. How did we not know about this?' Elliot says, his thumb scrolling down his phone.

'I don't know. Do you think Dad knows?'

'Surely not.' Elliot checks his watch as I check the time on my phone. It's too late to call him.

'Ready?' I ask, gritting my teeth.

Elliot claps his hands together. 'I'll do it. I can play it through the speakers.' Moments later it's like the walls are shaking. The song starts with a heavy bass, very different to the electro-pop sound of Dad's, and then his voice comes over the top, just as some laser-like sound starts ringing out in the background. 'Do you ... Do you ... Do you know me?' There's a silence and then the beat drops and all the different sounds come together, achieving something scarily impressive.

'Bloody hell,' Elliot shouts over the top. 'This is ...'

'Fucking brilliant,' I say back.

When it's over we sit in silence for a moment, my brain whirring.

'It could totally relaunch his career,' I say, at the same time as Elliot says, 'One for Dad's memory box.'

We lock eyes. 'You think Dad wants to be prancing about on a stage, now?'

'He'd love it! He's spent years giving up on his dreams for all of us. Now's his time.'

I think about how Mum was on the phone, seemingly close to another crash. The extra pressure it might put on me if

Dad goes for it – but it's worth it. He needs this. He needs to prove to himself that he's his own man.

Elliot's watching me. He opens his mouth and closes it.

It's not even the end of the first night, and it's happened. We've run out of things to say.

The rest of the trip is mainly spent using Jordan as a distraction, so my brother and I don't have to talk much. We get into a routine: I get up early with my nephew, because I'm wide awake with jet lag anyway. We play with building blocks and read books. I had no idea there were so many kids' books that are like daggers to the heart. My eyes have welled up at everything from a hippo dancing, to a little girl making paper dolls. Jordan is utterly oblivious, stabbing at the pages and asking completely irrelevant questions about why the flowers are blue or the hippo has a big nose. We have breakfast, then wake a very grateful Elliot up with coffee, before we set about sightseeing. We walk part of the High Line, take a horse and carriage around Central Park. We catch the train out to Williamsburg and get the ferry to the Statue of Liberty and Ellis Island. We're busy and I'm tired, and that combination means that for five blissful days I don't think too much about everything at home. I don't even pick up Erin's books, instead falling into a dead sleep the moment my head hits the pillow after a long day.

On our last day, Elliot takes a call from Carl as we're navigating our way through the centre of Times Square. Jordan's asleep in his pushchair, and Elliot pulls us into the doorway of Planet Hollywood, so he can hear.

'Hey, I've got five minutes, where's my big man?' Carl says.

Elliot screws his face up, turning the phone to show Carl his son, slumped over in his seat clutching, for a reason I'm still unsure of, a tape measure. 'Sorry, babe, he's crashed. Uncle James is exhausting him.'

Carl sighs. 'I'm in meetings over here now until beyond bedtime. Can you wake him?'

Elliot laughs. 'You know that's not a good idea.'

'I hate this.'

'I'm sorry.'

I step backwards, to give the impression of some privacy, even though I can still hear every word.

'I'm going to try and get home.'

'Please don't say that unless you can do it.' My brother's voice sounds like it might break.

'Okay.'

'Want to say hi to James?'

'I've got this meeting. Send my love.'

'Okay.'

Elliot turns, his shoulders low. His husband's sadness is etched on his face.

'Sorry about that,' he says. 'It's like he knows the worst time to call. Every time. And then he blames me and gets upset.' He runs a hand through his hair, looking down at his son.

'Maybe don't take on Carl's emotions as your own,' I say, hating to see my brother like this. 'You can't fix it for him.'

Elliot starts guiding the pushchair back onto the bustling streets. There are giant billboards all around us advertising everything from a new Billie Eilish album to the world's most famous fizzy drink.

'Like you do with Mum, you mean?' He fixes his eyes on me, anger flashing across his face.

I swerve to let someone pass. 'Woah. That was unnecessary.'

'True though.'

'Well, someone has to with Mum. It's different.'

'Is it?'

We turn right towards Broadway, where I take a leaflet for a musical I won't have time to see.

'What do you mean, "is it?" Of course it is.'

'You can't fix her either though.' His voice is low.

I can feel a lump forming in my throat.

'Maybe not, but I can make things better for her. You'd know that, if you ever came home.'

A smile, lacking any warmth, flashes across his face. He stops and does a slow clap. 'There it is. Finally.'

'What?'

'An admission that you resent me for being here.' He turns to face me, and I look at him standing there, his shiny Rolex blinding me. I think of his incredible apartment. This life where he gets to choose to do whatever he wants, day after day, while I'm on a train home to my parents the moment I need to be.

'I don't resent you for . . . *Fine*. Maybe I do. Maybe it feels shit to be the one who always has to look after Mum. To give up his life and go back to a different one.'

He leans forward. 'You took that on. No one asked you to. Not Mum. Not Dad. They've always told us to live our lives. It's what they both want for us.'

'Well, maybe you're able to do that without feeling guilty about it, but I'm not.' I screw the leaflet up into a ball in my hand, crushing as hard as I can.

'Obviously.'

'What?'

'How can you ever stop feeling guilty when you blame yourself for how she is?'

We're at a complete standstill now, on one of the busiest streets in New York City, glaring at each other. Swarms of people are having to walk around us and it isn't like it would be in London. There's no polite tutting here. Everyone is shouting at us to get 'out of the fucking way'. I'm too riled to care.

'It's hard not to blame myself when everyone keeps reminding me it was me being born that made our mum ill.'

Elliot shakes his head. 'No one reminds you of that. No one has ever blamed you for that. That's all on you.'

'You don't know that, because you left.' The words burst out of me. The ones I've been suppressing in every call we ever have. 'Mum threw it at me all the time. When you dropped off the face of the earth for those two years, it was like she finally had permission to tell me what she thought of me. She blamed everything on me. I kept trying to call and email you, but you'd cut us off. You'd cut *me* off.' The last words break as they come out, and I bite down on my lip.

'I had to,' Elliot shouts. 'I took that year off for you, James. I was there for you every day, waiting after school, and then Joel came along. You two were always off somewhere.' Tears glisten in his eyes, a smile on his lips. 'I was so happy. I knew you didn't need me any more, and I was fucked inside. I had all these feelings about who I was, and I didn't dare say them out loud. Mum was leaning on me more than ever. She kept saying I was the only thing that made her happy.' Guilt washes across his face, as he admits it. It doesn't surprise me, but it still hurts. 'I stayed because of you, and the second I could see you were okay without me, I ran. I couldn't be reminded of home while I figured myself out. I'd have come straight back and I'd never have dealt with it. I never would have met Carl. Never would have had Jordan. I had to do what I did, to be the man I am now. But I'm sorry. I really am sorry.'

I wipe the tears from my eyes. It's all I've ever wanted him to say, and I feel awful for having forced it out of him.

'I'm sorry,' I say. 'I didn't know you were going through stuff too.'

'Of course you didn't,' he says, his voice gentle. 'You couldn't focus on anything except getting through each day. I don't even know how you did that. I'm so proud of you.'

'I'm so proud of you,' I say, reaching out an arm that Elliot falls into, hugging me tight.

'Good. So can I have my brother back now?' he asks, turning and walking back towards his apartment as though we haven't just been blocking the streets of Times Square.

The brother from years ago would have told Elliot everything, and suddenly I want to. Everything back home with Erin is consuming me and I need help to find my way out of it.

'Consider him back,' I say, and I start talking. 'So, you won't believe what happened before we came here. You remember Erin? Obviously you remember Erin. Well . . .'

By the time Elliot and I make it to the airport, something's settled between us. Conversations have been laid bare. I feel as though I can be myself around my brother again.

Jordan insists on wheeling my hand luggage to check-in, which means the whole thing takes considerably longer than it should.

Elliot and I pat each other on the back, before I scoop up Jordan, holding him tight.

'Come here, little man,' I say, trying to hug him as he wiggles out of my arms to spin the suitcase again. 'Be good for your daddy, okay?'

Elliot bends down and picks up whatever fell out of my pocket in the struggle. It's the book I picked up for Erin at Barnes & Noble, during my trip.

'We've seen that film,' he says, placing the copy of *On the Road* in my hand and crash landing me back to the reality I've so successfully avoided.

21

Erin

There's still no book in the library, and it's been over a week. Rather than let that get to me, I'm trying my new and improved What Would Bonnie Do approach, which involves focusing on other things. Making the most of every day.

Georgia calls me as I'm walking to the local shops to put up posters for my English coaching. The weather is so unpredictable. I left the house in a jumper and jeans, and I'm already down to my T-shirt and dreaming of shorts.

'I've done it,' she says, breathing out as I scan back through all our conversations for the thing she's been wanting to do. 'I told Rishi.'

I stop outside the McDonald's on Camberwell Road. 'What? And?'

'He proposed.'

'Of course he did. That is *classic* Rishi.'

'Erin, you had two therapy sessions with him where you claim he didn't even speak. Stop pretending you know him.'

'Fine. Then it's classic you.'

'What's that supposed to mean?'

A bus pulls up beside me, emptying a load of people onto the street. They disperse around me.

'Well, it's like the time you spent the whole of Easter crying and freaking out about your exams, so Dad put together that whole revision plan for you, and then you got all A's, which you were always going to get anyway.'

My mind jumps to Savannah, who's got her GCSEs soon. She thinks she's going to do okay, but C-grade okay.

'You're making no sense. Are you hungover?'

I laugh. 'No. Anyway, that's irrelevant. Is this your low-key way of saying you're now both pregnant *and* engaged?'

She snorts. 'Absolutely not. I told him to get a grip. A baby does not have to equal a life sentence in an unhappy marriage.'

'Our parents thought it did.'

After she's gone, I reread my sign, checking it for any mistakes. I do not want spelling errors on a sign advertising English tuition.

Experienced tutor with a 2:1 degree in English Literature, available to help prepare for GCSEs or A levels. £50 per session.

I didn't include the quote Savannah offered me. I'm not sure 'she got me my first C+!' is the advertising I'm after. I've added an email address that I've set up just for teaching, and passed it on to Savannah via her dad as well.

I've already got four of her friends in the year below lined up for weekly sessions throughout the summer holidays. I'm worried that I just got lucky with Savannah, and tomorrow, when it's a different student, I might discover I'm awful at it. That I hate it. But until I know that, I may as well try. It's what Bonnie would do.

I've figured out that between the dog walking and tutoring, I can make enough money to stay in London. That plus the very generous cash gift Georgia gave me as an early birthday present. I'm still having weekly sessions with

Philippa, and she thinks that now Callum's moving out, it's a good idea for me to keep the stability of my London flat. She doesn't know the real reason I'm so terrified of leaving. I've kept it to myself that Bonnie lives in that room. That when I moved out of my flat in Stockwell and into the one in Loughborough Junction, there she was, waiting for me in the armchair, which came as part of the fully furnished agreement. I've never seen her anywhere else, and if I have to leave, I think it means I leave her too.

Cassie comes over in the evening to check out the flat. She messages on the way, apologising that she's definitely going to be early because the journey's even more of a dream than she realised. I take that as a good sign.

I've messaged Callum to tell him I've got someone looking at his room. He sends back a thumbs-up. This is the only exchange we've had since I stood topless outside my bedroom, throwing his T-shirt at him.

The bell goes as I'm finessing the flat. I've lit a scented candle in the sitting room and fluffed the cushions. Cleaned the kitchen surfaces until they shine and added some fresh flowers. I've opened the door to Callum's room to air it – did it always have that aroma, even when I crept in at night? I don't remember it, which worries me. Turns out love – or lust – goggles are a real thing.

When I open the door, Cassie is bouncing up and down, her tight curls springing with each movement. She's wearing oversized lilac trousers and a matching jacket, with a white crop top underneath. I'm envious of how well she knows how to dress for every season.

'Were you not tempted to stay in your awful job, purely for the commute?' she asks, walking into the kitchen and pointing with her thumb towards the front door, indicating the end of her dream journey.

'It's pretty good, isn't it?' I laugh, taking her jacket and throwing it on the back of an armchair.

She looks around the open-plan living room and kitchen, nodding. 'This is so much nicer than my place.' She opens the door to the fridge and throws her head back, letting out a sigh of relief. 'No labels on the shelves. Wait ... do you even ... share milk? I've been trying to convince the others that it makes so much more sense than all of us buying our own.'

'We do.' It's not something I ever thought I'd be proud of.

'Go on then ... show me the bedroom.'

'Be warned,' I say, leading her back towards the front door, where Callum's room sits just off to the right. 'It smells of man.'

Cassie screws up her face and then laughs, stepping in. 'There's space for a double bed *and* cupboards. I'm sold!'

She turns to look at me.

'Wait ... actually?'

'Yes! I was already sold on the housemate and the journey alone. The flat itself had a pretty easy job.'

I clap, walking towards her for a hug. 'I can't believe it.'

'Me neither!' She pulls a bottle of rosé from the bag on her shoulder. 'Now ... shall we open this to celebrate?'

'Definitely.'

I take the bottle from her and reach up for the only two wine glasses we have in this flat. I bought them after I moved in and found Bonnie here. I used to take the bottle into my room, and pour one for each of us. I stopped when Callum noticed me washing up two glasses once and looked at me for a really long time, before walking away. The significance of

The Book Swap

using this same glass for Cassie isn't lost on me, but I know Bonnie wouldn't be sad about it. She'd be so happy to know I've got a friend here. It's not Bonnie that causes me to stop for a moment before I turn around, holding the glasses out – it's me. It feels as though I'm leaving my best friend behind and I'm not sure it's something I'm prepared for.

Cassie sits herself at the little round dining table on the other side of the kitchen bar. It's not somewhere I've ever sat much before. When I first moved here, I'd eat the odd dinner there, angling the television towards me. But then Callum started to stay home more and more with his cycling shows on, and for some reason, because he lived here first, I felt as though he had more say over what we watched. I started disappearing to my room to eat, occasionally taking the other sofa if I didn't want to be on my own. I can see how different it will be living with Cassie, and I wish it could start right now.

In the morning, I try the library again. I'm getting desperate. As I pass under the bridge, I glance up the road, in case anyone's walking towards me. I still don't know if I'm ready to meet Mystery Man, but the more I read his answers, the more I want to. There's no one there so I go to the library, feeling less sure with every step that anything will be there – but I can see it. The bright red spine of *Beloved*, sitting next to another book. I wonder if he's been brave back, and chosen something that might hint at how he feels about me. I open it up to the back page. *Meet me in* On the Road? Reaching back into the library, I pick up the Jack Kerouac and flick through it, grinning as something falls out of the back, landing at my feet. It's a postcard with the words 'New York' on the front in a retro font, and when I pick it up and turn it over it says, *Really sorry this is late*. X

So he does think about me as much as I think about him. He's even written me a postcard. I look down at the page it was tucked into and see lines underlined in red.

'A pain stabbed my heart, as it did every time I saw a girl I loved who was going the opposite direction in this too-big world.'

All I can focus on are the words in the middle. 'A girl I loved.' Did he place the card there on purpose?

Flicking through the rest, it's as though he's added extra messages to make up for how late it is. Normally his margins are fairly sparse, but now he's filled whole pages.

Do we really think this is based on a true story? One man can't have gone through this much on a single road trip? Dean gets married THREE times. I'll be lucky to get married once.

There's a lot of rain in this book. Rain reminds me of some pretty bad times, so I just imagined it sunny. Recommend you do the same.

Switching back to *Beloved*, I turn over the last page, ignoring his answers to the questions for a moment and scanning right to the bottom. Mystery Man is no longer Mystery Man.

Mystery Man is called . . . Edward.

22

James

'Edward?' Joel asks, standing in front of me with pads on his hands as I slam my fists repeatedly into them.

I've filled him in on what happened on the bus, my trip to New York and my decision, after that trip, to lie.

In the end, after talking it through with Elliot, it was simple. I couldn't lose her.

'No offence, mate,' Joel says, letting out a breath each time my boxing glove makes contact. 'But James . . . is quite . . . a common name. Not sure Erin . . . would have presumed . . . you were the same person.' He forces the last words out as quickly as possible, putting his hands down.

I keep my arms up close to my body, the way we've just been taught. Another class Joel has hunted down in his efforts to try new things.

'I couldn't risk it,' I say, nodding for him to put his hands back up. 'Not after the bus. Anyway, it's not like it's an actual lie.' I slam my glove into his pad, in an effort to escape his judgement, as well as my own. He stumbles backwards, eyes wide, before regaining his balance.

I was actually christened Edward James Parr, but when Mum became unwell, she apparently took a real aversion to calling me Edward, and so I was always known as James. I reminded myself of this as I put the book back in the library, around 11 p.m., when I was sure Erin wouldn't check. Then

I walked around the park back to my flat, and to distract myself from the dishonesty, I sent the first three chapters of my book to Sophia Lindsay, the literary agent. This morning, I can't stop thinking about what she might reply. I'm hoping something along the lines of them being the best chapters she's ever read, and a desperate plea to see the rest of the book, to which the answer would be . . . no.

With just twenty thousand words left, all I can do is stare at the white screen until it's not white any more and my eyes are stinging. How can I write a book apologising for the past when I've just created a whole new reason to be sorry? It's as though I need Erin's forgiveness in order to continue, and I know I can't get it. Especially now.

Moving one fist after another as fast as I can into Joel's pads, a wave of sickness hits me. I can't believe I've been so stupid. If she finds out it's me, she won't just hate me for lying. She'll know that I've had to lie for a reason. Because I know that Margins Girl is Erin.

Sweat's dripping from my head but I can't stop my arms from moving.

'Jesus, James, chill,' Joel's muttering, keeping his hands up in front of his face as I slam another right hook into him. How could I not have thought about that? I'm so fucking selfish. Slam. Slam. Slam. All I thought about was buying myself more time.

I've still got it, somewhere. The letter I was going to give Erin the day she screamed at me in the rain. I was being selfish then, too. Thinking Erin would care that I'd fallen in love with her when her life had just been torn apart. I always get it so wrong.

'Okay, time to swap over,' the coach shouts, but I can't. I don't want a second of thinking about what I've just done.

The Book Swap

Ignoring the protesting in my lungs and the burning in my arms, I keep hitting. I know I deserve all the pain I'm feeling and more. I've let her down again. It's like no matter how hard I try, it's all I'm capable of doing.

My ears are ringing by the time I stop. My cheeks are burning hot as bile shoots up into my throat and I turn towards the floor, vomiting onto the ground. I gasp for breath, bent over as my whole body threatens to collapse right there, and I stumble, allowing myself to fall. Lying back, I throw my arms above my head, chest heaving as I stare up at the ceiling, covered in dark brown stains.

I wish I was like Jack Kerouac. Then I could leave a city, not worrying for a moment about the pain I'd left behind. There was a grotesqueness to the way his characters Sal and Dean lived, but right now I envy it: the freedom there is in continuing to escape your life.

'Fucking hell, mate,' Joel says, appearing over me. 'Are you trying to punish yourself?'

He has no idea.

The following week, Dorothy calls me into a meeting, landing it on me the second I walk through the door. She wants to reduce her workload by the end of the year, and asks me to become a director.

'You'd be taking over the reins, really,' she explains. 'You'd be the face of Big Impressions.'

There it is. The offer I've hoped for since I started here. If I could just get to that point, I'd be stable. Successful. Sorted. Joel appears in my mind. What he said about his own job, and how he'd never do it if he had a passion the way I did.

I ask Dorothy for time to think about it and, instead of

going back to my desk, I walk right past it and down the stairs, out onto the street.

Legs shaking, I sit down on the bench in the little park, resting my elbows on my knees. This is good for me. It's a good opportunity. The money will be a lot more than I'm on already. The people are fine. It's a decent job. I'm good at it. I don't know if I want to do it.

Scanning back through the last few years, I'm not even sure how I ended up here. I'm starting to wonder if everything I wrote to Erin in response to her questions is bullshit. Another lie. I told her everything happens for a reason, but how can a career in corporate training be leading me towards becoming an author? It isn't. It's purely providing me with the money to finance it. I've given that so much importance. Watched my bank balance grow, while allowing everything around me to fall apart.

If I could do anything at all, I'm not sure this is it, but what other options do I have?

Picking up my phone, I call Dad. I didn't get around to it post-run this morning, and now I have a desire to hear his voice. To add some normality to my life.

'It hasn't been good here,' he says, when we've got the fake pleasantries out of the way. 'Your mum was up all night for a few days. We've altered the medication and it seems to be working for the time being. She's a bit more stable.'

I know this cycle. They'll need me soon and my first reaction is relief. I'll have to delay my answer on the job offer. Leave London for a while. I close my eyes and lift my head to the sky, taking deep breath. Springing forward as I realise what else it means. No more book exchange. I'd be away from the library. From the one person who's causing me equal parts pain and joy.

'Do you need me to come?' I ask and I don't know what I want the answer to be.

'I can handle it for now. She hasn't crashed yet and she's at least responding to me when I tell her to rest. Well, she is now. She wasn't having any of it at four a.m. for a while.'

'You must be exhausted.'

'I'm okay,' he replies, the way I knew he would. The way he always does, no matter what's happening. Sometimes I'd feel so much better if he just complained a bit. Said something bad about her. He never has. Not once. I've only ever noticed the slightest tone of irritation in his voice.

'You should get some sleep now too, while you can.'

'I will, it's just ... there's a fair amount of clearing up to do.' That means Mum's absolutely trashed the place.

'I'll come home soon. See if I can help out a bit.'

'That would be nice.'

I swallow. I know what will cheer him up. 'I just got offered a director role at work.'

The moment the words are out of my mouth, I sort of wish I hadn't told him. Now there's no way I can turn it down. Except he doesn't respond the way I thought he would.

'Is that something you want?' he asks, and I find myself shaking my head.

'I don't know, but it's something I can do. Maybe that's enough.'

'Maybe. But there's lots of things you can do. Don't waste your heart's calling on saying yes to something, just because you know you can do it. The straightforward route isn't always the best one.'

I think about Dad, and what he's missed out on with his own calling, by focusing on Mum.

'Did you know some DJ's done a remix of your song?' I blurt out.

'I do.' He laughs, and I hear the familiar sound of water going into the mug. The 'tink' of the teaspoon against it. 'He messaged my agent. He—' He stops.

'He what?'

'Oh, he wanted me to go on some tour with him. Come out on stage and surprise the crowds. Something silly like that. They sent me through the dates, in case I was interested, and God, the man's playing everywhere.'

'You should do it, Dad.'

'Absolutely not.'

'But it—'

'No, James. Not with your mother the way she is. Not when the house is a tip and someone's got to sort it.' There it is. The only tiny sign he'll give that his life's in any way difficult.

'I can sort it.'

He sighs. 'You've got your own life to live. Speaking of which, a letter came for you this morning. I was about to send you a photo. An invitation from Frome College, to speak at their careers day. Apparently they have you marked as quite the success story.'

I frown. 'Me? Are you sure?'

'Yup. Addressed to you. They want a reply as soon as possible. Anyway, I'll see you soon. Better go wake up Henry the hoover and hope he's had more sleep than your mother.'

I try to laugh. I know he just wants to ease the tension, but I can't. Dad's doing it again. Giving up his life's dream. I can't watch him do it. I'll find a way to make this happen for him.

'Okay, Dad, bye.'

The Book Swap

He follows up with a photo, and there it is. The Frome College logo and an invitation for Mr James Parr to speak at the careers day in September. I imagine walking back into that college as a different man, with everyone I knew there now gone.

Leaving the park, I push open the door of the bookshop and walk inside. I know I need to tell Erin the truth. This can't go on. It means the next book I give her will be the one where I explain everything. Where I say goodbye, and I need it to mean something.

My watch vibrates, to announce an email, and I grab my phone, staring at the preview on the screen.

Hi James,
Thanks so much for sending this through. I look forward to reading it.
Best,
Sophia

23

Erin

16. How did you know you wanted to be a writer?
I've always known, I've just been too afraid to act on it. I've grown up in fear of not having enough money to live on, and I chose the path that would stop that from ever happening. I couldn't understand anyone who chose to follow their passion, whether they could afford to or not. I judged them for it. Answering this has helped me realise something though: I judged them because I was jealous. I wanted to do what they did, but I hadn't allowed myself to. If I'd started after school the way I wanted to, who knows where I'd be by now. But I know that's no one else's fault but mine. They were brave, and I wasn't.

17. Do you have brothers or sisters?
I have one older brother. I actually just came back from visiting him. We've grown apart over the years and your comments about your sister made me want to try and rebuild things.

18. Are you close to your parents?
I think they are the bravest and best people I know.

19. If you could live anywhere else in the world, where would it be?
Having just read On the Road *I'm now pretty keen on the idea of a road trip across America, but I've found myself running*

away from things I need to face recently, and I think I need to be braver now. For that reason I try not to imagine my life anywhere but where it is right now. (God, that was an intense answer? I should have just written Florida!)

20. Who is your favourite person in the world?
Right now, my nephew, because he makes me feel like a superhero. He also has the most eclectic taste in children's books and I'm a changed man from having read them. I might even leave you one for our next exchange!

'He is absolutely your boyfriend and the more you deny it, the redder your face goes.'

Cassie, Georgia and I are sitting in an Italian restaurant in Covent Garden called Ave Mario, to celebrate my thirty-first birthday. From the outside it's underwhelming, but on the inside it's filled with neon lights, big mirrors and hundreds of real, fresh flowers. It's breathtaking as you walk in, and the smell that fills it is almost as good as the food itself.

'You know the rules about birthdays, Georgia. You're not allowed to be mean.'

'Ah, but Cassie didn't know that rule, so she's exempt.'

Despite having never met before, by the time starters had arrived Cassie and Georgia were already chatting away. Now we're mid-mains and they've formed a united front, particularly when it comes to Edward.

'Do you think of him when you hear something funny?' Cassie asks. 'Like, "Edward would find this funny".'

'Oooh, good question.' Georgia is nodding like Cassie has just asked me something that could change the state of the world. Solve global warming. Begin world peace.

'Yes.' I push a piece of the silkiest ravioli I've ever eaten into my mouth, unable to focus on anything else except the taste.

'Knew it. Have you imagined what he looks like?' Cassie pokes a fork of carbonara towards me.

'Clive Owen,' Georgia interrupts with a mouthful of pizza, as Cassie claps her hands together.

'Brilliant.'

'A young Clive Owen,' I correct. 'Think *Closer*. *Sin City*. Dark hair. Chiselled. Piercing eyes.'

'That's so weird. That's exactly what my imaginary boyfriend looks like.'

I glare at Georgia. 'I wish I'd never told either of you.'

'Noooo, don't say that,' Cassie says, drinking some wine. 'I think it's so romantic. Honestly. People have met in way weirder ways.'

'Name one,' Georgia says, and I can tell by the way she's already treating Cassie like family that she likes her.

'Fine. When I was twenty I met a guy by walking off with his suitcase at the airport, and he chased after me. Genuinely got so excited. Thought it had to work out, but unfortunately, he was fucking boring, so . . .'

Georgia cackles and I laugh, using it as my excuse to add some clarity.

'You see. I can't get carried away. Edward could be awful. Boring, like suitcase man.'

'He won't be,' Georgia says.

'Oh, but I did meet my ex-girlfriend because of him, so—'

'Ohhhh,' I interrupt Cassie because I know this story, but I'd forgotten all about it.

'She was in the same bar, sitting alone and she'd been stood up, so I left boring suitcase man, and went and sat with her instead. We were together two years, so in a way . . . it worked out. She was the last person I dated who I met in real life. It's been depressing online date after depressing online date ever since.'

'I refuse to online date any more,' Georgia says, nodding. 'I mean . . . not that it would be a good look right now anyway.' She looks down and the three of us erupt into laughter. 'I met one too many terrible men and that was it for me. Deleted the apps. They weren't serving me any more.'

Cassie's eyes light up. 'I love that. They weren't serving you. That's so true.'

'Yup. Anything that isn't serving you, get rid.'

'I'm going to do it,' she says and I roll my eyes at Georgia being the voice of inspiration, the way she always is.

'But Mystery Man . . . he's serving you, right? Are you getting any clues that he feels the same?'

Heat rushes to my cheeks as my mind immediately flashes back to every single line he's underlined that's given me hope. I don't want to seem insane by quoting them all.

'Yes. Well . . . I think so.'

I look down at my bag. I've got *On the Road* and *The Bell Jar* with me, in case I pass the library on the way home. Both Georgia and Cassie follow my gaze, and for a woman who's now sporting a small bump, Georgia's on her feet faster than I was expecting, snatching at the straps of my handbag.

'No way,' I say, grabbing the other strap and pulling. 'It's private.'

'Nothing's private from sisters,' she says, clenching her teeth and pulling back.

'As someone who has three, I can confirm that's true,' Cassie says, shrugging as she wraps the last of her carbonara around her fork.

The Book Swap

'That's bullshit,' I say, yanking as hard as I can.

'Just show us one then,' she says, letting go so I fly backwards and into the hip of the handsome Italian waiter who's passing with some menus. He stops and rests his hand on my shoulder, smiling as he helps me back into my seat before walking off.

'If you didn't already have a boyfriend, that could have been your moment,' Cassie says.

After saying goodbye to Cassie, Georgia and I walk back to her car. Now that she's pregnant she insists on driving everywhere. Minutes before we reach her parking spot, she has to run in somewhere to wee and I wait on the bench outside, opening *On the Road* and scanning Edward's questions.

21. I can't believe I haven't asked you this yet. What is your favourite book of all time?
22. What's your philosophy in life?
23. What is your favourite memory of your best friend?
24. Would you rather go back in time, or forward into the future?
25. What's your best memory from your school years?

His last question is a weird one, but I like that it gets me thinking about the good times at school, instead of the bad. I pull a pen out of my bag and answer the questions as honestly as I can and then tap the pen against my lip as I think of five more of my own to write inside *The Bell Jar*. The first four don't even really matter any more; it's the last one I'm interested in hearing an answer to. Having spoken to Georgia and Cassie, I realise this can't go on. At some point, one of us has to put an end to it. Or a beginning.

30. Shall we meet in person?

I thought I'd feel nervous writing those words, but I don't. Adrenaline is pumping through me and I know that I'm ready. It's time to take all of this off the page.

Georgia comes back just as I'm putting the books back in my bag.

She lifts her fringe away from her face so she can be sure I see that she's raising her eyebrows, and I shake my head, laughing.

I DJ while she drives, and put on Beyoncé.

'If this baby can hear through the womb, it needs an education. The second it's out it'll be stuck listening to soft rock if you've got anything to do with it. I've got to get in early.'

'There's early, and there's pointless.'

I switch to Cyndi Lauper.

'Oooh, do you think it's a sign that it's a girl?'

'That you just put on "Girls Just Want To Have Fun"? I'm not sure that's classed as a sign.' We sing along anyway.

'So you're all set for your birthday Boxing Day in Frome tomorrow? Mum's booked the Italian. I felt too bad to say we were having Italian tonight as well.'

'Can never eat too much pasta.'

I start playing 'Just One Cornetto' and Georgia shakes her head, turning the volume down.

'Cassie's great,' she says, smiling across at me as we drive over Waterloo Bridge. The lights from the buildings are reflecting off the River Thames, and for the first time in a long time I recognise that London really is a beautiful city.

'She's been a really good friend to me.'

'Bonnie would have *loved* her,' Georgia says, and my chest tightens at the knowledge they'll never meet.

'She really would have. They're quite different, but the same where it matters.'

The Book Swap

I switch to Whitney Houston, my mind drifting to Bonnie. In ten days' time it would have been her birthday. It will forever be impossible to celebrate mine without thinking about hers too, and I don't think I'd want it any other way. The more ways I can keep her with me, the better.

I wonder what she'd make of this situation with Mystery Man. Would she have joined in with Cassie and Georgia, if she'd been there tonight? She'd definitely have teased me, but she'd be happy too. Because all she ever wanted was for me to be happy.

'Can we detour?' I say to Georgia as we approach my flat, and I direct her towards the library. Now I've decided I want to meet him, I'm ready for it to happen. Desperate for it.

'Can't believe I'm about to see it in the flesh,' she says, turning onto Cambria Road, and taking a parking space just in front of Eileen. 'Though she isn't quite as eye-catching as I'd imagined,' she goes on, screwing up her face.

'I sort of love how dishevelled she is.' I jump out of the car and run towards the library, putting the books front and centre. If he's anything like me, he'll check first thing in the morning on his way to work, when most other people are way too busy to stop and pick up a book.

'So, that was it,' Georgia comments as I climb back in. 'And did you declare your undying love for him yet, or does that come later?'

'No,' I say. 'But I did suggest meeting up. Happy birthday to me.'

She looks across at me, mouth wide open. 'Yeah, you did!' She shoves me on the arm and I grab it, pretending it's bruised, so she rolls her eyes and puts the car in reverse.

'Look, look, look!' She slows down, pointing out a figure as they cross the road towards the library.

I look from them, to Georgia and back again.

'Probably some drunk,' I say, unable to take my eyes off them. It's a man. Definitely. A man, in a Barbour-type jacket.

He bends down and open the doors, seemingly oblivious to the headlights from the car.

'Surely not,' Georgia says out of the corner of her mouth, as my heart starts racing.

He pulls something out and then stands up, patting the roof of the library in the same way that I always do. As though he's saying thank you.

Georgia inches the car forward, and I reach over, holding my arm out. 'Stop! He'll see,' I say, lurching forward as she presses the brake.

He turns and squints, staring straight at the car with two books clutched against his chest.

Thrusting myself back against the seat, my chest tightens so much I'm not sure I can breathe.

'Oh my God,' I mutter under my breath at the exact same time as Georgia speaks, her voice shrill with confusion.

'Is that . . . James Parr?'

24

James

There's a sense of relief as I see the two spines slotted into the library. Relief that it's all coming to an end, because when I put my next book in the library, I'm telling her everything. I'll lose her, but in doing that I'll set her free. I just need to figure out what the book is. I thought I'd know by now, but each one I choose doesn't quite say what I want it to.

Holding a hand up over my eyes, I clutch the books to my chest and squint towards the car, blinded, before the passenger door swings open, and the lights switch to half beam.

'I was starting to think I could forgive you.' I recognise the voice, stinging with anger, before I can make out who it is. Erin's walking towards me, looking so beautiful I can't look away. Her hair's falling in smooth waves around her face, and she's got dark make-up around her eyes so that, in the light from the headlamps, they're sparkling. She's wearing a long black coat and her lips, which are bright red, are set in a thin line. Her expression makes the one she had on the bus seem friendly.

'I'd convinced myself that I made it worse in my head. That you would have *never* intentionally hurt me. I'd even started hoping you might be at the memorial, so that we could *talk about it*.' She spits the last words.

Swallowing, I look down and back up. The anger falls from

her face, as it crumples. 'I don't understand what I've done to you,' she says, her words thick with confusion. Her features soft. 'I thought we were friends. *More* than friends, even. But actually, you must hate me. I don't get why else—'

'I don't hate you, of course I don't.' My stomach lurches as I walk towards her, arms outstretched. *How could she think that?* 'If anything it's—'

'There's no other explanation.' She looks around, and I'm trying to think how to correct her, but I know it has to be right. I've only got this one chance to explain myself. To finally get her to see me for who I really am. 'Do you enjoy it? Building up my feelings, then crushing them? Does it make you feel good? Give you the power you never had over the boys at school?'

I shake my head. 'No. I hated hurting you then, and I hate that I've hurt you now. It's the absolute opposite of what I want. How can you not see that?'

'What proof is there?' she shouts, her voice ringing out into the darkening night. 'All I see is one bullshit lie after another. Is your name even James? Or is it *Edward*?'

I flinch, guilt washing over me and rendering me speechless as she rolls her shoulders back, standing taller.

'How long have you known it was me? Have you been *following me*?' She curls her lip as though I'm someone to be disgusted by. All I want is for her to look at me the way she used to when we were in school. I start talking in a panic.

'Absolutely not. I swear I didn't know it was you until the bus. I—'

'The *bus*?'

'I saw you there once, but only your back.' I signal towards Eileen, wishing for a moment that she were a real person who could speak up and tell Erin it's the truth. *Believe the boy, Erin.*

The Book Swap

It's fucking true. 'Saw the coat and the bag and then I . . . you sat beside me on the bus and I recognised the bag, but . . .'

I can see that she remembers her behaviour. That she didn't give me much time.

'You could have said something. Then, or when I asked for your name.' She looks behind her, and when she turns back, her eyes are brimming with tears. 'I told you *everything* in the pages of those books. I gave you all of me.'

'So did I.' I take a step towards her. I need her to hear me. 'I've never admitted half of those things to anyone before.'

'But don't you see how that's different?' Her hair falls in front of her face and I instinctively reach up to tuck it behind her ear, getting so close I can feel the static of her skin against me before I drop my hand. God, I want to know what it feels like to touch her skin. Not like we did in school, but properly. To feel it beneath my fingertips. I've come close, so many times. 'You chose to reveal those things, knowing it was me. I never got to make that choice. You took it from me.'

Heat rushes to my cheeks as what she's saying sinks in.

'I'm sorry. I didn't know what else to do. If I told you, you'd never reply. It'd be over.'

She shakes her head. 'That was never your decision to make.'

The driver's door opens. I'd forgotten, for a second, that the car was even there. That for Erin to step out of the passenger seat, there had to be someone driving.

'Hi, James,' Georgia says, nodding at me. 'Come on, Erin.'

The second her sister's arm is around her, her whole body collapses.

'I swear I was about to tell you,' I say, my voice so pathetic I hate myself even more. 'I've spent all weekend trying to find the right book.'

Georgia half-carries Erin towards the car. I'm waiting for

her to say something back. Anything. Instead, her sister bundles her into the passenger seat and goes to close the door.

'I can't lose you, Erin,' I shout, trying to think about what I might have told her in the margins. Trying to find the strength to say it in person. 'Not again. You're right. We were more than friends, back then. I loved you. I was in love with you and I'm not sure that's ever stopped. I'm really sorry.'

Georgia freezes, holding the door slightly open. I guess it's in case there's anything Erin might want to say in return. Then Georgia nods and shuts the door.

I stand there, the books under my arm, as she climbs into the driver's seat and reverses slowly back up the road.

There was so much more I could have said, but I don't think it matters. Erin is never going to be willing to hear me out. Nothing I say can ever make up for breaking her trust. Twice.

'Fuck!' I shout into the air. 'Fuck, fuckety fucking shitty *FUCK!*' I glance back towards the library and I know that, while Erin most definitely hates me now, I've probably risen in Eileen's estimation.

Joel calls me on my way to work, just as I'm leaving Highbury & Islington station to mope my way into work again, and I know I have to answer. I don't even know when it was that I last spoke to him, but I know it was before everything happened with Erin. I've been too ashamed to speak to anyone since then.

'*Finally!* What the hell's going on? Wait. First. Guess where I am?' he says, before I can tell him anything.

'I don't know? Home?'

'Yes! How did you guess that?'

'You're in Frome?'

'Frome isn't home. I keep telling you this. I'm in Orlando. Taken a two-week holiday from work. My first in years. Figured I'd try and fit some actual living into this life of mine.'

Frowning, I pull the phone away from my ear to stare at it, and put it back.

'What? You didn't tell me that at boxing?'

He laughs. 'Are you joking? I was trying to. I couldn't get a word in with all those punches you were throwing.'

I think back to that day. It's like I knew something bad was about to happen.

'Erin saw me at the library,' I blurt out.

'Fuck.'

'Yeah.'

I feel the familiar racing in my chest. Stop walking to try and still it.

'I'm guessing . . . ?'

'She's as angry, if not angrier than when we were at school. I've totally fucked it.'

'You need to tell me these things. I thought I made that clear? I have many questions I'll come back to, but , speaking of school, did you get that invite to speak at the college?'

'How did you know about that?'

'I got one too.'

My heart starts racing even faster. All my thoughts of Erin, coupled with imagining walking back through the school gates. That and . . .

'That job offer you messaged about before you went quiet on me. Don't you *dare* take it. I've been thinking about you a lot this trip.'

'Yeah?' I can hardly get the word out. My chest is tightening as I listen, and I can feel my breath quickening. I start walking down the hill towards work. I need to keep moving.

'Yeah ... these ...' He's breaking up. '... Ted talks ... *One life, man ... Just wasting ...*'

'I can't hear you. Joel?' The phone goes dead and I stare at it. I don't know what he was going to say but I'm not sure if now's the time to hear it. It feels like too much. Like each thought is another block of Jenga, stacking higher and higher inside me, precariously close to toppling.

I've messed it all up with Erin. She'll never forgive me. When I last spoke to Dad, he said Mum had taken out a credit card to order all of the best equipment required for laying carpet. She was talking rapidly in the background, even once Dad had closed the door. All signs I need to prepare myself to get home. I've got to tell Dorothy if I want the job, and prepare a speech to prove myself back at college. Joel's jumbled words are on repeat in my head. My body starts to tingle and I feel light-headed, stumbling for a second. There's a flashing in my eyes and everything starts spinning. I actually feel like I might ...

When I open my eyes, I'm staring into the face of Helena.

'There we go,' she says, crouching beside me on the pavement, as though the months of silence between us haven't happened. 'Just try and breathe for me.' She takes a deep breath in and back out, nodding towards me to do the same.

Pulling myself up onto my elbows, I look around. There are a few other people standing over me, watching. My stomach hardens and I want to get up and leave, but my head's still swimming. I'm not sure I can walk yet.

'He's fine,' Helena shouts, but the crowd has already started to disperse. It's never as interesting once the person on the ground opens their eyes. 'He's my friend. I can take it from here.' She turns her attention back to me. 'My boyfriend

The Book Swap

owns a shop just here, and it's full of comfortable armchairs.' She grins. 'Come in and I'll make you a sweet tea. Try and get some colour back in your face.'

I move slowly to my feet and walk behind her, sitting down in the nearest chair I see. Helena disappears.

'You were only out a few seconds,' she shouts, answering the first question I have. 'I was just coming to put some chairs out and saw you go down.'

I look around me, taking in the shop as I wait for my face to stop tingling. For my ears to clear and the world to feel steady again. It's full of furniture, which is what's creating the musty smell, with a glass cabinet of jewellery in the corner by the till. *Helena's got a boyfriend, and this is his shop.* What are the chances?

Slowly, I can feel the blood returning to my head. She comes back, a tea towel over her shoulder. I thought it would feel awkward to see her again, but I'm grateful for the familiar face, and to Helena for taking control without seeming to need an explanation. She hands me a mug and I reach out to take it, clutching it between my hands.

'Thanks,' I say. 'For this – and for not leaving me out on the street, when you had every right to.'

'Right?' she says, her eyes lighting up as she laughs. She's in love. I can see it. Too happy to care about the guy who once messed her around. Especially now he's been punished by passing out in public. 'I'm kidding. It's no problem. Mike's at an auction so I said I'd open up for him. It was obviously meant to be.' The sparkle disappears from her eyes as she leans her head to one side. 'Are you okay? What happened?'

Somehow, it feels exactly right that it was Helena who found me. I don't deserve for her to listen, but I know she will anyway. I take a sip of the tea, enjoying the sweetness.

'My life's imploded. I feel like I might be losing my mind.'

I stare down into my mug, frowning. In a variety of different fonts, it says, 'Hold on. Let me overthink this.'

She catches me reading it and grimaces. 'God sorry. I should have gone for the "same hours in the day as Beyoncé" one, shouldn't I?'

Laughing, I settle into the chair and start talking. At one point she stands up and turns over the sign on the shop door. She leans on her hands, new silver rings twinkling as I speak. She gets up and makes more tea, and doesn't offer too much in the way of advice in response while I talk. She just listens. I cover Mum, and Dad's tour offer. Elliot and his loneliness. My job offer, and the talk back at college. Finally, I reach Erin. I owe it to Helena to explain it all. She shakes her head, and smiles at the mention of Erin's name.

'None of that stuff about you and Erin surprises me,' she says, when I wonder if I've said too much. 'You two were inseparable at school. With Bonnie of course, but I always thought . . . Well, I was surprised you didn't get together, put it that way.'

I bite down on my lip, staring at the ground. I was surprised too.

She leans back on the deep green velvet chair she's pulled over towards me. 'You know what I sometimes do when I have too much to think about. When I feel like I'm standing in the centre of a shit-storm?'

I shake my head, desperate to hear anything that might help.

'I just focus on the next thing. I start at the bottom of Maslow's hierarchy, and work my way up.'

She types something into her phone and brings up a picture of a colourful triangle, handing it to me. At the bottom of the triangle, it says 'Physiological needs'. Air. Water. Food. Shelter. At the word shelter I think immediately of my parents' house. This time they don't just need me, I need them too. I'm suddenly desperate to walk through that front door and see them. To have some moments with my mum, before I lose her for who knows how long.

'Thank you,' I say, handing the phone back. 'That's surprisingly helpful.'

Her face lights up and she stands, walking towards the door and turning the sign back around.

'I kind of owe you. Without you sending that message I wouldn't have realised where I was going wrong with relationships. Mike wants a future with me, and you're right . . . I hadn't had anyone in my life who wanted that before.'

'I'm really happy for you,' I say, meaning it.

'Me too. Well, I suppose I should try and make some money today.' She stands up and I do the same, stretching and turning around to get my jacket.

Stopping for a second, I turn back towards Helena.

'How much is this chair?' I look at it, taking in the soft brown leather. I feel bonded to it. It's enveloped me in its comfortable cushions for over an hour while I've spoken. Not once have I got pins and needles, or needed to shift position. It's sort of like it was made for me. 'I've just told it all of my secrets, so I feel like I owe it.'

'It's my favourite one too,' Helena says, leading me to the till.

'I'm really sorry, for how I treated you,' I say as I hand my card over.

'You were a shit.' She types the price into the card machine and holds it out to me. 'But I guess I was a shit to you in school. Sometimes there's too much history.'

I push my card in and type the pin.

'You and Erin, though. That's different. That's almost like the perfect amount of history.'

She hands me my receipt and I take it, my brain, for the first time in days, turning to the book I'm writing. *The Perfect History.* It could work as a title.

'Thank you.'

'Pleasure. And now we're even. I finally helped you up after a fall – the way I should have at school. And you said sorry. Good luck with everything.'

I nod, and leave. So, she did remember that moment in the dining hall the whole time we were seeing each other, she was just too ashamed to admit it – in the same way I'm ashamed of how I behaved in the years since. Maybe she's right. Maybe now, we're even.

I don't go to work. I get on the tube back to Brixton, having arranged delivery of the world's comfiest chair, all the time wondering what Erin's doing right now. Whether anything I said to her might have made a difference. Whether there's a chance, at some point, she might get in touch with me.

I open up my emails to tell Dorothy that Mum isn't well and I have to go back home. My heart jumps as I see Sophia's name in my inbox.

Hi James,
I've just read your three chapters and I really love where you're going with this.

You're right, it's very different to what I last read of your work, but it has the same qualities I witnessed before. The voice is really strong and I think you have a real story to tell.

I'd be delighted to read the rest of it if you're ready to send it over?
Best,
Sophia

The Book Swap

That book felt like it belonged to a whole other person, living a whole other life, until just moments ago. Now it's like it's slowly coming back to me.

It's only after I call Dad and start packing that I realise I still have the books Erin left in the library. I've been so distracted by what happened, I forgot why I was even there that night. I pick up *On the Road*, flicking to the back of the book, to where my questions are. I feel something a tiny bit like hope as I read the last answer.

25. What's your best memory from your school years?

I thought it might include a story about Bonnie, but she's written about that for question twenty-three. She obviously wanted to mix it up.

When I was in fourth form, it was Valentine's Day. All the girls in our year were so excited. Coming into different classes holding a rose, or a card. I thought it was awful and cheesy, but I was still a bit jealous. A few weeks earlier I'd lost this silver bracelet and I was so upset. Going on to everyone about how I couldn't find it. When I reached into my backpack in English, there was a box and a card in there. When I opened it, it was a really similar bracelet, and the card just had a question mark in it. I've always thought it was Bonnie. She always said it wasn't. I'll never know, but every time I think of that moment, it makes my heart dance a little bit.

Now reading her words fills me with the same feeling. Because it wasn't Bonnie. It was me.

25

Erin

'Erin, there's some food outside the door.'

Mum's voice sounds as though she's pressed right up against it, and I wait until I hear her footsteps disappear back down the stairs before I hoist up my tracksuit bottoms, tiptoe to the edge of my room and retrieve my dinner.

After Georgia and I came here for my Birthday Boxing Day, I climbed into bed and I haven't been able to leave. Georgia went back to London, checking over and over if I was sure I didn't want to go with her, but just like last time, my legs wouldn't do it.

Mum and Derek have been going to work, but making sure I'm fed before and after.

While they're gone, all I'm able to do is read through the notes in the margins of all the books James and I exchanged. He has all the books with his questions and my answers, but I have all the others, where he's answered back to me. I do believe him. I don't think he knew it was me at the beginning. I think the day he wrote that his name was Edward, that was when he found out. That's why his next questions were about my memories of Bonnie and school.

The hurt is twice as deep. To be betrayed by him once was bad enough, but twice has split me in two. Twice I've trusted him, and he's burned me in return.

The last time that I lay in bed, unable to leave, I lost out on time at school and time with Bonnie. This time, I'm missing out on being there to support Savannah before her results. I'm missing my teaching with the girls in the year below Savannah. They've got mocks to prepare for and I was going to be helping them. Cassie's moved in and I'm not even there in the flat. Everything was about to start again for me.

I've brought the framed postcard from Bonnie, and it's resting against the wall, staring back at me.

Don't forget to make all your dreams come true!

I open up the frame, pulling the postcard out. I trace the words with my finger, thinking about when she wrote that, and why. The first time I saw her again, after months of keeping my distance.

All of this feels linked somehow. I kept going back to that library because I needed the postcard back, and what was waiting for me changed my life. Squinting, I turn the card over, scanning my eyes across Piglet and Pooh. It's almost like Bonnie's behind it all. My search for the postcard led me to James — but that makes no sense because she hated him too, after what he did. She told me she ignored him at school. She didn't speak to him again. Shaking my head, I put the postcard down on the bed. I've been inside this room too long. I'm starting to think about things that don't make sense. I didn't want this postcard to lead me to James. I needed it because it's the only sign I have that Bonnie forgave me for everything that happened.

I'll accept every bit of pain that comes because I know it's the punishment I deserve, for abandoning Bonnie when she needed me the most.

When I look back, I'm not even sure how it happened. I went to visit her in Frome the way I promised I would on that very first weekend, after she told me about her diagnosis. I took food. Signed up to every possible streaming service that promised bad TV like *Real Housewives* and *Below Deck*. Things that would distract her. That we could watch together to take her mind off everything.

I was expecting Bonnie to be the same, but even within that week something had changed. I didn't know how to connect with her any more. Things I said to make her laugh weren't landing. She didn't seem to want me to hug her, or to talk about our lives. There were no threats from her. No 'do this or I'll tell everyone the mystery floater in the girls' loo that wouldn't flush for three days was you.' Her mind was somewhere else. Of course it was. I understand why now. I don't know why I couldn't then. How I could be so blind?

Each time I went back home it was worse than before. It was still the early days of the chemo, but some days I'd turn up at the house and her mum or dad would have to gently turn me away. They would say that she was too sick, or she wasn't up to seeing anyone. Bonnie had never rejected me before – and she was the one person who I thought never would. It brought back everything I'd felt about my mum, and James. I didn't know how to cope. When I did see her, she'd make excuses or drop hints for me to leave early. Her face would sometimes fall at the sight of me. I started making my own excuses. I would say I was busy with a boyfriend, or Charlotte was keeping me late at work and booking me for events at the weekend. Actually, I was offering myself forward for anything and everything that came up. Booking weekends away and assuring myself that Bonnie didn't need me. If she did, she'd ask.

By the time her dad called me on that day in August, I hadn't been back in months. I'd messaged. Sent voice notes.

She replied when she could. I did everything it took to be what I thought was a good friend, from afar. I can only admit this now, but I was waiting. Waiting for her to get better. Waiting for her to be the Bonnie from before.

Instead, her dad told me the opposite. That I should get back to Frome. Bonnie was asking for me. The chemo wasn't working, and she'd decided to stop the treatment, and live as many good days as she could without it. I always thought in the films when people received bad news over the phone and sank to the ground that it was unrealistic. Heightened for dramatic impact, but it's exactly what I did. I crumpled to the ground, an animalistic sound escaping from my mouth as my mobile fell beside me.

I raced back. She'd asked for me. If she wanted me there, there's nowhere else I'd rather be.

That was the night we went to The Griffin and she gave me the postcard. The night she was the old Bonnie, just for me.

Now, in a few weeks' time, it's the memorial and the anniversary of her death. Yes, I was there. From the day we met at The Griffin, I hardly left her side, but it was all too late. She deserved so much more from me. A friend who was there for her through all of it, not just the ending. Someone who sat beside her through every single chemo session, holding her hand and telling her how much she meant to them. Who picked her up and kept her company, expecting nothing in return. I was naive, and I was afraid. I couldn't admit that my best friend was dying, and if I couldn't see her, I didn't have to believe it.

I can never forgive myself for doing that to her, and I'm sort of glad the universe won't either. That it keeps breaking my heart, so I remember how I broke hers.

★ ★ ★

The Book Swap

I wake up the next day to someone banging on the front door.

'Postie,' they shout, before banging again.

I wait for Mum to answer, but I can't hear her downstairs. I check my phone. That would make sense. It's gone eleven in the morning. The postie can leave any letters or parcels on the doorstep.

The door bangs again, harder this time. Turns out it's quite a different service in Frome.

I pull on my grey tracksuit bottoms, and wander down the stairs, rubbing my eyes.

More banging. For fuck's sake! Can't they come back tomorrow? Fixing on my best 'you've interrupted me' smile, I open the door a crack. The second I do, it gets shoved towards me and I fly backwards.

Georgia comes bursting in, kicking the door shut behind her and marching into the kitchen.

'No way,' she says, turning around to face me, her eyes landing on my tracksuit bottoms. 'You're not doing this. Not again.'

Folding my arms, I lean against the wall.

'I can do whatever I like.'

'Actually, you can't. This cannot be your cycle. Something bad happens to you and you shut yourself off in those trousers that belong in the bin. In fact' – her eyes widen as she advances towards me – 'take them off.'

'No.'

'Take them off right now.'

'Absolutely not.'

She starts marching, arms outstretched, six months of baby bump protruding towards me.

She reaches for the waist of my trousers. 'Stop it,' I shout, trying to move out of the way.

237

'Do not attack a pregnant lady. It's dangerous,' she yells, getting her thumbs into my tracksuit bottoms and pulling them down as I scream.

'You've gone insane.'

'Maybe.'

I kick my feet against the legs of the trousers, shaking them down to stop my sister from fully undressing me like some kind of giant toddler. She tears off the final leg, rising up with wild eyes, her hair sticking up in the air.

Walking back to the kitchen, she throws them into the bin, eyes darting around the room before she walks, with determination, towards the fridge.

'What are you doing?'

She rummages around and reappears, victorious, clutching a tube of ketchup. She holds it over the top of the tracksuit bottoms and squirts out the entire tube, loud fart noises echoing through the room as she goes in for another double-handed squeeze. Making a circular motion with the last drops of the bottle, she swings it in the air before throwing it on top of the trousers, slamming the door shut, and clapping her hands together.

Shaking my head, I walk back up the stairs and into my bedroom, climbing into bed. Georgia comes after me and stands over the bed.

'Get up,' she says.

'No.'

'Get up.'

'Why? I've got nothing to get up for.'

'You do. There's a thing called *life* that's been waiting for you for a fucking long time now.'

'Why are you making this your problem? Just leave me alone.'

The Book Swap

I pull the duvet up to my neck, shrinking back against the wall. All the fire has gone from her eyes, and instead they fill with tears.

'I can't. I won't. Not this time.'

Lifting my head to the ceiling, I roll my eyes in frustration. Every so often Georgia gets this wave of guilt about what happened after we found out about Mum. After James saw her with Mr Carter when she was meant to be picking up our fish and chips.

Georgia chose to stay with Mum after the break-up, on the weekends when she was back from uni. I chose Dad. She didn't know how bad I'd got. How after one day at my new school, Matravers, I didn't want to go back. I locked myself in my room for weeks. Even Bonnie couldn't help me.

By the time Georgia came back for a weekend, I was close to failing my exams. I didn't want to, I just couldn't find the strength to leave my room. I heard her on the phone to Mum, saying she'd decided to live with Dad. With me. If it wasn't for her I'd have failed everything. I might never have left that room again, but she doesn't remember that bit. Just the bit where she wasn't there.

'I can't watch this happen again,' she says now.

I can feel my body vibrating against the icy wall behind me as I sit in my T-shirt and pants, watching my sister wipe at her eyes. 'First with Mum. Then James. Then Bonnie. Then your job. Now James again. At some point you've got to break the cycle. Respond in a new way. Today is that day.'

She's right and I know she is, but it's tiring, having to find the strength each time. To pick yourself back up when once again someone's broken your heart and your trust.

'We don't have to talk about him, if you don't want to, but—'

'I don't want to.'

'Okay. Just . . . he was so young, Erin. Back then—'

'I said I don't want to.'

'If anyone's to blame, it's Mum,' she says, and I sit forward, mouth slightly open.

'I can't believe you just said that.'

'Well, it's true.' She shrugs. 'But she's just human. She made a mistake. We all make them, and in the long run it sort of worked out better for her. For everyone. They're happier. Mum and Dad were never happy.'

She stands up and opens my wardrobe, throwing me a pair of jeans. Keeps her back to me and looks around her while I pull them on.

She reaches into the wardrobe again, throwing me a bra, a white V-neck T-shirt and a long navy jacket, before sitting on the bed.

'Is this even about James?' she asks, her eyes landing on the postcard from Bonnie.

She picks it up, turning it over to read the message and holds it up to me.

'How's the living your dreams going?'

'Actually spectacularly well,' I say, putting my bra on under the T-shirt I slept in and then pulling on the clothes Georgia threw at me. Not bad choices. I might even have gone with them myself, on another day. A day where I intended to get dressed. 'I tried,' I say.

She nods, her head tilted to one side.

'I did the whole "What Would Bonnie Do" thing. I was actually getting somewhere.'

'You were. You have. But I wonder . . .'

'Uh oh.'

She laughs. 'Do you think it's time to start asking yourself what Erin would do? She's pretty smart too.'

'She's a total failure.'

'I know you think some of this stuff was Bonnie, but it wasn't. Not really. Taking the risk with the margins guy. Teaching Savannah . . . That stuff was you. And correct me if I'm wrong, but what you promised Bonnie – it wasn't that you'd live her life for her, it was that you'd make the most of your own.'

She stands up, reaching into the chest of drawers and turning around with a pair of socks.

I hold my hand out to catch them, but Georgia throws them, hard, at the side of my head.

'Ouch.' I unfold the socks and move to the edge of the bed, wrestling my foot into one of them.

'I'm going to ask you one more time to get up.'

'I seriously don't understand why you pay for me to have therapy and then you try and give it to me for free.'

'I've literally never met anyone more annoying in my whole life.'

'Ditto.'

I pull on the other sock, and Georgia watches.

'Thank you,' I say, unable to look at her. 'For coming here.'

I push my feet into my Converses, and tie up the laces.

'Thank you for letting me in.'

'I actually let in the postman.'

'I know.' She stands up and walks towards the door. 'Right, quick toilet break, as per, and then we're off to do some living.'

She disappears to the bathroom and I watch her leave. I've never felt luckier to have her as my sister than I do right now.

When I hear the door click open, I stand up.

'Okay, let's attempt some of this living you speak of.'

She reappears in the doorway, eyes wide and face pale.

'There was blood.'

I spring forward. 'What?'

Tears fill her eyes. 'When I wiped. Just now. I don't know what to do . . . I'm not sure I've felt it today. Oh my God . . .'

I rush towards her, holding on to her.

'Let's go to the hospital,' I say. 'We'll go. We'll go right now.'

Georgia sinks down onto me and pushes the car key into my hand.

26

James

Dad swings open the front door and pulls me in for a hug as I drop my bag at his feet and wrap my arms around him. I've been searching for this feeling the whole time I've been in London, but it turns out I only get it here. The settling of everything in my body. The knowledge I can finally let it all go.

'Jesus,' I say, as my eyes go from Dad's shoulder to the rolls of carpet lined up down the length of the hallway, beside the stairs.

'Pop in here a sec,' he says, leading me into the kitchen. Radio 2 is blaring from somewhere else in the house, and he pokes his head out of the kitchen door to look around, before closing it behind him and lowering his voice. 'Your mum's attempting to lay the carpets herself. She chatted to the guys who do it at work and watched a load of YouTube videos. Just wanted you to know before you see the state of the place.'

Nodding, I look around the kitchen, grateful for the tiled floor.

'Let's hope she doesn't get a job in a tile shop next.'

He raises his eyebrows and smiles. 'It's good to have you home.'

'Good to be here. I'll go say hi.'

Opening the door, I follow the sound of the radio, treading over the carpet down the hall and making my way into the sitting room.

I'm pretty sure my mouth hits the once-carpeted floor. The furniture has been pushed into the dining room behind me and on the ground is some cold grey stone. There's a bucket in the corner with all sorts of serious-looking equipment laid beside it. A small shovel-like tool, some sander-looking thing, a tape measure and a giant scalpel.

Mum appears behind me, wiping her hands on some blue overalls I've never seen before, which is a bad sign in itself. She gets fixated on an outfit in her manic phases, and I think the overalls might belong to this episode.

'I didn't realise you were here already, JJ.' She reaches up her arms and wraps them around me and I can see from her eyes that she's not really here any more. She's the other person now, and I can feel a lump in my throat that I've missed my chance to spend time with Mum. There's no point in telling her to stop or to question what's going on. She won't listen and I don't want to be the enemy so soon after arriving.

'Looking very professional,' I say instead, and she pushes her wild hair away from her face, grinning. 'What can I do?'

The amazing thing about Mum when she's like this is that she can actually do anything she puts her mind to. She doesn't look as though she's slept in days, but she knows the names of all the tools. Has read up on exactly how it's meant to be done, and she's working at such a speed that I wouldn't be surprised if she does manage to carpet the whole house within the week, even while I know deep down it will never happen.

'We need to put down the underlay – soft as a cloud, apparently – and then you and Dad can bring up the carpet. We went with cream for this room in the end.'

'Sounds good.'

The Book Swap

I walk to the far end of the room where the underlay appears to be ready to roll out. Mum leaves so I wait, staring at everything she's done. I don't know how Dad's put up with it. The television is squashed in with the dining table, the sofa and the armchair. There's no way of actually watching it comfortably. I presume once this is done, all of that furniture will be moved in so she can do the dining room.

Wandering out, I head up the stairs, checking to see if anything's been started up here yet, and I shrink back in horror at the sight of my bedroom. The carpet's been torn up and someone, presumably Dad, has tried to do the best job they can at making the room look presentable without its original flooring. It looks like a palace compared to Mum and Dad's room though. Bits of chipped floorboard and some sort of wooden border with spikes coming out is running around part of the perimeter, and then just stops. A tearing sound comes from behind me and I cross over into Elliot's room, where Mum's on her hands and knees, pulling backwards on the light grey carpet.

'Mum,' I say, frowning. 'We were going to do the underlay?'

'That can wait,' she says, her voice forced as she puts all of her body weight into ripping up the only comfortable flooring left in the whole house. I crouch down beside her, holding on, and together we tear it back, dust and foam flying everywhere as we stumble and land on our backs in the far corner of the room.

She turns onto her side and locks eyes with me.

'Satisfying, isn't it?'

'Very.'

'How's London?' She always says the word like it's some faraway land. Some imagined city from a fiction book.

'It's okay. I got in a bit of trouble.'

She pushes herself up, dusting her hands down on her overalls.

'What kind of trouble?'

I think back through everything that happened. Try to boil it down to a sentence she'll have the time and patience to listen to.

'I got talking to Erin, who I used to go to school with, but it was through notes and she didn't realise it was me. She thought I'd tricked her.'

She frowns, standing up. 'Just tell her you weren't tricking her. Tell her the whole truth.'

She gets up and leaves the room, her feet thundering on the stairs. She's actually right. Shouting after Erin that I love her isn't the whole truth, it's only the beginning. Erin needs more than that to be able to forgive me. I need to help her to understand what I did and why I did it. It might not change anything, but it's worth a shot.

I stare at the doorway where Mum just was. It's very obvious she isn't telling us the whole truth either. Standing up, I go downstairs and into the kitchen, where Dad's still where I left him, staring out of the window.

'Mum's not taking her medication, is she?' I say, pulling him out of his world and back into this one.

Dad looks like he's been caught stealing.

'She said it was giving her a stomach ache.' He lights up at an idea. 'You could offer to cook for her. She won't accept anything I give her in case I've hidden pills in it, but maybe . . .' He trails off as he realises one meal with medication won't fix anything. That he's asking his son to spike his mother's food.

'Where is she? She came down here?'

'I imagine ...' Dad says, walking back out of the kitchen, over the rolls of carpet and towards the lounge, where he stops in the doorway, his head tilted to one side. I follow his gaze, seeing Mum wedged onto the sofa beside the dining table, fast asleep.

Dad takes a blanket from behind the sofa and puts it over her and together we tiptoe back to the kitchen, and I close the door behind us.

'I have a feeling we're about to become experts in fitting carpet,' I say, and Dad laughs gently.

'Your mum's been playing the videos so loudly, I think I already am.'

I thought I might have timed it so that I was back just as Mum crashes, but tonight as I'm in bed trying to sleep, I can hear scraping and banging downstairs. Footsteps and doors slamming as she goes in and out of different rooms. Eventually the smell of frying onions makes its way from the kitchen, up the stairs and under my door. I haven't seen her like this since my school years, and I wonder how many times Dad's told me she's fine, whilst living through these moments. He needs a break from it. Deserves a break, and I want to give it to him. What was it he said on the phone when I called for advice about my job offer? He said not to waste my heart's calling by saying yes to something easy. That the straightforward route isn't always the best one. Well, I want to give him the opportunity to follow his heart's calling. To take the best route for himself for once.

In the morning Mum's back in her overalls, carrying chairs from the dining room out into the garden, with Dad calmly receiving them from the door and placing them on the patio.

I help her lift the table, knowing there's no way we'll get the sofa out there.

'Help me push that,' she says, nodding towards it.

'Shall we do the underlay in here first?'

'Later.'

We lift the sofa back into the sitting room, followed by the chair and television. Before I can even wheel the table with the TV on it out of the way, she's down by the corner of the room, tearing at the cream carpet.

'I found this under your bed,' Dad says, putting his hand into the back pocket of his jeans and handing me a small square envelope. 'When Mum got at the carpet.'

Taking it, I turn it over. It says *Erin* on the front in the handwriting of a younger James. It's still sealed. That's Dad for you.

'Thanks.'

I take it inside, staring at it for a while before running my finger gently under where it's sealed and taking the letter out. Scanning the words, I remember it all. Sprinting home so fast that I vomited on the path outside on my way to the front door. Finally, I was safe inside. I ran straight upstairs and wrote everything down in that letter.

Dear Nothing, it started.

I can't believe despite our great love of The Perks of Being a Wallflower *this is my first letter to you. I really hope it won't be my last.*

Even knowing the group of boys could be minutes behind me, I could only think about Erin. I wanted to apologise for what I'd done. To say the one thing I thought might make her feel better.

Sometimes, in the years after we stopped speaking, I wondered if I'd made up how close we were. If perhaps it was just me who felt it, but reading this letter makes everything clear. We had in-jokes. Nicknames. Moments.

Remember the day I told you that you and Bonnie had changed my life and I would do anything for you? Well I need you to hold that in your mind, while I say this next part, because it's true, no matter how it may look.

How could she just walk away from it all without giving me a chance to explain? If not on the day, then at some point in the future. How has she made me feel like it's the worst thing anyone ever did to her, even now? I've spent years rewinding to that moment, hating myself for what I did, but if she knew why, she might have understood. And she never asked. She made it all about her, despite knowing what I was going through. We could have fought the bullies together, but instead she left. She left because she didn't want to experience what I was experiencing.

I go back downstairs and find Dad sitting at the diningroom table as though it's always been out in the garden. He's staring at the apple tree, deep in thought.

'Dad, if you need a break from all this. A long one—'

'I don't need a break. You know, you and Elliot used to love climbing that tree.' He points towards the apple tree.

'I remember.'

'I don't know when it stopped. One day you were just inside playing video games or watching telly and that was it . . . you never climbed it again.'

'I guess that's called ageing.'

He sighs. 'Happens so fast. When El was born, a midwife told me to enjoy it. That "the days are long, but the years are short". I've never forgotten that.'

'And now, here you are, with a DJ wanting you on tour. Your best years could still be ahead of you, Dad.'

He turns to look at me, frowning. 'You make it sound like I was complaining. It's the opposite. I miss it. I miss it all.'

I stare at the tree with him, trying to think how to word it.

'I want you to go on the tour. You deserve it. To live your best life. To fulfil your dreams.'

'I am.'

'If we go by the advice you gave me on the phone, you're not. You're taking the straightforward option, but not necessarily the right one.'

Dad lifts his head as the sun comes out from a cloud, shining down on us to the backing track of the tearing of carpet behind us.

'I thought you'd do that,' he says, closing his eyes.

'Do what?'

'Take my advice and make it about me.'

I look over at him. He somehow looks older than he did when I last visited. His hair's in the standard ponytail, and I can see dark brown age spots on his skin, which I'm not sure were there before.

'In what way?'

He turns to look at me. 'My heart's calling wasn't being a pop star. It was being a husband. A father. All that showbiz stuff . . . that was my straightforward route. I could have done it without even trying. That's why I didn't take it.' He smiles across at me, reaching out to pat my hand. 'Every challenge this life has thrown at me has taught me more about myself and the world than singing ever could.'

'But—'

'I don't expect you to understand my choice,' he says. 'But I do wish you'd respect it.'

The Book Swap

'Can someone give me a hand in here?' Mum shouts from some distant room, and Dad jumps up the moment he hears her voice, squeezing my shoulder before walking inside.

Standing up, I walk down towards the apple tree and reach a hand onto the trunk, pulling myself up onto the lowest branch, which wavers under the weight of a grown man. I look up, holding my hand out to grab hold of the next branch up, pulling myself onto it, my right foot slipping against the tree. It felt a lot easier when we were kids.

'Helloooo . . . can someone help me please?' Mum shouts from inside. Frowning, I lower myself back down the tree. I thought that was where Dad had gone, but it can't have been. Slipping down from the last branch, my hand rakes its way down the bark, my left shin making contact with the trunk as I try to land.

'Fuck!' I stare down at my hands, cut up from a climb I did a thousand times a day as a child.

'Coming,' I shout to Mum, running up towards the back door. She isn't in the sitting room, so I tread my way across the fucking rolls of carpet, which couldn't be more in the way.

Just as I reach the end and jump off, I catch sight of Dad's feet, sticking out of the kitchen door.

'Dad?' I run towards him and he's lying on the ground, his right arm clutching the left side of his chest. His face is almost grey. He's squeezing his eyes shut.

'Call an ambulance, son, please,' he whispers through laboured breaths, and I can't help but think: *this can't be it*.

Memories of Dad fill my mind as I reach for my phone. Dad standing at the bottom of the apple tree, telling me and Elliot where to put our feet. Dad turning up at uni with a Tupperware of food, and me trying to force him back out of the door before he's even had a cup of tea. Dad reading us *The Very Hungry Caterpillar*, an arm around each of his boys, his voice raised to drown out the sound of Mum hammering away in the back garden as she tried to build a fence that was never finished. Dad turning up at the school gate to surprise me with the new car he'd just bought, and me walking straight past him like I didn't know him. Dad, just now, desperately trying to make me understand him – when all I've ever done is see him through my own eyes, and not his.

I clutch hold of all of those memories, and his hand, and dial 999 for an ambulance.

27

Erin

Pushing my foot down on the accelerator, I drive as fast as is safely possible towards Bath Royal United Hospital.

Georgia stares out of the window and everything in me wants to do the same thing I tried with Bonnie. To distract her. To chat. To try and make her feel better, but I know that isn't the right thing to do. Sometimes people are going through something you can't relate to, and you just have to show up. I didn't do it for Bonnie, but I can do it now. I can do it for Georgia.

As we drive along the A36, an ambulance overtakes us, sirens blaring. Should I have called an ambulance? I don't know how serious this is or what it means.

Georgia pulls out her phone and starts typing something. She'll be googling. *Don't google*, I scream inside my own head, but I say nothing. This isn't my experience.

I'm trying not to spiral. The world can't be this cruel. She can't lose this baby.

It's like it's rush hour by the time we reach the hospital and cars are driving around, trying to find somewhere to park.

'You go to A&E. They'll tell you where to go. I'll come find you as soon as I've found a space.'

Georgia steps out of the car, holding her bump. She walks away from me, glancing back, her face ashen, and I nod. She can do this.

I drive to the other end of the car park, further away from the entrance, whispering a 'thank you' as I spot a bay, and move towards it at the same time as a car flies in from the other angle, taking it before I can reverse in.

I beep my horn.

'I was fucking reversing in there,' I shout, getting out and slamming the door behind me at the same time as I hear theirs open. 'That was my space.' Spinning around, I walk towards the driver, who slams their own door shut and turns towards me.

My heart thumps in my chest.

'This can't be happening.' I'm laughing without humour as I take in the man looking down at me, hair dishevelled, dark bags and his eyes wide as they dart back and forth. So different from the way he looked at the library, but still, without question, James. 'Of course you're the type of person to take someone's parking space at a *hospital*.' I shout the last word as he stands opposite me, running a hand through his hair. Seeing him like this, out of context, he looks different. I'm not sure I've ever realised how tall he is. How much broader he's become since school. At the library I was too angry to notice. On the bus I did everything I could to get away as fast as possible. This time he's in front of me, all six foot of him, his jeans slung low, and a navy hoody pulled over a grey T-shirt.

He holds his hands up, the palms grazed with dark blood. As he does so his jumper lifts for a moment, exposing the skin of his torso. I look away.

'Please don't,' he says. 'There are other spaces. I don't have time for this.' He turns and walks off towards the hospital and I run after him.

'Move your car. My sister's in there.'

The Book Swap

'Oh my God, Erin,' he shouts, spinning around and glaring at me. 'There you go again – making it all about you. Forming a judgement without taking just one *second* to find out what's actually going on.'

I stop, stumbling backwards. He's never raised his voice at me before. Never looked at me this way. His nostrils flared and eyes bulging.

'What are you talking about?'

'Don't bother to ask me *why* I'm at the hospital. Just jump right on in with your accusations, just like you did back at school.'

'I had good reason to accuse you then.'

'You never asked me *why*,' he shouts. 'Didn't give me even a second to explain myself.'

I don't know how to respond to the James who won't say sorry. Behind us, someone's beeping their horn, trying to get past my car.

James pats his jeans, moving a hand to his back pocket and pulling out an envelope, holding it up in front of me.

'This is what I wrote to you the day I found your mum. It tells you everything. How eight of them pushed me to the ground. How they all got their dicks out and were about to piss on me. How telling them about your mum gave me one whole minute to get away. It's all in here. My dad found it and . . .' He looks over towards the hospital, swallowing. 'This is the apology you wouldn't let me give. And now, instead of just taking this one, it's like you expect them all the time. You expect a lifetime's worth of apologies in all of their different forms. You even think I should move my car for you.'

'I—'

'There's no point in me apologising,' he says, throwing his arms out. People are getting out of their cars. Shouting over to us to move. James keeps going. 'You don't forgive people.' He lowers his voice. 'It was all over the margins of those books.'

My ears start ringing and I try to refocus because he's still talking. 'Not Gatsby, not Estella, not Sal and Dean. The second they did something you didn't approve of, that was it. Written off for good.'

My chest rises and falls. If he's going to go there, then so will I.

'You can talk,' I say back. 'Nothing anyone did in those books was good enough for you. They could be working four jobs, be millionaires, be pursuing their lifelong ambition and you judged them for it. Made them sound like failures. Sometimes just one small achievement is enough. Just making it through the day is enough. After what happened, that was all I could do. Is it any wonder I couldn't forgive you? I trusted you more than almost anyone, and you broke it.'

He blinks, licking his lips.

'And now it's happened again. You lied about your name.' Tears sting my eyes as I finally tell him the truth. How I wasn't just angry because he hurt me, but because he was one of the only people who I thought never would. 'You tricked me.'

He sighs. 'I was never trying to trick you, Erin.' He looks down at his feet and back up, running a hand through his hair before fixing his eyes on mine. 'I was trying to keep you.'

A jolt of electricity races through me as an explosion of car horns sounds through the car park. James looks at me for a moment longer, before placing the letter in my hand and running towards the hospital.

Shaking, I mutter apologies to the drivers and climb back in, moving slowly forward just as a car ahead of me reverses out of their space.

The Book Swap

I go in nose first, not willing to risk losing it, and then I kill the engine, clutching the wheel with both hands, the letter still gripped in one. I read my name on the front, immediately recognising the handwriting from all our exchanges. Staring at it, I think about what he just said. That he told them so he could escape. *It was never about destroying me. It was about protecting himself.* I put the letter inside the glovebox, and pull out my phone.

Georgia's messaged me.

Meet me at the maternity ward.

I scan the words, wondering what they mean. She's only six months. It's too soon to be having the baby. I want to ask her, but I know not to. I just have to be there.

Locking the car, I open the map on my phone, searching for the maternity ward, as a woman comes running down the car park.

'Where's my husband?' she shouts. 'I need to find my husband.'

There's an ambulance towards the end of the car park, and she charges towards it, banging on the back windows.

'Is he in there? Gareth.' She's got both fists on the glass, slamming them as hard as she can.

I approach her. She spins around, and the same wild expression that just met me in James stares back at me.

'Are you James's mum?' I ask.

I've never met her, but sometimes he'd tell us a little bit about her. Not a lot, but enough that this, coupled with her shouting Gareth's name, allows me to figure it out. She must have been in the car. Why would James just leave her here? I push the thought away. I'm doing it again. I'm immediately judging him for behaviour without waiting for an explanation.

'My husband's had a heart attack,' she says, clinging to my arm, and heat pulses through my body. That's what James meant. Of *course* he's here for a reason, and the reason is that his dad might die. I didn't even think to ask. 'They took him, and I . . . I . . .'

She bursts into tears and I clutch her towards me, leading her in the direction James went.

'He's a bastard. A bastard, that boy,' she says, spitting the words out as she lets me walk her. 'Always has been. They don't change. He's not like his brother. Oh no. Elliot's a good boy. He's a very good boy.'

I squeeze my eyes shut and keep walking. I lead her towards the double doors, walking through them. I look around. James is on a chair to the right. He's got his head in his hands, and for a moment he looks so like the James from school. Vulnerable. Worried. He flings his head up when he hears the doors and all of that washes away. We lock eyes, and he stands and walks towards us.

'Come on, Mum.'

'You get away from me,' she shouts. 'I don't want you touching me, I want my husband. I want my husband,' she yells in the direction of the receptionist, and he wrestles her gently away from me, walking her towards the seats.

Blushing, I turn away. I don't want to embarrass him by staying and I can't look at him anyway. Not now I know why he's here. I'm too ashamed. I ask the receptionist for directions to the maternity ward and follow the signs through a separate door.

James's mother is still shouting as I walk away. Wanting her other son. The good one.

He was going through all that at school. His mum being ill and the bullying. He only had me and Bonnie, and then I cut him off. I made Bonnie do the same.

The Book Swap

I've been so selfish with so many people in my life. With Bonnie. With Georgia. With James. Even, maybe, with Mum.

When I reach the maternity ward, I'm ready to say my sister's name at reception. Be directed to a bed. I'm preparing myself for the worst. Ready to give her whatever it is she might need. Everything I never gave Bonnie.

'Erin,' she says from one of the seats in reception, standing up.

I walk over and hug her. 'Have they not seen you yet?' I spin to the receptionist, accusatory.

'No, they have, I can go.' She's got a slight smile on her lips as I follow her back out and follow signs towards the car park.

'What's going on?' I ask, running after her.

'I'll tell you at the car.'

'Tell me now. Is everything okay?'

'It's all okay,' she says, resting her hand on her bump, and I let out all the breath in my body.

We reach the car, and I open the passenger door for her. Once we're sitting, she turns to me, biting her lip.

'I'm so embarrassed,' she says.

'Why?'

'It was bloody haemorrhoids. Literally bloody,' she adds, allowing a small laugh.

'Oh, thank God.'

'I was so worried, and the whole time it was my arsehole. I thought something was happening to the baby and it was just my anus bleeding through the strain of carrying it.'

She waits for me to join in on the joke, but I'm not ready to laugh. I'm still taking it in.

'I swear to God the *weirdest* shit happens when you're pregnant. My vagina is so swollen, it's like I've got a trout pout down there. Honestly. If you saw it, you'd think it was Donatella Versace.'

I'm still trying to catch my breath. She stops making jokes and looks across at me.

'Can I be honest about something?'

'Of course.'

She stops, resting both hands on her bump. 'It's the first time I've felt connected to this baby. I've spent the last few months so unsure if I even want it, but the moment I thought I was losing it . . . Well, now I don't just want it, I'm desperate for it.' She stretches a hand out across her stomach. 'I can't wait for it to arrive.'

A feeling rushes over me that I can't quite place. A weight in my chest.

'Me neither,' I say. 'And I can't wait for you to boss it as a single mum. You're going to be amazing.'

We lock eyes, both filling with tears.

'God, Erin,' she says, shaking her head. 'The amount of time we spend fixating on all the bad things about someone. I've wasted months finding reasons not to want this baby. I could have just been loving it instead.'

A lump forms in my throat, and I know what the weight in my chest is. It's James. Memories are piling in before I can stop them. James falling against me at the house party. James on the bus, big eyes staring down at me. James shouting after me as Georgia reversed away from the library. James just now, with a locked jaw and blazing eyes.

'I think . . .' I say. 'I think I know exactly what you mean.'

Georgia reaches across and takes my hand, squeezing it.

* * *

The Book Swap

When we make it back home, Mum comes rushing out of the house towards us as we climb out of the car. We called her on the way back, explaining what had happened.

She reaches us, taking hold of Georgia and hugging her.

'She's okay,' I say. 'Everything's okay.'

Derek appears behind her.

'Thank God,' he mutters, and I can see real concern on his face. The three of us lead Georgia inside and she heads straight up the stairs to bed.

For a second I go to follow her, but that isn't the promise I've made with myself. There's something else I need to do instead.

'Can we have a word, Mum?' I ask, as Derek widens his eyes and disappears into the kitchen.

Mum nods and leads me into the sitting room, taking a seat on the sofa. I sit beside her.

My eyes land on her face and I almost can't do it, but I can see James in my head, standing in the car park, shouting at me to listen. I didn't – and I think I've lost him because of it. I don't want to lose my mum – I've just been so afraid that I already have.

I take a deep breath.

'I'm sorry,' I say now, staring down at her hands, clutched together on her lap. 'I've never asked you for your version of what happened. I can't promise I'm going to understand it, but you deserve to tell me.'

Mum's eyes fill with tears, and I blink away my own.

'If I could change the way it all came out, of course I would,' she begins, locking her eyes on mine. 'If I'd known the hurt it would cause you. If I'd known what I'd put poor James through, blaming himself for you leaving.'

I frown. 'How do you know about that?'

Mum shrugs. 'He used to meet up with Derek sometimes, after college the following year. He had this book idea he wanted to talk about. It was very good, apparently. It was an apology, really. To you ... That poor boy. What he went through at school ...'

My chest tightens. *Everyone knew but me.*

'I fell in love with Derek. It was as simple as that. It's no excuse, but your dad and I had been unhappy for years. He even admitted it himself in the end. And I'm so sorry for what happened as a result of that, but I'll never be sorry that I met Derek. Never.' Her eyes cloud over. 'I couldn't stay, Erin. Not after what I put you all through. It wasn't fair. Of course I wanted to take you both with me. I tried. I wanted more than anything to have you both home with me, but you didn't want to come, and I couldn't make you. I just had to hope that one day you'd forgive me.' She lets out a small laugh. 'I didn't realise it would take *quite* so long.'

I smile back. 'It still might take some time,' I say, and pain fills my mum's features. 'But I'm trying,' I add, still thinking of James, and her face relaxes.

'Then that'll do,' she says, picking up my hand and squeezing it.

Derek brings a tray in, carrying a teapot and two mugs.

'I've taken one up to Georgia. She's fast asleep.'

'Thank you, my love,' Mum says, smiling up at him.

I nod towards the coffee table.

'I see you finished the book then, Mr Carter – Derek. What did you think of it?'

He grins and picks it up. 'I thought it was as close to perfect as a book can be. There was actually one paragraph that I wanted to talk to you about.'

The Book Swap

He picks the book up off the table, the way he used to from his desk at school, and excitement starts to build within me the way it always did. I want to know which parts of the book he enjoyed. I always wanted to know. He licks his thumb and forefinger and flicks through the pages, bending it back at the spine.

'*There isn't a disconnection in the world that can't be healed by forgiveness,*' he starts, quoting the moment where the protagonist realises she needs to stop blaming her family for her mental health. It's a poetic and beautiful piece of writing.

We lock eyes and laugh, the way we used to in class sometimes. I'd look at him and think about the joy he seemed to get from teaching. *One day*, I'd think. *One day, I want a job like that.*

28

James

I can't believe what just happened. Mum's finally crashed beside me, asleep, with her head resting on my arm as I replay everything with Erin.

Maybe I was unfair on her. I took all my anger and frustration out on her. Everything that had happened after I called for the ambulance.

'What's going on?' Mum had shouted, running down the stairs to see paramedics carrying Dad out on a stretcher.

Normally it's Dad and me together deciding what's going to be best for Mum. What information to tell her – and what to withhold. My heart felt torn in two. Half of me wanted to jump in the car and chase after Dad to the hospital. The other half needed to make sure Mum was looked after. I didn't know how to do both things, when there was only one of me.

For the first time that I can ever remember, I called Elliot, asking for help.

'We're coming,' he said, hanging up.

I didn't know how much to tell Mum about Dad. My gran's death is what triggered Mum's worst depression. The one that had her bedridden for months. That was the year I saw Bonnie at the bus stop. Dad would know what to say. He always does.

'Elliot's coming home, Mum,' was all I could think of, and her eyes lit up, the way I knew they would.

We drove to the hospital, the journey so familiar, and yet so different. This time, it was Mum beside me, not Bonnie. I kept looking over and expecting to see her there. She'd have been chatting away. She'd somehow have been able to make me laugh. To distract me with a story about her and Erin, or London, or her work.

Clutching the steering wheel, I tried to imagine what was happening to Dad in the back of that ambulance. All I knew is they'd be fighting to save his life.

'He's going to be okay, Mum,' I said, but maybe that was just for me. 'He was still conscious. The ambulance came quickly. I found him early.' I didn't add that he couldn't die. Not when I hadn't told him that I was sorry.

'If he isn't okay, it'll be your fault,' Mum said, looking across at me, her eyes dark. It was the version of her that scared me the most. 'You were harassing him.'

I kept my eyes on the road. Tightened my grip on the wheel, palms stinging from my fall down the tree.

'I wasn't harassing him.' I indicated left onto the A36 and crossed over the River Avon. It was Bonnie's favourite part of the drive.

'You were. You wouldn't leave him alone. On and on you go, about his music career.'

'I just didn't want him to miss out.'

'Then you shouldn't have been born,' she spat. 'Your father turned down a tour that year. A whole record deal for an album, to look after you.'

Swallowing, I fixed my eyes ahead of me.

'That isn't true,' I said to Mum, needing it not to be. Her jaw locked. She was saying the worst things imaginable, and she knew it. She didn't care. 'It was to look after you.'

I could hardly see the signs as I drove past a cemetery on

the right, and on to the hospital. Bonnie and I always commented on how cruel it was. To put a cemetery so close to a hospital, that you had to drive right by it on the way. She used to laugh about it. She found humour in everything, right up to the end.

'And then, after all of it, you shouted at him and now he's in hospital.'

'I didn't shout.'

'You may as well have.'

Anger ripped through me, and the words came flying out of my mouth before I could stop them.

'If you hadn't torn apart the entire house so Dad was living in ruins, he might not have been so stressed,' I shouted, seeing a parking space ahead and slamming the car into it. I shouldn't have shouted. I knew it wasn't my mum speaking, but she was trying to blame it all on me. 'Dad had to look after me, because you couldn't. There's just as much chance *you* did this to him.'

Someone started beeping their horn and I got out of the car, slamming the door shut. Then I looked up, and there was Erin, and all the leftover anger I had because of Mum transferred onto her.

I can't think about it. Not now. Not while I sit and wait for news of Dad.

All I can think about is whether Mum's right. If I could have caused this somehow. If my pushing Dad about his gigs was opening old wounds. Breaking his heart. But earlier, he said the opposite. That it was the best decision he made. He's made peace with it all, there's only one person who hasn't. Me.

Wiping at my eyes, I glance over to the receptionist, who's whispering to another employee, looking in my direction. I can see her mouthing 'Gareth Parr' as her colleague mouths back, 'Do You Know Me?'

I've never understood how Dad could let it go, because I couldn't. I let that one chapter of my book hang over me for years. I was never going to give up on it, even though it's obvious I should have. That the moment I did, better things happened to me. Dad said the same today. He hasn't just accepted his choice, he's happy with it, and I know that means I have to be too.

We get odd updates throughout the night, as we wait on those rock-hard, plastic chairs. He's in critical care. They're doing all they can. They'll be out when there's more news.

Eventually, at some point the next day, in between chasing Mum around the waiting room and lying her down on the chairs, my brother appears.

'I just spoke to reception. Someone's coming soon.'

It feels so good, to have someone else sharing the burden. Mum's asleep on me, and I gently lower her down onto the seat I was sitting on, standing to hug Elliot.

'Thanks for coming.'

'Of course.'

'What happened?'

I tell him. I start with the carpets, and the table in the garden. Me climbing the tree. Mum shouting. The ambulance. The drive with Mum. I tell him everything.

'Did you really shout at him?' Elliot asks, his voice low as we both watch Mum.

Shaking my head, I look towards the doors, desperate for a doctor to walk through and tell us something. Tell us Dad's okay.

'I didn't, I swear. I just told him he should go on the tour, and I'd—'

'Why wouldn't you let that go?'

'Because he deserves to live the life he was going to, before I came along.'

Elliot nods towards the next chairs over, and lowers himself onto one.

'He gave that life up long before you were born. He gave it up the day he moved to Frome. You do know Dad didn't *want* to be a pop star? He was glad to meet Mum and have an excuse not to do it.'

'I know he says that, but I don't believe he means it.'

'Of course you don't.' Elliot rests his head against the wall, glancing towards the double doors and back again. 'Because you only have one measure for success, and being a father doesn't count.'

His words land hard against me, choking me. I want to say that it isn't true, but I think I'd be lying.

'You know,' says Elliot, looking down at his phone, a photo of Jordan staring back at him. 'I'm proud, every single day, that I'm a full-time parent, just like Dad. To me, this is success.' He nods towards the photo. 'Raising him. Watching him grow. Being there for him every time he needs me. Do you remember there ever being a moment that we needed Dad and he wasn't there? Because I don't. He chose to be there, for everything. I can only hope to be half as good a dad as he was. Is. And I don't care what you think of it. You make all these digs about me getting a job, or Dad restarting his career. All of that's on you, not us. I'd put on a Domino's outfit in a heartbeat if it meant putting food on my son's plate. I'd clear the streets. I'd clean toilets. When you're a parent, you do whatever it takes.'

Swallowing, I jig my leg against the ground. It's true. Dad was there even when I didn't think I needed him, and always when I did. I don't know why I didn't respect that.

'Your view of achievement is so skewed.' Elliot fixes his warm brown eyes on me. They're just like Mum's are, when she's well. 'You work your arse off in a job you hate, telling yourself you're succeeding because you earn good money and you keep getting promoted. Take a risk on what it is you *actually* want. You can't have success without some failure, so stop being so afraid of it.'

I don't know why I've spent all these years convincing myself that two years of no contact means my brother doesn't know me. Doesn't understand who I am. He sees me more clearly than anyone, he's just never felt the need to point it out, the way I do. It's not that he always runs out of words, he just chooses not to use them.

'For what it's worth, I think you're an amazing dad,' I say, because I should have told him when I visited. I should have told him so many times. 'I was in awe in New York. Everything you did for him. It's . . . He's lucky to have you.'

'I know.' That's the tessa about Elliot. He doesn't need validation the way I do. He never has.

Mum wakes up and Elliot's on his feet immediately, rushing to her side. Placing a hand on each shoulder to steady her. It is such a relief to have him here. Not to be the only person responsible for Mum.

A doctor appears and speaks to the receptionist, who nods in our direction. All three of us stand and walk towards her.

'He's had what's called a non-ST-elevation myocardial infarction. An artery's partially blocked,' she explains, leading us through the double doors.

'Is he—'

'He's going to need a lot of rest. A good diet. Short walks every day if he can manage them. Daily blood-thinning medicine. He'll need to stay here for a coronary angiography.'

'But he's going to be okay?'

'Would you believe he's wide awake right now, singing "Do You Know Me?" to one of the nurses?'

Elliot grins, looking across at me. 'Of course he is.'

'No stage performances for him for a while, though,' the doctor adds, laughing.

'Oh, there's no fear of that, don't worry,' I say, following her into a room, where Dad is sitting up, resting against a pillow, linked up to a load of different machines.

'Here they are,' he says, smiling at us before turning to the nurse, who's fiddling with something on his monitor. 'My family.' His words ring out with such pride that if I didn't understand what Elliot was trying to say, I do now. There's no greater achievement in Dad's life than us, and there never could be.

Walking towards him, I sit beside the bed and hold his hand.

'Thank you, Dad,' I say, swallowing, and he looks at me, his eyes shining.

'Nothing to thank me for,' he says – and he knows, without me saying more, what I'm thanking him for. 'Best job I've ever had.'

29

Erin

'So, to be clear, we don't hate James now?' Bonnie asks from her chair in the corner of my room.

She's younger. She's the Bonnie from school. The Bonnie who wouldn't leave my side after the first time James hurt me. I want to throw my arms around her. Smell the coconut scent of her skin and the Lush body spray she smothered herself in. I want to feel the comfort of her as she strokes my hair and tells me that it's all going to be okay. That I've always got her.

'I fear it's quite the opposite,' I say, tracing my finger along his handwriting in the letter.

'Always was,' she says, laughing.

It's been a few weeks since I saw James outside the hospital. He didn't tell me everything that was written in the letter before he gave it to me outside the hospital. He let me find out the rest for myself. That he was in love with me. That all of the feelings Charlie felt for Sam in *The Perks of Being a Wallflower* were the same as how he felt about me. That even if we never ended up together, it was just as I'd said to Mr Carter that day. That Charlie loving Sam the way he does opens him up. That's why he grows. It was the same for James, he said. He didn't just love the book because he related to it. He loved it because it reminded him of me.

I imagine myself reading this letter back at school, after everything that happened. Whether it would have changed anything. Whether I'd have finally known what it would feel like to kiss him. Somehow, because we were always with Bonnie, we never found out, and then the friendship was over.

It's her yearly fundraiser next month and I've got no idea what to dress up as. I've been asking her, but she's remained silent on the matter.

There's a knock on the door and Cassie waits for me to shout before coming in. I turn from the bed to smile at her, and she grimaces as her eyes land on the books on the bed, and the letter beside them.

'Still rereading all his notes? Otherwise known as torturing yourself.'

I nod and hand her one as an example. I hand her *The Great Gatsby*.

She frowns, scanning something at the back of the book. She pulls at her top lip, her glasses sliding down her nose. Closing it, she hands it back to me, pushing up her glasses.

'There I was thinking you were just changing the lives of these school kids, but it sounds like you kind of changed his life too. You reminded him he wanted to be an author. That's big stuff, Erin.'

'He did the same for me. Reading that answer was what made me realise I wanted—' I stop. I haven't told anyone but James – Mystery Man James – about my dream of becoming a teacher. It feels too fragile. As though if I admit it out loud it will crack.

'What?' Cassie asks, walking further into my room and sitting down in Bonnie's chair. I sit bolt upright, almost going to stop her, but it'll seem insane. *You can't sit there. It's where my dead best friend sits.*

'I want to be a teacher,' I say, distracting myself with a confession instead. Cassie's face lights up and she claps her hands together.

'You'd be amazing at it,' she says. 'You're already doing it. With Savannah and her friends. With James. You're more than halfway there. Plus . . .' she bites her lip, 'Miss Connolly has an excellent ring to it.'

I shift my gaze from Cassie, to the framed postcard from Bonnie. *Don't forget to make all your dreams come true!*

Cassie's eyes land on it, too.

'I think she'd be so happy for you,' she says. She has no idea of the importance of those words, delivered while sitting in Bonnie's chair.

'I wasn't always a good friend to her,' I confess. 'When she got sick, I didn't see her. I was afraid.'

I wait for judgement to cross Cassie's features, but she stands up and walks towards me instead, taking me in her arms the way I'd wished Bonnie could a few moments earlier. She doesn't smell like Bonnie. She smells of vanilla, and the Gucci perfume she insists on showering herself with, but I'm just as grateful for the hug.

'Of course you were afraid,' she says. 'None of us know how to handle something we've never been through before, all we can do is learn from it. Use it to better ourselves.'

Nodding against her, my mind goes to Georgia. I've really tried to be there for her the way I wasn't for Bonnie. It isn't enough, but it's something.

My phone rings and I jump when I see who it is, holding it up to show Cassie. Taking a deep breath, I answer. It's a video call.

'Hey,' Savannah says, her lips in a straight line. Her eyes dull.

I swallow. 'It doesn't matter,' I say. 'You have worked *so* hard, and whatever result it is, I'm still so proud of you. Okay?'

Cassie clenches her teeth together, staring at me.

'Okay.' Savannah nods, looking beyond the camera. I should have gone with her. Been beside her when she got the results to give her a hug, but I know that isn't my job as a teacher. I just set her up as best I can. It's all I can do. 'Well that's lucky because I got a B,' she screams, breaking into a huge grin before cackling.

'You little—' I stop myself from swearing at a minor, and start laughing instead. 'You got a B,' I shout, a smile breaking onto my face that I'm not sure will ever leave.

Cassie starts jumping up and down, doing a silent dance.

'Thank you,' Savannah says, chatter breaking out in the background of the video. Someone's shouting about going to get ice cream. 'I couldn't have done it without you.'

'And I couldn't have done it without you,' I say back, meaning it. Without Savannah's dad picking up that book and leading me to her, I'd never have found out what it is I want to do with my life. I owe it all to her. 'So thank you right back. Now go celebrate.'

'I will,' she says. 'Bye, Erin.'

'Bye, Savannah.'

She's gone and I bite down on my lip as I look at Cassie.

'Miss Connolly's only gone and smashed her first teaching job,' she says, hugging me. 'Let me go and get us some food. We can find you a teacher training course to sign up to over my famous spag bol.'

She stands up and leaves the room, my heart rushing with love for her, and gratitude that she lives here now instead of Callum.

The Book Swap

The moment she's gone, Bonnie's back. I grimace. 'Did she squash you? Sorry.'

'Please don't be sorry. I'm not sure I've ever been happier. Except . . .' She looks down at herself, sitting back in the chair. She's in a bright green jacket, with black-and-white trousers. 'I'd *never* wear this. If you're going to keep me alive in your imagination, can you at least make it accurate.'

I shake my head, grinning. 'I knew you'd help me eventually.'

Bonnie frowns, staring at me, as I pick up my phone. I know exactly what my costume will be for this year's fundraiser.

30

James

The moment I see Frome College ahead of me, all the familiar feelings come creeping back. Sweat forms on my upper lip and I roll the sleeves up on my shirt. I don't know why I'm even doing this. Why I agreed to it. It made sense at the time to face my fears, but now the moment's here I don't think I can.

A group of boys are hovering at the entrance and I stop, just for a second, flashbacks racing into my mind. On a different day, when I was still at school, that sight would have been enough to make me turn back around. Now, Joel appears, breaking up the circle to wave at me.

'Out of my way please, boys,' he says, and the group disperses. 'It looks so much smaller than I remember it being.' He signals behind him with his thumb, walking towards me and pulling me in for a hug. 'The classrooms. The people . . .'

I laugh, shaking myself out of the memories. 'I guess we're bigger these days.'

'Exactly.' He locks eyes with me, and I get what he's doing. He's trying to change the place before I walk into it. Make it somewhere different, so I don't feel the same.

'Let's do this,' I say, walking ahead of him. He slaps me on the back and runs to walk beside me. Always so competitive.

'Actually, mate, it's just you,' he shouts back.

I stop. 'What?'

'It's quite hard to do a speech about the job you're in, when you've quit.' His face breaks into a grin as my mouth hangs open.

'You what? You *quit?*'

'Yup.' It's the most I've seen him smile in weeks. Maybe years. 'It was bullshit. All of it. I thought I was *living*, in London. Can you believe it?' He looks across at me. 'I actually thought I had a life, but all I ever had was a job. Money and stability. I went back to Orlando hoping it would feel like home. It doesn't. Nowhere does.' He looks down at his feet, scuffing his shoe against the ground. Pretty sure it's a Yeezy one. The ones that cost hundreds of pounds. 'That's when I realised, if I want a home, I've got to build it myself. It's up to me.' His eyes are wide as he turns to me. 'You've got so much to be grateful for, mate. A job doesn't mean anything. But love. A place to call home. A passion. That's life. That's living. The rest is just filler. And in case you're wondering, yes . . . I'm hoping I inspire you to do the same. Force you out of that comfort zone of yours and get you doing what you actually want instead.'

A group of students walks past us and into the hall we're due in any minute.

'But for now . . . go lie through your teeth.' He hits me on the back and walks ahead of me into the hall, pushing his shoulders back as he's greeted by the head teacher, Mr Marsden.

I always thought Joel was totally in control of his life, but it seems like it was the other way round. His life was in control of him, until just now. He's done the brave thing, again. He's quit on something that isn't working for him. He's set himself free. I looked up to him for going after what he wanted with that job, back when we left school. I thought

The Book Swap

it was what I wanted too. I'm not sure it's what either of us want any more.

The hall's swarming with teenagers. There are so many of them that I can't even fixate on one group. They look so young. Jumping off chairs and pushing into each other. Laughing and shouting across the room. How could I have let a group of kids, who had no idea what they were doing with their life, control what I did with mine?

Mr Marsden approaches me, shaking my hand.

'James, great to see you back here. I was surprised when I saw what job you were going to be speaking about. Always hoped you'd go into something English-related, but my students always surprise me.'

Smiling, I take in how much his face has changed. How grey his hair is. How wise his eyes still look behind his thick-rimmed glasses.

'I still do the odd bit,' I say. 'Don't give up on me yet.'

'Glad to hear it,' he says, leading me backstage. 'Doesn't have to be long, just try and keep them interested. Inspire them.'

Nodding, I look down at the A4 page of notes I've typed out. I'm not sure 'interested' was what I had in mind when writing it. I scan the words I've been writing over the past few days. The words I've been practising with Dad. The words I've bored Elliot with and murmured at Mum while she's been sleeping.

I hardly listen to the other talks. Mr Marsden calls my name and I walk onto the stage, standing in front of the microphone.

Elliot assured me I wouldn't be able to see the audience, which is total bullshit. The second I look out, I can see rows and rows of bored teenagers staring back at me.

I cough, and begin.

'I fell into my job in what was a surprise to a lot of people, but most definitely myself,' I say, which is the only bit I know off by heart. Now I look down at my sheet. 'See, I actually wanted to do something else. I wanted to write books, but the world can lead you in mysterious ways, and before you know it, you're a partner at a corporate training company. I know . . .' I say, catching sight of the rolling eyes in the front row. Sweat starts to form at the back of my neck. 'It doesn't sound glamorous or exciting, but . . .' One of the boys I saw waiting at the front of college is directly in my eyeline. He turns to his friend and whispers something. It's starting. The piece of paper starts shaking in my hand as I wait for it. The song they made up about me. They must have heard about it somehow. Know who I am.

'Come on,' someone shouts, and I swallow, staring back down at the words on the page, which are swimming in front of me. I can't make them out. 'Achievement'. 'Success'. 'Pay rise'. Everything is moving and I can feel my breath quickening. A younger Erin appears in my mind. She's standing on this very stage reading an excerpt from *The Hunger Games*, as Bonnie and I watch from the audience. It's the bit about hope being stronger than fear.

I take the deepest breath I can, in through my nose and out through my mouth, the way Helena taught me after she found me on the street. The day she taught me about Maslow's hierarchy. At the very top of the triangle is fulfilling our own potential.

'You know what,' I say, dropping my hand, which still holds my speech. 'Some of you might make brilliant corporate trainers. Some of you might end up with a shit job – sorry – because you spent your entire time at college laughing at the people working hard, while you did no work at all.' I fix my eyes on the boy who was laughing. 'It doesn't really matter what it is that you end up doing, or how you get there. It just matters that you love it. That you wake up every day and cannot wait to get started.' I can see Joel standing at the very back, hands in his pockets, staring at me. 'I'm not going to stand here and tell you that you have to do something that's well paid, or well respected. If you're good at what you do, and you work hard at it, then whatever it is, you'll make money. You just won't sell your soul to get there.'

Someone in the middle of the crowd laughs, and another starts clapping.

'I told you, sir,' someone shouts.

'Just . . . whatever it is right now that you're thinking about doing, that thing that seems untouchable, or embarrassing or too difficult to pursue – don't give up on that. Keep hold of it. Remember it. Get yourself a group of friends here who won't let you forget about it. Even just one friend.' I find Joel again and nod at him, smiling. He grins back and gives a thumbs-up. 'Because when the time is right, you'll be ready. And you'll go for it. And you'll wish that you'd started sooner.'

Looking around the room, I can see everyone's face on me, but it doesn't feel the way it used to. I don't feel small, or embarrassed, or a laughing stock. I'm just me.

'Good luck,' I say and Joel starts whooping and clapping from the back until everyone else starts to join in.

I walk to the back and watch the rest of the talks, then say my goodbyes and leave with Joel. We pass by the art block, where I witnessed the moment that led me to betray Erin. Joel squeezes me on the shoulder as we walk. Out through the front courtyard and past the hall, which was the setting for so much of my bullying. The chanting. The punching. The chewing gum. The humiliation.

Out towards where the bike racks used to be. The ones that I'd walk towards with fear pumping through my chest, every day. I just had to make it past them and start running, or jump into Elliot's car. They're gone now, a flower bed sitting in their place, bursting with colour.

31

Erin

The Cheese & Grain is swarming with Bravehearts and Bob the Builders, boxers and bunnies. One inflatable big boob is wandering about, with the largest, most unrealistic nipple I've ever seen. There's ballerinas and brides, Batman and *Baywatch*, and I'm standing amongst them all, dressed as Bonnie.

I asked her parents to send me an outfit I remember her wearing a lot. A pink Chanel top, with a pink fur jacket and light blue jeans, topped off with gold hoop earrings and a gold Chanel belt, with white trainers. She always told me that if someone gave her back all the money she spent on clothes, she'd just use it to buy more clothes. It's what made her feel most like herself.

The only thing missing tonight is Georgia. She stayed at Mum's, claiming that being sober at a memorial is too depressing, even for her, even if she has the perfect fancy dress outfit without even trying. Baby Bump has got to win extra points, for being a double B. Cassie's come instead. She said she's heard so much about Bonnie, she wants to get as close to meeting her as possible. She's slicked all her hair back so it looks shorter than it is, and is wearing a pair of shorts, a white shirt and a tie. She's come as a boy, and I know Bonnie would approve.

I direct her to the bar as I scan the room for the first two people I need to see. They're in the corner by the stage, tearing up raffle tickets.

'Thanks for sending this,' I say, approaching Bonnie's parents, who look up at me and smile. Her dad's eyes glaze over as he takes me in.

'I remember that one well. I hated how much of her midriff was on show.'

'I'm hating it too, if that helps?' I reply and they both chuckle.

'I'm so sorry that I wasn't there for her.' The words I've been so afraid of saying out loud come so easily. 'I wasn't the friend Bonnie needed, and I know that.'

They exchange a look, before nodding. 'We were disappointed,' her mum says. 'When you stopped visiting. But we know it wasn't just you. She was pushing you away. All of us, really.'

Biting my lip, I nod, tears filling my eyes. 'I shouldn't have let her. I should have showed up anyway.'

'We saw your mum quite a lot during that time,' Bonnie's dad says, as I frown. She's never mentioned it. 'She had a theory about your struggles with abandonment. She told us that if we needed to blame anyone, we should blame her. But there's no blame here, Erin. Bonnie wasn't alone. She had people around her. Good people.'

I nod. It should have been me too and I know that, but it's something I'll have to live with. I'm just glad there were others who had the strength I didn't.

'You came back, too. You came back when it mattered the most.'

The three of us hug and I turn to see Cassie waving at me from a table, holding up a bottle of wine.

'Wow,' Cassie says, looking around the room. 'People really make an effort.'

'You didn't meet Bonnie, but she wouldn't expect any less.'

It's hard to concentrate. Now I've spoken to Bonnie's parents, all I can do is think about James. Every time the door opens, my eyes dart towards it in case it's him. I'm not even sure if he's coming, but I have to believe he is. If he doesn't turn up, everything I've prepared is for nothing.

'I think I might have fallen a bit in love with Frome,' Cassie says, looking around the room. She nods towards a bumble bee, who throws his head back and laughs, before pretending to buzz around the group he's with.

'All Londoners do!'

'Would you ever move back here?'

I've actually always loved it here. The beautiful little streets, so different and distinctive. The pubs that are full of character, and characters, each with such opposing personalities. The gentrification in recent years is something people like Mum and Derek love to complain about, while lapping up all the new restaurants and independent shops that have opened because of it. I had some of my happiest times here, and it's where I feel closest to Bonnie. We had great times in London too, but this town is where we cemented our friendship. Formed our unbreakable bond.

'Maybe one day,' I say and Cassie grins.

'Not before you've had a few more months with the best flatmate of your life, obviously.'

We lock eyes, bringing our glasses together for a cheers.

'To you,' Cassie says. 'And starting your teacher training. Can you believe it? One year from now you'll officially be known as "Miss".'

'And to you, incorporating a business. One step closer to ditching Charlotte for good.'

We grin at each other, and take a drink, just as Bonnie's parents take to the stage dressed as Bananas in Pyjamas.

This year her dad does the welcome speech, grateful that we're coming back year after year to remember their daughter. He tells a story about Bonnie running towards the sea that so perfectly sums up her enthusiasm for life that everyone's laughing and crying before he even speaks the final words.

'I'm grateful that she lived and I'm grateful for what she taught me. We love you, Bonnie, and we always will.' He reaches an arm around his wife and squeezes her shoulder, before standing tall and announcing the talent contest.

'Wow,' Cassie mouths at me.

They launch into the contest with Bonnie's sisters, looking so much more grown up than last year as they open with a dance. Someone sings a version of 'Candle in the Wind', which is so bad that everyone starts to turn away from the stage, unable to keep looking. A group of girls I don't recognise sing a Spice Girls song and a younger boy plays drums in a gorilla suit like the Phil Collins advert. Where's James?

Bonnie's dad reappears on stage, inviting the next act up. If James isn't here, I can't do it. Standing up to leave, I hear my name. 'Erin Connolly.' Bonnie's dad is staring right at me and I can't let him down. Not again. I've got no choice. Even if James isn't here, I have to go up. Reaching into my bag, I pull out a book and start walking.

There are murmurs as I take the steps closest to our table. Maybe because they know who I am, or because of who I've come as. I step towards the microphone.

'I'm going to be reading an extract from *The Perks of Being a Wallflower* – a book Bonnie loved.'

A hush falls around the room. I open the book, hands shaking. I know the words off by heart, but I need the book now. To look down, instead of out into the audience. Coughing, I start to read. I read the passage where Charlie, Sam and Patrick fly through the tunnel together in a car. The moment where the three of them cement their friendship.

> 'Patrick started driving really fast, and just before we got to the tunnel. Sam stood up, and the wind turned her dress into ocean waves. When we hit the tunnel, all the sound got scooped up into a vacuum, and it was replaced by a song on the tape player ... Sam screamed this really fun scream, and there it was. Downtown. Lights on buildings and everything that makes you wonder.'

I reach the last paragraph and stand up straighter, pushing my shoulders back. Cassie grins at me, giving me a thumbs-up. I try to find James, but I can't recognise anyone. I just have to project my voice and hope he understands that this is for him. This is the best way I can think of, to tell him how I feel.

> 'Sam sat down and started laughing. Patrick started laughing. I started laughing.'

I'm not reading about the three of them, I'm reading about the three of us. About me, and James, and Bonnie. Our friendship. I want him to know I remember it.

Ahead of me a group of blueberries part down the middle and someone slowly appears through the centre. For a second I catch my breath, because all I see is Bonnie's clothes. Her treasured Louboutin heels, the maroon jumpsuit that I almost chose to wear myself, and red lips framed by a bright blond wig. Stumbling over my words, I try to finish my sentence. Close my eyes. Recite it from memory.

'And in that moment, I swear we were infinite.'

My voice wobbles on the last word, as I think about me and James. About everything we've been through together. How it has to be true for us. We're infinite. Our relationship has no limits. It can't be measured. We will always exist together.

Swallowing, I close the book to signal the end of the reading and give a small curtsey. Cassie stands up and starts clapping and whooping so loud that everyone else realises I'm done, and a quiet ripple of applause makes its way around the room.

I didn't do it for the applause, but I'm still somewhat hurt that the reaction will barely register on the noise meter. None of that matters for long though, as the person dressed as Bonnie takes another step forward towards the stage, wobbling as they do on one foot and then the other, like a baby giraffe.

Leaning back on my flat-heeled trainers, I laugh, because of course it's him. Somehow, our fancy dress outfits have matched yet again.

Walking to the edge of the stage, I take the steps and nod towards James for the sake of Cassie. Then, heart pounding, I walk towards him, preparing to say everything else I've been planning.

His eyes are clouded, his red lips twitching at the corners.

'We were infinite,' he says, his eyes looking nowhere but at me.

Swallowing, I nod. 'We always will be, whatever happens.' I scan his face for a hint of how he might be feeling. I need him to know I've changed. 'Your dad, is he . . .?'

'He's okay.'

Just being in front of him, my whole body is vibrating with energy. All I want is to reach out and touch him. To know how it feels to finally hold his hand.

Someone on stage picks up the guitar, playing the beginning of 'While My Guitar Gently Weeps', and James's face breaks into a small smile.

'I can't believe you got up there and did that.'

'Neither can I,' I say, swallowing. 'I read your letter. I'm so sorry for how I behaved. Some might call it . . . self-centred.' I screw my face up, and he raises his eyebrows.

His eyes move to my lips and back. I don't understand how I turned him into someone so different in my head. All for one mistake. What would Bonnie think, if she could see me now? Here. Would she think I was mad for forgiving him, or mad for holding onto it all for so long?

I look away, catching sight of Cassie at the table, a man dressed as a Buddha having taken my seat opposite her. They're both trying to pretend that they're not watching us.

'You'll be pleased to know I've been making a lot of apologies recently. My mum. You. Bonnie's parents . . .'

'Why them?' he asks, his eyebrows knitting together.

'For not being there for Bonnie.'

'You don't need to apologise for that – she understood.'

His pale blue eyes are fixed on my face, staring down at me as I process what he's saying. I watch as his expression changes. As he shifts from empathy to panic.

Bonnie's dad finishes announcing the final act of the talent contest and out of the corner of my eye I see Cassie approach before retreating backwards, followed by the Buddha. Behind her is the wall plastered in photos of Bonnie. I shake my head.

'What do you mean?'

'I was with her.' He's watching me to make sure I hear his words. 'Through the chemo. I took her to nearly every session, and no she was *not* happy about it at first, okay? She hated me. She made sure she punished me for the entire journey but she had no choice. Her parents couldn't do all the trips. She needed the help.'

I'm trying to listen. Trying not to respond until I hear everything he has to say, but it's not making sense.

'She'd have told me.'

'She couldn't. The forgiveness thing,' he says, lifting his arm up towards me. I flinch. I'm trying to piece everything together. James and Bonnie. Jealousy catches in my throat. The two of them, together, without me, when I should have been there.

'Bonnie forgave you, Erin. She understood why you weren't there. Was grateful, actually, that you wouldn't see her like that. That you'd remember her the way she was before the cancer.' He lets out a laugh. 'She used to say that to me. That I would always hold the worst memory of her, and you the best. That between the two of us, we held all of her. We made her whole.'

Bonnie never mentioned him. Not once. Not in the voice notes or in our last drink together. I can't help but feel like she's tricked me somehow. Like they both have. Hanging out in secret. Making a pact not to tell me. Everything starts swirling in my stomach. The drinks. The nerves at getting up on stage. The image I can't get out of my head, of James and Bonnie as a duo. We were never a duo. If I'd known we could be, maybe I'd have done something about how I felt about James at school. I just presumed I couldn't. That it was the three of us or nothing. Bile shoots into my mouth and I start running towards the toilet, holding my hand over my lips. I

The Book Swap

burst into the cubicle, and past the group of bunnies reapplying their whiskers in the mirror. I throw up into the toilet as, in my pocket, my phone starts vibrating.

Dabbing my mouth with toilet roll, I pull out my phone. It's Georgia.

'The baby's coming,' she says, the moment I pick up.

32

James

She's gone. I wasn't concentrating on what I was saying. I was so distracted by her reading that I said the first thing that came to my mind when she mentioned Bonnie. I was always going to tell her tonight. I'd planned it so much better than that and now I'm walking towards Joel, having just seen her run out of the door and away from me.

The way I'd planned it, I hoped it would have reset everything between us. It would have finished what was started outside the hospital. Instead, I blindsided her. I made it sound like some sort of secret we were keeping at her expense.

'Everything okay?' Joel asks, pulling up his giant Buddha pants.

I lick my lips, shaking my head. 'I don't think so. She's just gone.'

'What the hell did you do this time?'

I stare towards the door. Maybe I should have run after her, but I don't have a good history with Erin accepting my apologies. She needs time.

'I told her about Bonnie. I don't think she took it well.'

'But she knows the truth, at least? No secrets between you now,' Joel says, always trying to find the positive.

'Nothing at all between us now, I don't think.'

He's right though. Even through all the confusion written on her face as I tried to explain myself, the pain in her eyes when I spoke about Bonnie is what stood out most of all. If in some way I've eased that, then all this is worth it. It's worth it, even if I've lost her.

'I was so sure this was going to end up as one of those big love stories,' Joel says, shaking his head.

'Me too, mate. I guess it was meant to stay in the past.' I rub my forehead, trying to wipe the pain away with it. All I've ever wanted is Erin. Why is it that every time we get close, I manage to do something to destroy it? I've spent so long hoping that one day we might be together, I've lost track of reality. She'll never be able to forgive me. Not now.

I think about the book I'm writing. I've been stuck on the last chapter, and it's suddenly become clear why. I needed to know how it all ends, and now I do.

Leaving the memorial, I pull off these ridiculous high heels and walk home in bare feet, parting with Joel at the bottom of Catherine Hill. I creep up the stairs to my bedroom and go straight to my laptop, and start typing. I write the ending that's needed, not the one I wished for. Then, before I can chicken out, or let the fear take over, I hit reply to Sophia's email, and attach my novel. I call it *The Perfect History*.

In the morning I wake up early and go downstairs to make a coffee. Elliot, Carl and Jordan are sleeping in and Mum isn't coping with Dad back in hospital. He's gone in to have a stent fitted and Mum's been in her room since she found out. I've been teaching Elliot what needs doing. Allowing him to make up for the time he's missed, while giving myself some time to heal from Mum's words.

As I wait for my coffee, I go onto YouTube, finding the

videos I need. Then I carry my mug through to the sitting room, where I push the television and chair back into the dining room and finally start rolling out the underlay.

At some point, Elliot appears. He's in his pyjamas, and it reminds me of when we were kids, coming down in the morning to watch TV together.

Without saying a word, he walks to one end of the sofa, which I hadn't been able to move alone. I take the other end and we carry it out of the way, and return to the underlay. Together, we roll out the rest, and I hand him the knife to trim it. Then I throw him a roll of adhesive, and we start at separate ends of the room, taping it down.

'How was last night?' he asks, eventually.

'Erin got up on stage, and said she forgave me,' I reply.

Elliot knows everything now. 'That's great.'

'Then she found out about Bonnie and left.'

He pauses. 'Ah. Just give it some time. At least it's all out in the open now.'

'I guess. Although given how long it took her to forgive my last mistake, I'm not sure.'

He frowns, resting his hand against the ground. 'Caring for Bonnie the way you did was not a mistake. It won't take her long to realise that.'

I look over at him, so happy to have my brother back.

It falls quiet again. We keep going.

'I'm sorry, that I haven't been here with Mum. It's bloody hard work. Harder than you made it sound.'

We're moving closer towards each other, as we keep sticking down the underlay.

'You know she said something interesting to me last night? She said her mother had electric shock therapy.'

I pause, looking at him. 'Granny?'

'Yeah. She was really unwell for a long time. Her mum before her too. You didn't do this to her, James. It's just one of those things. It's just who our mum is.'

Frowning, I stare at the ground. Can that be true? That maybe she'd have become ill anyway, even without me?

'I don't know how to process that information just now,' I say. It's all I've ever known. It's the story I've always told myself.

'Then wait until you hear this,' he says, leaving me to deal with the stuff about Mum in my own time. 'Carl's looking at jobs here. And so am I.'

My head shoots up and I'm unable to wipe the grin off my face.

'For real?'

'What are you more excited about? That we might come back, or that I'm finally getting a job?'

I shake my head, laughing. 'I'm very aware you already have a full-time job. You made that clear.'

'Good.' He sighs. 'He's loving it. Carl. All the time he's getting to spend with Jordan. He's like a different person here.'

'That's great.'

'It is.'

We're side by side, pushing down the last bit into place and he nudges me.

'Don't get too excited yet though. It might not happen.'

'One day at a time.'

'One day at a time.'

We go back out to the hall and try to pick up the cream carpet Mum chose for the sitting room. Fuck, it's heavy! We end up heaving it through with a combination of pushing, shoving and pulling. Once it's in, we roll it from the edge of the dining room to the end of the sitting room and by that point we're both out of breath and I have sweat covering my forehead. I throw myself onto the carpet, lying on my back. It really is soft, like a pillow.

Elliot joins me and we stare up at the ceiling, panting. We lie there in silence long enough for our breathing to return to normal.

Jordan comes running in, his hair all ruffled from sleep.

'Uncle James, please can you read me a story?' he asks.

'I can do one better,' I say, pulling him down onto me. 'I've got one of my own to tell you. It's a little bit about your dad, and a little bit about your grandad, and *you*, my friend, are my target audience, so I need to make sure you like it.'

He squeals, leaning back on me, and Elliot looks over to us smiling.

'I'll go take Mum her pills,' he says, leaving me to start my story.

I came up with the idea a while ago, as I fought writer's block. I prefer having more than one idea, anyway. This way, if Sophia doesn't like what I've written, I've got another. It's about a stay-at-home dad who's a part-time superhero.

'Danny wasn't like other boys,' I begin, trying it out. 'Because Danny's daddy had superpowers.'

'Yippee,' Jordan shouts, jumping in the air – and for now, that's all the approval I need.

Six Months Later

33

Erin

'You sure you don't need a hand with anything?' Georgia shouts from the sitting room, little baby Wren fast asleep against my sister's boob, as I finish packing my flat.

'Your moral support is everything,' I shout back.

Every time I see Wren, I'm right back there. Grabbing Cassie and dashing out of the memorial and into a taxi. The hospital, where I found Georgia having contractions, clutching onto Mum's arm. The labour room, where we fed her snacks and water as she shouted expletives at us, grabbing at the gas and air while screaming that she can't do this any more. Minutes later, baby Wren made her arrival, red-faced and angry as she stole the hearts of all three of us with one loud scream.

Georgia couldn't take her eyes off her daughter, but the moment I was allowed, I pulled Wren gently towards me, resting her in the crook of my arm. I looked down, taking in her tiny, perfect face, my chest expanding. That was the moment I knew how it felt to be infinite. I didn't need to drive through a tunnel in a car, I just needed to hold my niece. She was wearing a little hat, which crinkled as she frowned. She was making different noises as a multitude of expressions swept across her face. A pout. Surprise. Very cross. Totally relaxed. Peaceful.

I've never felt anything like it. The space that opened up within my heart and flooded it with a whole new type of love.

There I was telling myself I didn't know how to feel things, after Bonnie. It turns out it's possible. So very possible to feel grief, and love, all at once.

'Mum's so excited you're moving back.' Georgia appears in my doorway with her boob back under her top and Wren now flat out with her mouth open.

'She is,' I say in a high-pitched voice reserved only for my niece. 'Still gave her a final slagging off in therapy.'

'Of course you did.' Georgia laughs.

'She didn't say, but I think Philippa's going to miss me.'

'She's definitely going to miss my money.'

Ever since Cassie mentioned the idea of me moving back to Frome, I couldn't stop thinking about it. What it would feel like to return there and do something I've always dreamed of doing. I'm going to finally go back to Frome College.

Derek told me about one of the English teachers retiring at the end of the school year. They're looking for a replacement, and it ties in with the end of my course. While I can't be sure I'll ever do as good a job as Derek did with me, it feels right to try. To continue his passion for the subject. To get back the years there that I missed.

Georgia hands me Wren, and walks into the room, looking around.

'It looks so empty in here.'

I stroke Wren's cheek, heart swelling at the softness of her skin. The perfect features. How peaceful she always looks. It's as though the love I have for her has helped ease the pain of losing Bonnie. Not a lot, but enough.

'So, I'll take her home in the car and meet my removals people, and then you come over tomorrow and we'll go from there?'

'You bet.'

I was worried my news would devastate Georgia, but instead she sank with relief. It turned out she'd been considering a move herself ever since Wren was born, but didn't have the heart to tell me. She wanted to be closer to Mum and Derek, and all the help they're so desperate to give in the grandparenting department, so she's moving too, with Rishi's approval. He's been trying to escape London life and will follow Wren anywhere. Georgia and I are both staying at Mum's until we find somewhere. All of us, back under one roof. It's what Mum wanted after everything that happened – but just a few years too late.

It's worked out for Cassie, too. She's moving in with her new boyfriend, Joel. She got chatting to him at Bonnie's memorial and they bonded over their best friends' unusual exchange on the dance floor. After all her wishing, Cassie finally met someone, in person. Joel took her on a first date the next day and, when she gave him her speech about wanting something serious, he threw his head back and sighed with relief. He'd just returned from some life-changing trip to America and was all about making the most out of life. About building a future with someone.

It was on that date he told Cassie what James had said. That there was nothing between us and whatever was there before needed to be left in the past. That he'd gone to the memorial to tell me the truth about Bonnie. He wanted to end things and move on with no more secrets between us.

I needed Cassie to tell me, but I couldn't keep hearing about James after that. I asked her not to mention his name again, so I could be happy for her at all times, without it being wrapped up in missing him. Now our conversations are a careful balance of mentioning Joel's name while erasing the name of the best friend that's normally attached to it.

Beneath the shock of finding out what happened with James and Bonnie, all I'll ever feel is gratitude. For all of it. In that moment, when I saw him dressed as her, telling me that she forgave me, I didn't see him any more. I saw my best friend. I saw Bonnie. I heard her voice. I let myself believe it, just a little. After all, Bonnie wasn't perfect either. She lied to me about James, and somehow that makes everything a little better. It's a relief to remember her as a human again, instead of as a saint.

That isn't the main reason I'm so grateful, though. I'm grateful to James, for being strong enough to be there for Bonnie when I couldn't be. Now, when I imagine her going through treatment, I don't have to picture her alone. I see James beside her, holding her hand. I see the two of them talking and laughing, the way they used to at school. The way they'd probably have continued to if I hadn't insisted on breaking up their friendship. They found each other again, and I'm so happy that they did.

I help Georgia put Wren into her car seat and insist on carrying her out and strapping her in. Once I've waved them off, the weather's so nice I decide to walk. To go on a trip down memory lane and say goodbye to my little neighbourhood.

I make my way along Southwell Road and up Cambria Road, under the tunnel. The walk I used to do, up to five times a day sometimes, hoping for something from Mystery Man. From James.

For old times' sake, I walk towards the library. Eileen's looking worse than ever. One of the doors has hardly any paint left on it, and a piece of the roof has come off. The wood underneath looks like it's rotting. The sides are peeling and soon there'll be no colour left at all. Eileen would hate it.

The Book Swap

I bend down and open the doors, the same rush of adrenaline flooding me, even through memories. I lived my whole life here for a while. Maybe I'll take one book with me, as a memento.

Scanning through the titles, I pull out one that I think I've already read, check out the blurb on the back to confirm it, and then return it. As I look across the top shelf, my eyes land on one that makes my heart jolt. *The Perfect History* by Edward James Parr. It can't be – but it's too much of a coincidence to be anything else.

Opening the first page, my heart starts racing as I read the dedication.

To Erin. These extra wide margins are for you.

Shivering, I flick through the pages and it's true. The margins of this book are wider than all the others. There's space for so many notes.

This book is written by James, and his first name is Edward. On the spine there's a publisher's logo, while on the front, in a different font beneath his name, are the words 'Uncorrected Proof Copy'. An early copy of his book. He's done it.

I check the back of the book as I always did. In writing, beneath the words 'The End' it says:

Erin Connolly: I've loved you since you first reached your hand out to me in the dining hall. Since the house party. Since I left that bracelet in your bag on Valentine's Day. Since I saw you in the bookshop on the day of Bonnie's memorial last year. Since the glass in your foot. Since I picked up To Kill a Mockingbird, *not knowing, but knowing now, it was you. Since the bus. Since I told you outside of this very library how I felt about you. Since the hospital. Since you stood on that stage and read* The Perks of Being a Wallflower. *Since forever. Since always. I'm sorry it wasn't a happier ending for us. I wish it could have been.*

My head starts swimming. I don't understand. He told Joel we should be left in the past, but now he's saying that isn't what he wanted. Not only that, but he's finally solved the ongoing mystery of the bracelet. It was him. It's always been him.

Staring back at the library, my stomach starts to harden. I'm wondering if I've got this all wrong somehow. Again. And now I'm about to give up my life here and move back to Frome. I leave tomorrow.

Closing the doors to the library, I look around me before walking away, breaking into a run as I get closer to home.

What we had was something real. Maybe it could be again. Why else would he leave me this book? Despite all of my behaviour, here he is, trying again. I don't deserve him, and I know that – but God, I want him. I want a man in my life who has his strength. His compassion. His open heart and honesty. I thought it was too late, but I'm starting to wonder if it isn't.

I put on the kettle and send a photo of the book to Cassie. She's at Joel's and I've got the flat to myself, to find out what James is thinking. To see what the future might hold. Cassie replies.

Cassie: OMG!!! The love story is BACK ON. I'm grilling Joel for the ACTUAL truth as we speak. He now 'isn't sure' if James wanted to leave it in the past or not. Apparently your name's been banned since the memorial. MEN!!! They drive me insane.

The Book Swap

So he couldn't hear about me, either.

I make a cup of tea, then curl up on the sofa under a blanket and start reading. I'm hooked by the first sentence, and I can't stop.

Everything about our story is in these pages, littered with apologies and explanations. I've fallen in love with the characters, and I know it's because I've fallen in love with James too. That I never stopped, not really. I didn't know how to love again, but the events of the past year – and Wren's arrival – have changed all that. It's made me realise that I'm ready. That I've got enough love within me to not let go of Bonnie in my attempt to love someone new. It can exist together. All of it.

I read all night, wiping away tears so many times but especially at the end. The book doesn't finish the way I want it to. I wanted Carmen to forgive the man who loved her. I wanted them to try again and I don't know how much to read into the fact that she doesn't. Why did James write that ending? Is it for everyone, or just for me? To make me realise how stupid I've been? How much I've lost? Of course we're meant to be together. We always were.

I've just got time to return the book before I leave for Georgia's. I've filled it with notes. Underlined every sentence that meant something to me. I've underlined most of the book.

Turning to the blank page at the back, I reach for a pen and write one question. The bravest question I've ever written.

Meet me in happy ever after?

I put the book in my bag and stand up, knowing there's one more thing I need to do. The thing I've been avoiding. The only thing that makes moving hard.

I push open the door to my bedroom, one half of me in the present, and the other in the past, on the day I entered Bonnie's hospice for the final time.

That day I wasn't ready. Her parents had called me in the morning, saying I needed to get there as soon as I could. That she'd taken a turn for the worse overnight. That it was time. It wasn't making any sense. We'd been laughing the day before. Playing Uno. I'd painted Bonnie's nails her favourite turquoise. I'd spoken to her about what she could wear for our next pub outing. She hadn't corrected me. Hadn't implied for a second that it might not have been possible.

'No,' I forced out, entering her room when it was my turn to be with her.

I clenched my fists when I saw her. She was in bed, eyes closed, taking one laboured breath after another.

'No, no, no, no, no . . .'

I ran to her side, picking her hand up as gently as I could. Her skin was thin as tracing paper. Her nails still a bright turquoise. It had only been one day.

'Bonnie, it's me. It's Erin.' I waited for her to open her eyes and grin at me. To give one of her deep, husky laughs. Instead, an eyebrow twitched, her forehead furrowing for a second.

I bit down hard on my lip. We had more time. This wasn't my moment to say goodbye.

'Water?' I asked, reaching for the bottle, but she turned her head slightly away.

She wasn't even drinking any more.

'I'm not doing it,' I said, shaking my head hard, lip wobbling. 'I won't say goodbye. I refuse. It's just a bad day. You just need some rest, before you get back out.'

I waited for her to open her eyes. She squeezed my hand lightly.

'Bonnie please. Please don't go.' I wanted to shake her. If her mum and dad hadn't walked back in I might have. My head dropped to the bed as I wrapped my arms across her body, sobbing into the sheet that covered her. 'You can't go,' I begged.

Today, she's in the chair in my bedroom and the Bonnie I was searching for in her face that day is back. She's colourful. She's alive. I don't often see her this way. The way I knew her, before the cancer.

The sparkle is in her eyes. Her hair bouncing in curls. Her face warm. She grins at me, the way she used to when she'd meet me after work. Every time she saw me.

'I never said goodbye,' I say. 'I'm so sorry.'

My room's now bare of all my things. Only the furniture belonging to the landlord remains, Bonnie's chair included.

'It's okay.'

'It isn't. But if I said it out loud, it was real.'

'I know.'

I scan her face, so happy to see her this way.

'I get it now. I'll never be ready to say it, will I? I just have to say it anyway.'

She smiles. Nods her head. 'I'll be glad to get out of this chair to be honest.'

I laugh through my tears as she winks at me.

'I need something though. A way of knowing you're still with me.'

She looks out of the window and back at me. 'I'm always with you. I'm in you. Around you. Part of you. Like . . . Like the Snowman.'

I frown, not following.

'You know in *The Snowman* where he's just a heap of clothes and a pile of melting snow at the end, but he isn't gone. Not really. The snow keeps falling. The boy's got a constant reminder of their time together.'

I nod.

'I don't want to be snow though,' she says, screwing up her face. 'I'll be the sun. Every time the sun is shining, that's me. Okay?'

She's looking sleepy. I forgot how she had this knack of just napping whenever she felt like it. You'd be on the sofa having a chat and then you'd look over and boom. Eyes closed, mouth open.

'Okay,' I whisper, nodding. I lick my lips, ready to say it. To say everything I should have said that day. I don't know how to start.

I look down at the floor beneath me. A crack of sunlight breaks through the window and lands at my feet.

Lifting my eyes, I laugh.

'Told you,' Bonnie says. 'There I am.'

I pause.

'Bonnie?'

'Yes, Erin.'

'I will never love anyone the way I love you.'

'I know,' she says, standing up. 'Ditto.'

'Even after everything?'

'Especially after everything.'

I nod. I know it's time. I have to do it.

'Leave right now or I'll tell everyone about the time you turned up to school with no knickers on and cried on your lunch break.'

'Goodbye, Bonnie,' I laugh, raising my voice and turning

my back on the chair. I walk towards the door and open it. 'And thank you. There aren't enough thank-yous in the world for what you gave me.'

I turn one last time, needing to see her. My Bonnie.

'The pleasure was all mine. And Erin? I'm so proud of you. Don't forget to make all your dreams come true!'

A smile breaks across my face and I know that while I'm not okay at all, one day I will be. And for the days that I'm not, there's always the sunshine.

Walking out of my room, I close the door behind me, and press my hand against it, knowing, without needing to look, that she's gone.

I hold the book under my arm and walk back up the road, towards the library.

34

James

I spent so long trying to find the perfect last book to give Erin, I didn't realise I already had it. That I'd written it myself.

I was able to write it because of the girl in the margins, who encouraged me and educated me and gave me the self-belief I needed. The book isn't just an explanation for Erin, it's a thank you.

To be honest, I'm a bit offended by how long it's taken for someone to choose it. I put it in the library over a month ago and I've been checking several times a day ever since. I've even witnessed someone pick it up and read the back, and then return it, which doesn't bode well for future sales.

Every time I go there, I've got a spare copy with me, just in case. If it's gone, I'll put another one there, until I know it's Erin who's taken it.

And now I know she has. No one else did, but that doesn't matter. It was only ever meant for her.

I know she's taken it because I told Joel it's the only time he's allowed to mention Erin's name to me. If he finds out she has the book, he has to contact me immediately. He takes great delight in it, catching me as I sit at home in the world's comfiest chair, pondering a new book idea.

Joel: Erin has the book! ERIN! ERIN ERIN ERIN ERIN ERIN. She has THE book. Erin has your book.

Joel's got a job working for a homeless charity now and has way more time on his hands than he used to. That, combined with Cassie, has made him happier than I've ever seen him.

It's late in the evening when he messages, and it might take Erin days to read it. She might not even put it back. I've no idea what she feels about me, and I keep telling myself this could just be our goodbye, but I have to know for sure.

I set my alarm for five a.m. and when it goes off, I wheel the giant suitcase with everything I need through Ruskin Park and towards the library. I won't miss much about London when I move back to Frome, but I'll miss this park. I feel like, along with Erin and the library, it helped me to write again. I googled the man the park was named after. John Ruskin. He was an author, but he didn't write just one type of book. He wrote every type imaginable. Fiction. Poetry. Art. Even children's books.

My Dad the Superhero has just been sent to a publisher's. Maybe it won't get picked up, but I've already had one copy made, just for Jordan.

He, Carl and Elliot have moved back to the UK. It's what prompted me to make the final decision on my Big Impressions job, and, rather than take the promotion, I did a Joel and quit. I thought Dorothy might be really angry with me, but she stood up, smiled and hugged me. She said she was glad I'd finally decided to follow my dream and she's even keeping me on the books as a freelancer, so I can do training on the side, while I look for work in Frome. Basically, the step I was so terrified of taking has actually given me the life I've always dreamed of, and I'm not sure I'd have done it if it wasn't for the people around me. Erin relit the fire in me. Joel reminded me how much I loved writing. And Elliot made me realise I was living my life in fear of failure and that's really no way to live.

I'm excited, too. To have just one place to call home. A place where I get to see Mum and Dad whenever I want, not just when they need me. It turns out sometimes I still need them too.

Reaching the library, I open my suitcase, then stand back and take a look at Eileen. Rubbing my hands on my jeans, I crouch down. I pick up my hammer, placing it under the grey tiles and lifting them off as gently as I can, then placing them on the ground beside the library. It's amazing how much of a skilled handyman it can make you, when you have to recarpet an entire house.

Once the tiles are off, I take out a spatula and start peeling away the old paint. I've developed such a character in Eileen now, it's as though I can see her face flinching as each piece of paint flakes away onto the ground.

'Brighter days are coming, Eileen. I promise.'

I take out sandpaper and sand down the library. My fingers are red raw by the time I've done the whole thing. It's getting lighter now as people start walking past me and under the tunnel to work. I run my hand along the wood to check it's all smooth.

Taking two tubs of paint out of my suitcase, I open the library doors and pull all the books out, carefully placing them where the paint was sitting. First I take the lid off the pale yellow, which I matched with a paint app, and apply the first coat. While it dries, I put masking tape around the glass panels of the patterned windows, and open the can of vibrant blue for the door, running my brush carefully along the wood. Then, I fit the roof. I hammer nails through the grey sandpaper-like tiles, making sure there are no gaps for water to get through.

Standing back, I take a look at my work so far. I think Eileen would be happy. It looks as good as new. Finally, I feel like I've repaid her for everything she's given me.

Pulling a pre-made bacon sandwich out of my suitcase, I sit on the wall behind the library to eat it, spinning around as I hear footsteps coming under the bridge. A man stops and stares at the library, then me. He has a teenage girl with him and he points towards the shelves.

'That's where I found it, Savannah. Right there. Wasn't quite as smart-looking back then though.'

'I'll take that as a compliment,' I say, smiling.

He looks at his watch. 'Funny time to do it.'

They're gone before I can reply.

I wonder if Erin's reading the book right now. If she'll at least give me that final chance to explain myself. Everything I haven't been able to say in her presence is in that book. Between that, and my notes in the margins, she has all of me. Now it's up to her.

I need to do another coat, but it needs time to dry. I look through the books in my suitcase and choose *Rachel's Holiday* by Marian Keyes, settling down beside the library.

At some point, my phone rings.

'All okay?' I ask, seeing my parents' landline.

'All good,' Dad says, back to his old ways. 'I just got a royalties cheque from PRS.'

'Oh yeah?' Smiling, I pull myself up so that my back's straight against the brick wall behind me.

'Reckon I've got enough money here to buy so many copies of your book, you'll top the charts!'

'That's great, Dad! But maybe spend it on a holiday. Something for you.'

The Book Swap

'There's enough for that too. Your mum's already started researching.'

Worry rumbles through my stomach, but if she's getting ill, it at least feels more manageable now, with Elliot here to help.

'You deserve it. Hope you've sent your thanks to DJ Tenderbass?'

'I have. He's coming round for a cuppa when he plays the Cheese & Grain.'

I laugh at the thought of a world-renowned DJ at Mum and Dad's kitchen table, having a cup of tea, but I'm starting to learn that things are never as straightforward as you think they'll be. Sometimes opportunities come much later, or in a totally different shape, or not at all.

'Well, say hi from me, and congratulations again, Dad.'

At some point the sun appears from behind a cloud, shining down on me with such intensity that I feel like I'm under a spotlight. Eileen is my co-star, dazzling the world with her makeover. The sun arrived out of nowhere, and I don't know how I know what it means, but I just do.

My heart starts racing, a smile breaking across my face as the footsteps start echoing from under the bridge and towards me. They aren't a surprise. I know they're coming just as I know who's responsible for the shadow that now falls over the pages of my book, spilling darkness across my notes in the margin.

Squinting, I raise a hand to cover my eyes, and I look up.

'I loved it,' Erin says, holding out my book, and I stand to take it from her. Our first in-person book swap.

I flick through it, not sure what I'm looking for until I see the words written on the blank page at the back.

Meet me in happy ever after?

Dropping the book at my feet, I reach out and put my arms around her. She moves towards me, until she's close enough for me to do something I've imagined doing for half of my life.

As I bend my head towards her, she lifts her face to meet me and my lips are on hers immediately, unable to wait a second more. I pour everything from the last fifteen years into it, making sure she's in no doubt as to how I feel about her.

My entire body feels as though it might sink to the ground. I've got no control over myself any more. It takes everything in me to stay standing. To keep hold of her.

Distant footsteps pass behind us as she parts her lips and I move closer still. I'm not sure if I'll ever feel like I'm close enough to Erin. It's always been that way.

'I didn't like the ending of your book,' she whispers when we pull apart, her forehead pressed against mine. 'This one is much better.'

'I've always been ready for it. I've just been waiting for you.'

'You told Joel we should be left in the past.'

Shaking my head, I hold her hands and pull them towards my chest. 'I thought that's what you wanted. It was never what I wanted. I want you, Erin. I've only ever wanted you.'

She reaches up and kisses me again. Softly. Gently. Once. Twice. Three times.

'I want you, too,' she says.

Wrapping my arms around her, I look down towards my suitcase.

'I've been saying a quick thank you to Eileen,' I say, nodding towards the paints and reaching for a paintbrush. 'Want to join me? She needs another coat.'

The Book Swap

Erin takes the paintbrush I'm holding, my heart thumping against my chest as her hand touches mine.

She grins and dips the brush into the yellow, as I stand beside her with my own brush of blue.

'Hey, Eileen,' Erin whispers, smiling.

I move to stand beside her, running my brush along the front of the door.

'I can't stop thinking about how much Bonnie would love this,' Erin says. 'Thank you for being there for her.'

'It was the greatest honour of my life,' I say, meaning it. A load of memories come flooding in, the way they always do. The way I hope they always will. 'Is it true you came to school one day with no pants on?' I ask, and Erin's mouth falls open.

'What else did she tell you?'

I pretend to think about it.

'We had a lot of time to talk. I'm pretty sure I know everything. I hold all of your stories, Erin.'

Dropping her brush on the ground, she pulls me towards her by my T-shirt, kissing me again and again on the mouth, as the sun moves behind the clouds. I wrap my arms around her, and hold her as close to me as I can.

It's too late to change the ending of my book, but as the warmth of Erin's body spreads through mine, I see a whole new story stretching out ahead of us. A sequel. One with a much happier ending.

Acknowledgements

Firstly, in writing this book, it was brought to the very forefront of my mind just how many books exist in the entire world (seriously . . . there are LOADS!), and if you've got this far, it means that out of all of them, you chose mine. As a debut author that's such a huge privilege, and one I don't take lightly. Thank you.

For every uplifting and encouraging podcast or book that exists on becoming a writer, there's always the other ones. The ones that announce the statistics. That tell you how difficult the journey can be. Those statistics only serve as a constant reminder to me of how grateful I am for my agent, Jemima Forrester. Not just how fortunate I am to have an agent, but how very lucky that in a world of such compromising percentages, I got you, Jemima. You are a force. You truly care for your authors and your passion for this book and for my writing have given me the greatest cheerleader I could ask for. Your wisdom and belief in me. Your support and encouragement. Your brilliant brain for plotting and for funny lines. Nearly everything I'm proud of in this book started through conversations with you. To quote Erin, there aren't enough thank-yous in the world for what you gave me. Seriously. And that's not even including the hours of gossip and TV chat over ceviche. Further thanks to everyone at David Higham Associates.

Thank you to my smart and brilliant editor, Amy Batley, for noticing every moment where this book could be improved, and for pushing me to do my very best. Your eye for what shapes a story is so sharp and *The Book Swap* wouldn't have become what it did without you. Your insightful notes in the margins changed everything, and helped me to make sense of anything that wasn't quite working. Having you by my side through each draft of this book was like jumping from an aeroplane, knowing I was wearing the safest parachute that existed (I'm not sure that analogy works, but I'll trust you to suggest something that makes it better if it doesn't!). Thank you for totally getting Erin and James and for always knowing what they needed. To Lucy Stewart for all the encouragement, support and reassurance, and for such brilliant notes in record time. I love working with you. And to the entire hard working and wonderful team at Hodder & Stoughton: not only are your cakes delicious and your rooftop views enviable, but you are the most warm and welcoming team to meet up with.

To international editors around the world – I am beyond blown away every time I think about Erin and James out in different countries and languages, because you have chosen this book. Thank you.

While most of the authors of the novels included within these pages are no longer with us, it has been such a joy to re-read so many classics while writing *The Book Swap*. Much like James's book, this one was better for having learned from some of the best.

To my friends who so bravely shared their stories with me, which helped to shape the lives of Erin and James. To Emily Sharkey, Sophie Berkeley and Raj Duhra. Thank you for trusting me with things so personal to you.

The Book Swap

To the little library in a dark corner of Loughborough Junction – thank you for existing, and giving me the setting for this book.

Thank you to those of you who gave me the confidence to keep writing, early on. To Katy Loftus, to Jericho and the Festival of Writing, to Cornerstones and Tessa Shapcott, to the Romantic Novelist's Association and the New Writers Scheme, to Debi Alper and to the author Julie Cohen. Julie – your generosity helped to shape me as a writer, and I'll be forever grateful for the insight you gave me into your brilliantly creative mind. I read and loved your books before I met you, and only after I met you did I learn what a phenomenal teacher you are, too. Many of the things I use in my writing are there because you taught them to me. How to plot and create believable characters. How to always dig deeper. How to 'make shit happen'. Your constant asking 'but why?', that now shapes the way I think. I have learned so much from you.

To authors who have been so generous with their time and advice: Lia Louis, Lynsey James, Freya Berry, Christina Pishiris, Cesca Major, Lorraine Brown and Helen Selvey. And to Marian Keyes for writing books that made me realise just what was possible. I wanted to become an author because of you. Your books showed me that words can breathe life and laughter into a reader, and I've tried to do that with my writing ever since.

To author Alison Bloomer – your early notes were so helpful. Thank you for encouraging Erin to be a little more feisty and for proving that every book is made better by the appearance of mini Haribo.

To Charlie Covell for reading an early draft of *The Book Swap* and for being so encouraging.

Tessa Bickers

To Sally Phillips for such willing early support. You have always been so kind to me.

To my friends who don't mind when I disappear for weeks into another world, and are still there waiting when I pop back out, desperate for entertainment and *a lot* of wine. In particular to Em, Zsuz, Rosie, Vicki & Stumpy – you are my rocks throughout this and everything in this book about friendship is dedicated to you all. Thank you for the unconditional love and the laughs. I'm so lucky to have had you all in my life for nearly thirty years!

To my step-mum, Jude, for teaching me about love and loss. For showing me that when someone dies, they aren't truly gone. For displaying the strength through cancer that helped me to create Bonnie. I think of you every day, and I always will.

To Grandad – the first author I ever met, who was the original pantser. *'My next book is about a man who hides a very dark secret.' 'Ooooh. What's the secret, grandad?' 'Well I don't know, I haven't written it yet.'* I hope having another Bickers author in the family makes you proud.

To Mum, Dad and Charley – I wouldn't choose any other family to be a part of. Thank you for the hilarious group WhatsApp, all the laughter and all the love. And in particular, thank you, Mum, for reading every draft of every book I've ever written, right back to the age of 11. You've championed every choice I've made, and I couldn't have made any of them without you. Thank you for being by my side through life, cheering me on.

To Maria – thank you for your endless and never-tiring love and support. For allowing me to talk nonstop about the characters in my head, and gently suggesting something that will change everything, and make it better. For putting up with my personality transplant when I have a deadline and for encouraging me to take a short walk when I haven't stopped tapping at my keyboard for a few hours. So much of you is contained within the pages of this book, but especially the love. And to Penny, for being the greatest reality check and for keeping my feet firmly on the ground by telling everyone from strangers to your teachers that *'my mummy used to be a waitress, but now she's just an author.'*

And to Bea Fitzgerald – this book wouldn't exist without your phenomenal brain. I owe you everything.

Reading group questions

1. 'First and foremost, *The Book Swap* is a love story.' Do you agree with this sentiment? What do you think was the most enduring theme in the book?
2. After the first chapter, were you shocked about Bonnie? What do you think about Bonnie being represented in this way?
3. Grief – in many forms – is an important emotion in this book. What did you find you were most moved by?
4. Do you think Erin and James found it easier to communicate with each other and reveal their deepest emotions because they didn't know who the other was? Is there a freedom to this anonymity?
5. Both Erin and James have complicated relationships with their families. Do you think they were right to hold grudges over their parents – or do you think they should have given them more slack?
6. Are there any decisions in the book you disagree with? Do you think James should have revealed he knew who Erin was before he did so?
7. If you were to pass on one message from this book to a friend or family member, what would it be?
8. If you were to leave just one book for a stranger in a free library, what would it be?